W9-CIK-319

TEXAS FOREVER

This Large Print Book carries the
Seal of Approval of N.A.V.H.

TEXAS FOREVER

JANET DAILEY

WHEELER PUBLISHING
A part of Gale, a Cengage Company

GALE
A Cengage Company

Farmington Hills, Mich • San Francisco • New York • Waterville, Maine
Meriden, Conn • Mason, Ohio • Chicago

LIBRARY OF CONGRESS CIP DATA ON FILE.
CATALOGUING IN PUBLICATION FOR THIS BOOK
IS AVAILABLE FROM THE LIBRARY OF CONGRESS

ISBN-13: 978-1-4328-6794-2 (hardcover alk. paper)

Published in 2019 by arrangement with Kensington Books, an imprint of Kensington Publishing Corp.

Printed in Mexico
1 2 3 4 5 6 7 23 22 21 20 19

With special thanks to Elizabeth Lane.

CHAPTER ONE

August, the present

The brutal August sun sank behind the Caprock Escarpment, streaking the cliffs with hues of gold, bronze, and deep blood red. Like silken draperies set afire, the tattered clouds blazed, then slowly melted into twilight. Shadows deepened, flowing down the narrow canyons to flood the parched foothills with the black of a moonless night.

A gray fox slipped out of its den, ears alert for the sound of a scurrying mouse or lizard. Bats darted on silent wings, catching insects in flight. A golden eagle glided to the rocky edge of a high precipice, folded its powerful wings, and settled for the night.

On the dust-swept plain below the escarpment, the sprawling heart of the Rimrock Ranch lay shrouded in unaccustomed silence. Cigarettes, dots of red in the darkness, glowed outside the bunkhouse, but the usual banter of the cowhands was absent.

7

Even the horses and cattle seemed subdued.

The windows were dark in the imposing stone and timber house that Bull Tyler had finished for his bride fifty years ago. On the broad front porch, two figures sat in rustic log chairs, placed close together.

Will Tyler, the ranch boss and head of the family, was nursing a can of cheap Mexican beer. He stared into the darkness beyond the porch rail, saying nothing.

His daughter Erin, now nineteen, sat watching him. Her father was far from old — not yet fifty. But time and grief had aged him beyond his years. Already mourning his wife, he'd been crushed today by the sudden loss of his oldest friend. Not that he'd shown it. Even after the sheriff and his deputy had driven off, he'd expressed no flicker of emotion nor shed so much as a tear. All the more reason for Erin to be worried about him.

"I still can't believe Jasper is gone," she said, hoping her father would open up and talk. Keeping his grief bottled inside was only going to make him feel worse.

After what seemed like a long silence, Will cleared his throat. "I just wish the end had been different for him. Even at ninety-three, crashing an ATV into a gulley isn't the way you want to go." He took a swallow of the

8

Mexican beer Jasper had always liked, as if he were drinking it as a sort of tribute. But even that did nothing to ease his inner pain. With a muttered curse, he crushed the unfinished can in his fist and flung it over the porch railing, where it would be picked up by a stable hand in the morning. "I never could understand why Jasper fancied this god-awful two-bit beer. It always tasted like horse piss to me. Still does."

Erin smiled at the feeble joke, sensing the anguish behind it. For as long as anyone in the Tyler family could remember, Jasper Platt had been the heart and soul of the Rimrock Ranch. He had worked for Will's grandfather, Williston Tyler, and for Will's father, the legendary Bull Tyler. To Will and his brother Beau, Jasper had been like a second father, watching over them as they grew to manhood, and teaching them all the skills they'd need to be good cowboys.

Even in his old age, when arthritis would no longer allow him to sit a horse, Jasper had served as honorary foreman to the ranch as well as friend and confidant to three generations of Tyler men.

Erin had adored him. To her, Jasper had been like a loving grandfather. She couldn't imagine the Rimrock — or her own life — without his wise, crusty presence. She'd

9

been in denial about Jasper's age and the certainty that he wouldn't last much longer. But when he'd failed to show up for breakfast that morning and when circling vultures had led searchers to his body, barely a mile from the heart of the ranch, the shock had been unimaginable. It was still sinking in that the old man was gone.

After examining the scene, Sheriff Cyrus Harger had declared his death a tragic accident. What else could it be? Surely, at Jasper's age, a stroke or heart attack could have caused the ATV he was riding to veer off the rocky trail and plunge to the bottom of a desert wash. The sheriff and his young deputy, who'd checked out the scene, had agreed that there were no suspicious circumstances. Will, to whom Jasper had given power of attorney, had turned down the suggestion of an autopsy. It would only delay the funeral, he'd insisted, and it would be a needless violation of the old man's body.

Still, Jasper's death had left unanswered questions.

"I begged him not to go out alone in that damned ATV," Will said, "but I know he liked hunting birds, and he hated being told what he shouldn't do. The sheriff said he died sometime between six and eight last

10

night. He would have been on his way home about then."

"When did you realize he was missing?" Erin had gone to a movie in town the previous night and hadn't come home until after her father was in bed.

"As I told the sheriff, he wasn't around at supper time, but that wasn't unusual. Sometimes he just warmed up leftovers and ate in his duplex. Later on I was busy making phone calls and didn't check on him." Will's voice roughened with emotion. "Lord, if I had, maybe we could've found him in time. This is on me."

"Don't talk that way, Dad. However Jasper died, chances are you couldn't have done anything." Erin reached across the space between their chairs and squeezed his hand. Without the truth, her father would always blame himself for the death of his old friend. Maybe finding that truth would be up to her. She would be busy until the funeral was over. But after that, she would take some time to look into the so-called accident.

"Were you able to reach Uncle Beau?" she asked, changing the subject. "Will he be here for the funeral?"

"He'll be flying into Lubbock on Friday with Natalie and their daughter. I offered to

11

pick him up, but he said they'd rather rent a car." Will's jaw tightened. "I'm guessing he'll want to leave right after the funeral."

Will's younger brother had grown up on the ranch. He'd left to join the military, then moved back after their father's death. But ranch life, and being bossed by Will, had grated on him. Three years ago, after a final blowup between the brothers, Beau had left the Rimrock to take up his former job in Washington as a senior agent for the DEA. He and Will had never made peace. But that didn't keep Erin from missing Beau's charming, fun-loving ways.

A night breeze had sprung up, its hot breath stirring the parched grass and peppering Erin's face with fine dust. This summer's drought was as bad as any she could remember in her nineteen years. The water holes had gone dry, and, as the creaking windmill reminded her, even the wells were getting low. There'd been talk of cutting back the Rimrock's herd of white-faced Herefords, selling off the steers and older cows early to save water for the ranch's precious breeding stock. Selling before the animals reached prime weight in the fall would mean less money for the ranch. But it would be better than watching cattle die of thirst.

Only yesterday, over breakfast, she'd listened as Will and Jasper discussed what best to do. And now, like a candle blown out by a breath of wind, Jasper was gone.

"Someone else is coming for the funeral," Will said. "You've never met her, but she's an old friend. I called her tonight, and she said she'd be here. I hope you won't mind if I volunteered you to pick her up at the airport. She's in her sixties, and I could tell she was nervous about driving a rental car in city traffic."

"I'll be happy to pick her up," Erin said. "But who is she? Why haven't I heard anything about her before?"

Will took his time in answering. "Her name is Rose Landro McCade. I haven't seen her since I was a boy. But she's not the sort of person you'd forget. Toughest woman I've ever known, and probably the most stubborn, too."

"I can hardly wait to meet her," Erin said.

"Rose can tell you a lot about the old days. She and my father scrapped like a couple of wildcats, but they never lost their respect for each other. And Jasper loved her like a daughter. They had a special bond, those two. When I spoke with her, even after all these years, I could tell how hard it hit her that he was gone."

13

"What happened to her? Where did she go?"

"She married a Wyoming rancher and never came back. I guess they had a good life, raised a couple of girls. He's passed on, and their daughters are grown now, so Rose is alone. I'm hoping she'll stick around for a while. She can stay in the empty side of the duplex. Maybe you can get it ready for her — something pretty on the bed, clean towels and soap in the bathroom, some snacks in the fridge . . . even some flowers, once she lets us know her arrival time."

"She must've been special."

"She was — is. She wasn't around here long, but she was like a big sister to Beau and me." Will paused, remembering. "I'll never forget the night Rose almost gave her life to save us. If it hadn't been for Bull, all three of us, and the man she ended up marrying, could have died."

"That sounds like quite a story. How come you've never told me about it?"

He exhaled, took a pack of Marlboros from his pocket, and tapped one into his hand. "Some stories are best saved for the right time. I'll leave the telling to Rose."

His lighter flared in the darkness. The tip of the cigarette glowed as he inhaled.

"I wish you wouldn't —" Erin stopped

herself from lecturing him. This wasn't the time for it. Years ago, Will had given up smoking to please his wife, Tori. But when she'd died of cancer four months ago, he'd taken up the habit again, as if to say *So what if it kills me? What's the point in living?*

"I suppose you've called Kyle," he said.

"Yes. He offered to come over, but I told him I'd see him at the funeral. Until then, I won't be much company."

Kyle Cardwell, whose father managed the neighboring Prescott Ranch for the syndicate that had bought it from the family, had been dating Erin since she'd finished high school. Last night, after their weekly movie date, he'd pulled his SUV off the road, slipped a small velvet box out of his pocket, and asked her to marry him. The diamond was impressive — at least a full carat. But Erin couldn't imagine wearing it to muck out the stable or wash down a horse, which was how she spent most of her days.

Stunned, she'd mumbled a reply. "I'm only nineteen, Kyle. I need time to think about this."

"Take all the time you need." His Hollywood smile had flashed in the darkness as he dropped the ring box back into his pocket. "But I hope you won't keep me waiting too long. I love you, Erin, and I

15

can't wait to make you mine. Now come here and kiss me."

After a few minutes of necking, she'd asked him to take her home. For the rest of the night she'd lain awake, weighing her choices. Maybe she should've said yes. Kyle was twenty-two, handsome, respectable, and well-mannered. Her father liked him and had hinted that he wouldn't mind having a grandchild or two. Why not do what everyone seemed to expect of her?

Why was she still unsure?

Was Kyle meant to be her husband, to love and honor and cherish? What if she were to refuse him? Would she live to regret it for the rest of her days?

And what about her own plans, her own dreams of breeding and training a stable of fine horses? Would she have to put those dreams aside when she became a wife?

Toward morning, she'd fallen into a fitful sleep — only to be awakened by Will with the news that Jasper was missing. An hour later his body had been found in a desert wash, under his wrecked ATV.

Kyle's proposal would have to wait.

Rising from his chair, Will crushed the cigarette with his boot and kicked it over the rail, onto the gravel below, then glanced at the luminous dial on his watch. He stood

16

for a moment, peering out into the darkness.

"What is it, Dad?" Erin asked. "Is something wrong?"

"Can't say for sure." Will shook his head. "I was expecting the new man I hired last week. He said he'd be here by tonight, but it's getting late, and I haven't seen hide nor hair of him."

"A new man? And you didn't tell me?"

"Sorry. Slipped my mind, I guess." Will sank wearily back into the chair. "Sky knows he's coming. The man's a farrier."

"A farrier? Just to shoe horses? That's going to cost us, Dad. And with the drought on, there's no money to sparc. We've been getting by for years with the cowboys shoeing their own horses, and Sky taking care of the rest."

"Sky doesn't have time. And neither do the cowboys, especially with the roundup coming up. Hear me out, Erin. I talked this over with Jasper, and he agrees —" Emotion stopped the words in his throat. He took a deep breath. "He *agreed* with me. We need a man who can keep our horses decently shod and in top condition. A good farrier's like a doctor, and he has to know almost as much. He looks at their gait, their alignment, the whole animal. Then he trims

17

the hooves for the best weight distribution and chooses a shoe to fit the horse's needs."

"That's still going to cost money."

"True. But I had a couple of hands quit last month to go on the rodeo circuit, so that's two less to pay. And I figure that in the long run, having a farrier won't cost us any more than having the cowboys take time from work to slap shoes on their mounts, then having horses go lame because they didn't do the job right. We could get by with fewer horses if they were all in good shape. And if we had to sell off part of the remuda, we'd get a better price if they were well shod and in prime condition."

"I understand where you're coming from," Erin said. "But a farrier would have to be paid a lot more than a common ranch hand. Can we afford a full-time man just to shoe horses?"

"We've got more than sixty horses in the remuda, as well as the brood mares and stallions," Will said. "When roundup's on, those cow ponies go through a lot of shoes. There should be plenty of work for him, at least through fall. And we already agreed that if he runs out of work here, he can take outside clients."

"As I recall, the last stranger you hired didn't work out so well," Erin said. "He stole everything that wasn't tied down."

"Don't remind me." Will shook his head. "But it won't happen again. This man was recommended by a customer. I met him a couple of weeks ago, when I picked up a truckload of hay from that big outfit east of the Prescott place. He said he'd been on the road since spring, going from ranch to ranch. I think he liked the idea of a steady job with a roof over his head. Quiet sort. He struck me as the kind of fellow who'll do his work and never make trouble."

"We'll see." Erin had always trusted her father's business sense. But since his wife's death, Will's judgment seemed to be less acute. Was it the shock of grief, a passing distraction, or only her imagination? Whatever the cause, she found herself questioning the decisions he made.

Like this farrier Will had hired. He could turn out to be just fine. But the fact that he hadn't shown up as promised wasn't a good sign.

"Why don't you get some rest, Dad?" she suggested. "You've had a hellish day, and tomorrow won't be much better."

"At least I can try. What about you?" He stood and turned toward the door, then hesitated, as if reluctant to leave her outside alone.

19

"I'll be along later. If your man shows up, I'll introduce myself and point the way to the bunkhouse."

"You're sure?"

"I'm sure. I'm too strung out to sleep."

"All right, but don't stay up too late. His name's Maddox. He'll be driving a black Chevy truck with a shell on the back and a two-wheel trailer behind. You can tell him there's a couple of empty rooms and a bath on the second floor."

"Don't worry, I'll keep an eye out for him. If he pulls in after I've gone to bed, that'll be his problem."

As her father went inside, shutting the front door behind him, Erin settled back in the chair and closed her eyes. After the emotionally draining day, she felt as if the earth had dropped away under her feet. In her growing-up years, three strong people had always been there for her — her mother, her father, and Jasper.

Tori, her beautiful, golden-haired mother, had slipped away four months ago, just weeks after her cancer diagnosis. Now Jasper was gone, too, and she sensed that her father was sinking into despair. He was putting on a brave face, but she could see the shadows that ringed his eyes and the slump of his once-proud shoulders. Erin knew the signs. It was as if she were losing him, too.

How could she even think of getting married when Will needed her? Her losses were his losses, perhaps even more deeply felt. This was no time for him to lose his daughter, his only child, to another man.

She had her answer for Kyle. Any talk of marriage would have to wait.

Erin greeted the decision with a sigh of relief. Until now, she hadn't realized how much pressure Kyle's proposal had put on her, and how unprepared she'd been to say yes and let him put that stunning diamond ring on her finger. Maybe later, she thought. Maybe in a year or so. But not yet.

As moments passed, she could feel herself relaxing in the chair. The peaceful sounds of night crept around her — the *chirr* of crickets under the porch, the faint creak of the windmill, the murmur of horses in the paddock, and the far-off wail of a coyote. Little by little, she began to drift. . . .

The security light, mounted with a motion sensor on a leg of the windmill, flashed on, startling Erin awake. She jerked bolt upright in the chair, blinking in the brightness as she struggled to focus her sleep-dulled mind. What time was it?

A black pickup towing a small trailer was

pulling into the ranch yard. That would be the farrier her father had hired, arriving late, without so much as a phone call to let anyone know when he'd be here. What was his name? Matlock? No, Maddox, that was it. Pushing to her feet, she took a deep breath and strode down the steps to meet him.

Luke Maddox let the truck's engine idle a moment while he watched the Rimrock welcoming committee walk toward him. He'd expected Will Tyler to come lumbering out of the house, ready to rip a piece out of his hide for showing up after midnight. Instead, here was this woman — a pretty one at that. She was dressed like a boy, in jeans and a plaid shirt. But there was nothing boyish about her lithe, confident walk, her willowy figure, or the honey-colored hair that fluttered in the wind.

She looked young — too young for him, Luke reminded himself. So why did he find himself wishing he'd bought a pack of breath mints before leaving that poker game at the Blue Coyote in town? He would've been here sooner, but what the hell, he'd been winning. Tyler couldn't fault him for that — not as long as he showed up ready for work in the morning.

Mildly intrigued, he opened the door of the cab, swung his feet to the ground, and waited as she approached him. Close up she was even prettier than he'd expected. Maybe younger, too. Boss's daughter, he guessed from her confident manner. Strictly off limits if he didn't want to get butt-kicked off the ranch by her father. But glory be, he couldn't be fired for looking.

Bold and direct, her eyes took his measure before she spoke. "Mr. Maddox?" Her raw, husky voice was too womanly for her age. "I'm Erin Tyler. I told my father I'd stay up and wait for you, but that was hours ago. We'd just about given up on you. I hope you had a good reason for being so late."

Boss's daughter. He'd been right. Princess proud and as sassy as a blue jay.

"I had about three hundred good reasons," he said. "But I won't be starting work until morning. Till then, I figured my time was my own."

One dark eyebrow arched upward. "Well, Mr. Maddox, there's a room waiting for you — door number five, on the second floor of the bunkhouse." She gestured toward a frame building on the far side of the yard. "There's a bathroom up there, too. Just remember that the men won't take kindly to your making noise when they're trying to sleep. Chores at five, breakfast at six. If you want to eat, be up on time and ready to help out. We're running a ranch here, not a hotel."

Sassy as jalapeño sauce. *Picante,* as the Mexicans would say. That was the word for her. "I'll keep that in mind," Luke said. "Where can I park this rig?"

"Over there by the barn for now. The foreman will be here tomorrow. He'll get you set up with a place to park and work." She started to walk away, then paused, turning back toward him.

"I'm afraid you've come at a bad time. We've had a death on the ranch, a loss to us all. Nobody will be in the mood for joking or bad language. Please keep that in mind and be respectful."

Luke nodded, and she continued.

"The funeral will be on Saturday. The ranch workers who knew the man will be invited to pay their respects. You'll be expected to work as usual."

"Understood. The name's Luke, by the way. I'm guessing you don't stand on formality with the hired help." Luke tried to keep the sarcasm out of his voice, but the sudden narrowing of her eyes told him she hadn't missed it. "Anything else?" he asked.

"I'd say that's enough for tonight. The

24

foreman can answer any questions you might have in the morning. His name's Sky Fletcher. I'll make sure he knows you're here."

Erin turned and began to walk away. She'd said enough. It was time she went back in the house and left Luke Maddox to get to bed on his own. There was something unsettling about the man, and it wasn't just his size — although six-foot-three inches of solid muscle was impressive enough. It wasn't even his arrogance. A virile, masculine energy seemed to radiate from him. It crackled in the depths of his sardonic black eyes and flowed subtly, like an invisible aura, over his rugged features, thick, dark hair, and stubbled jaw.

Erin had lived and worked with men all her life. She was neither shy nor nervous around them. But something told her she'd be smart to keep her distance from this one. When she looked at him, a cautionary voice whispered, *too hot to handle.*

She hadn't heard him get into his truck, which probably meant that he was standing there, watching her walk away. *Damn the man!* It would serve him right if she turned around and caught him ogling her backside — except that he probably wouldn't care.

She'd walked a dozen paces and was about to take another step when he suddenly shouted, "Look out!"

Faster than she'd imagined a big man could move, he lunged for her, seized her by the waist, and yanked her backward — just in time to keep her from stepping on a five-foot bull snake.

She lost her footing and fell back against him. His body was rock hard, his clasp like an iron vise. He smelled of tobacco smoke, horses, and man sweat.

"What the hell?" His grip eased as the snake slithered off into the shadows and he noticed her calm demeanor. "Did I just save your life or did I make a fool of myself?"

"I'm sure you meant well. But don't worry. I'm fine." More startled than scared, Erin righted herself and pulled away from him. He was still staring after the snake.

"It didn't bite you, did it? Do you want me to get a shovel and kill the thing for you?"

Erin managed to laugh. "Heavens, no. Henry's harmless as long as you leave him alone. He lives under the grain shed and keeps the mice under control. He discourages the rattlers, too. They don't want to mess with him. Mostly he stays out of sight. But tonight he probably thought he had the

26

place to himself."

"*Henry?* Are you saying the damn thing's a *pet?*"

"Not really. More like one of the crew. Watch out when you move your rig. I don't want to come out here in the morning and discover that you've run over him."

"Don't worry. I'll give that monster a wide berth." He shuddered. "Damn, I hate snakes!"

"Then you're in the wrong state. Maybe you need to move to Alaska. Sleep tight, Mr. Maddox." Turning away, Erin strode toward the porch, willing herself not to look back at him.

She remembered how a much smaller Henry had first shown up, and Jasper had talked Will into sparing the snake so it could live under the shed and feed on the mice that were pillaging the stored grain.

That had been three years ago. Now Jasper was gone — and with his passing, it was as if winds of change were blowing across the Rimrock. New challenges. New decisions. New dangers. And new people.

Tilting her face toward her shoulder, she inhaled the strangely erotic scent that clung to her shirt. The blend of horses, smoke, and sweat evoked the memory of a hard body and strong arms. But it was only for a moment. Her parents had made it clear that fraternizing with the hired help was a bad idea. And she had a boyfriend — a nice, respectable boyfriend she'd probably marry one day. Just not yet.

As she mounted the steps, Erin heard the truck start up. She didn't look back.

CHAPTER TWO

Rose Landro McCade pressed against the window of the United Airlines plane on approach to Lubbock Preston Smith International Airport. From the air, she could see how much three decades had changed the countryside. Subdivisions sprawled over what had been open prairie. Skyscrapers towered above the downtown area. Freeways crisscrossed the landscape.

Rose had thought of this trip as a homecoming. But that home, she realized, would not be the place she remembered — not even the people.

But then, she had changed, too.

This would be the first time she'd traveled by plane since she and Tanner, the love of her life, had flown to Hawaii on a long-awaited second honeymoon. They'd returned to the news that Bull Tyler, aging, crippled, and in pain, had died in their absence. Now Jasper had followed him. At

29

least this time, she would have the chance to pay her respects.

Two days had passed since she'd gotten Will's call. Rose had remembered Will as a boy. But it was a man with a weary voice who'd given her the news that Jasper had passed away in what appeared to be a tragic accident. Even now, she felt the pain of loss like an icy stab to the heart. She hadn't seen Jasper since her wedding day. But in her memory, he'd always been strong, vigorous, funny, and wise — and always her steadfast friend.

"The funeral is set for Saturday," Will had told her. "After the service, we'll be taking Jasper to the Hill Country to bury him next to Sally's grave. She was —"

"Yes, I know," Rose had said. "She was the girl who drowned before their wedding. He told me he'd never loved anyone else." Rose had wiped away the first of many tears. "I'll be there as soon as I can get a flight. Jasper was my best friend. I want to say a proper good-bye to him."

"You can fly into Lubbock," Will said. "Let us know when you've got your flight. Erin can be there to pick you up."

"Where has the time gone? I can't believe she's old enough to drive."

"Erin's nineteen and very much her own

person," Will said. "You'll enjoy getting to know her."

"That sounds lovely. I was going to get a rental, but I wasn't looking forward to driving a strange car on the freeway. How will I know your daughter when I see her?"

"You'll know her," Will had assured her. "Erin is the image of Susan, my mother."

Rose's thoughts spun back to the present as the plane touched down on the runway and taxied to the gate. Clutching her carryon, she let the crush of deplaning passengers — like cattle going down a chute, she thought — carry her through the Jetway and out into the terminal. There was a moment's unease as she spotted the BAGGAGE CLAIM sign and followed the arrows. Would Will's daughter be waiting? Would they recognize each other?

She'd kept in touch with her Rimrock family, mostly by way of occasional Christmas cards. She knew that Will had married, divorced, and remarried the same woman — strange that he hadn't mentioned her just now. She knew that a third Tyler son had turned up — Sky Fletcher, born of Bull's brief affair with a Comanche woman. She knew that Beau was married with a young daughter, and that he'd returned to the ranch for a time, but eventually had gone back to his government job. Ferg Prescott — the scheming neighbor Rose and Bull had both detested — was long gone. So was his son, Garn, who'd sold the Prescott Ranch to a syndicate before going into politics. Sky had married Garn's daughter, joining the two rival lines. And that, Rose thought, was the sum total of what she knew. Everything else would be a surprise.

Passing into the baggage claim area, Rose checked the flight numbers above the carousels. The luggage from her flight was already unloading, but she had yet to spot her old brown leather suitcase. She was waiting impatiently when she happened to glance through the crowd to the far side of the carousel. Standing a few feet back was a tall, slender young woman in jeans and a white tee, her dark blond hair brushed to the side in a single braid. In her hands was a cardboard placard with a single name on it — ROSE.

Erin hurried to meet the woman striding toward her. There could be no mistaking Rose McCade. Will had described her as he remembered, from her petite stature and dark eyes to the birthmark that blazed down the left margin of her face. But given Rose's age, Erin had expected someone elderly, a person who might need a hand getting out of the airport to the car. Apart from her silver hair, twisted and pinned atop her head, Rose was a total surprise.

Dressed in trail-worn jeans and boots, with a denim jacket, she was a wiry bundle of energy. Her face, bare of makeup, was tanned and weathered from days on the Wyoming range, but her smile was as youthful as her step. Her only ornament, besides her wedding ring, was a pair of miniature silver horseshoe-shaped earrings.

She stopped an arm's length from Erin and stood looking up at her. "Goodness, you make me feel old," she said. "I knew your grandmother when I was a girl. She was about your age then. You look just like her."

Erin found her voice. "Welcome home to Texas, Rose. Thank you for coming all this way."

They hugged, awkwardly at first, then warmly, both of them aware of the deep connection they shared. Rose wasn't family, but she was the closest thing.

"Let's get your bag and be on our way," Erin said.

"There it is." Rose pointed out a well-used leather suitcase. Erin grabbed it off the carousel and guided Rose outside to short-term parking, where she loaded the suitcase in the back of the dusty station wagon that had been her mother's. She'd actually had it washed that morning when she bought gas in town. But this summer, after months of drought, there was no escaping the fine dust that settled on everything.

Moments later, they were on their way, pulling out of the parking lot and onto the highway. "Let's hope we can beat the rush hour traffic," Erin said. "I promised Dad I'd have you home in time for dinner. He'll be so glad to see you."

"How is Will?" Rose asked. "I haven't seen him since he was a boy. But I remember how serious and responsible he was, even then. I'm guessing that Jasper's death hit him hard."

"It hit all of us hard," Erin said. "But I think it was the worst for Dad, especially since my mother passed away just four months ago."

"Oh, no!" Rose exclaimed. "He didn't tell me. I'm so sorry."

"He doesn't like to talk about it." Erin had learned to hide her own grief, even though it was always there, like a cold, raw pain that never went away. "It was cancer. She was only forty-three. Dad was devastated. And now, with Jasper gone, it's like he's been knocked down and gut kicked twice." She glanced at Rose. "I'm really glad you've come. Seeing you again is bound to raise his spirits."

"I hope so." Rose gazed out the window at the traffic, then changed the subject. "Lubbock has changed a lot since the last time I was here. I'm guessing the ranch has changed, too."

"Not as much as you'd think," Erin said. "The house is still there. The barn was rebuilt after a fire, but it's in the same place. The old sheds and corrals are pretty much the same, just fixed up."

"How about the people? I remember Bernice and what a wonderful cook she was. But she was only a few years younger than Jasper. I don't suppose she's still around."

"Bernice retired and went to live with her daughter. She passed away a couple of years ago. We hired a Latina woman, the wife of one of our cowboys, to take her place. Her name's Carmen. She's good at her job, but she doesn't live in the house, like Bernice did."

"And the chickens? I loved those chickens. Jasper and I built their coop together."

"Sorry, no more chickens. There's a supermarket in Blanco Springs. We get our eggs and chicken meat there now."

Rose sighed. "Too bad. There's something about raising chickens that's good for the soul. And goats, too."

"Sorry, no goats either," Erin said.

"Too bad." Rose fell silent as she gazed out the side window. They were on the freeway now, with the flat caprock plain stretching to the horizon on either side of them. The pastures, croplands, and cotton fields, watered by deep artesian wells, were green. But the stretches of open country offered little more than yellowed grass, dry scrub, and blowing dust.

"It's so dry," Rose remarked. "The Rimrock must be hurting for water."

"This is the worst drought I can remember," Erin said. "Are you familiar with that parcel up on the caprock, with the wells?"

"I am." Rose smiled. "As I recall, Bull won it in a poker game. I always suspected him of cheating, but that was Bull for you. To him, the land was everything. Land and family. Nothing else mattered." She paused. "Sorry, you were going to say something about the parcel."

Erin pulled out to pass a lumbering cattle truck. "We've counted on that caprock land to save us in a drought, but this year we've overgrazed it. There's water up there but the grass is almost eaten off. If we don't

36

pull the cattle off soon, it won't grow back. We're trucking water to the mountain tanks, and the water table's in danger of sinking below the wells that supply the house and lower pastures. Even the horses . . ." Erin pressed her lips together and shook her head. "Aside from selling our stock early, we're running out of options."

Rose brushed Erin's arm with one small, work-worn hand. "I can tell you're as passionate about the land and animals as your father and grandfather were. You're a Tyler, Erin. You'll find a way to get through this." She was silent for a moment. "You haven't mentioned the creek — the one that flows from the aquifer under the caprock and runs along the property line with the old Prescott Ranch. Surely that wouldn't go dry. Do you still run creek water into that old stock tank, the one that Bull dug years ago?"

"We've replaced the tank with a metal one," Erin said. "But yes, we still fill it from the creek. There's not enough water for a big herd, but that creek is vital to the survival of the ranch. The plan is, if worse comes to worst, and we have to sell off everything but breeding stock, we'll pay a grazing fee to run them on that government land beyond the ranch boundary and water them from the tank and the creek." She glanced at Rose. "I'm surprised that you know so much about the ranch, especially that creek."

"You shouldn't be," Rose said, "unless Will hasn't told you the story."

"Told me what story?" Erin felt a vague, tingling premonition.

"That strip of land along the Rimrock side of the creek belonged to my grandfather. To shorten a long story, I was with Grandpa when he was shot trying to defend it from the Prescotts. Bull showed up in time to save me, but it was too late for Grandpa. Bull buried him on the property, under an old fallen tree."

"Yes — I've seen that headstone. It's mostly covered in dirt and cow droppings now. I've always assumed it was some old-time settler buried there. So, that's your grandfather?"

"I was fourteen when he left that parcel to me. Bull took me in and took over the land. Years later, after I threatened to join forces with Ferg Prescott to get it, he deeded that land back to me on condition that the Rimrock always be given access to the water. I kept my part of the bargain. But I expected better for my grandpa's memory."

"I'm sorry," Erin said. "I wish I'd known about it."

"You couldn't have known, dear. All this happened long before you were born." Rose's voice took on a determined tone. "My grandpa gave his life's blood for that land. And if his grave isn't being given the care and respect it deserves, I'm going to have to do something about it."

"If you need help cleaning the place up and restoring the grave —"

"Thank you. I may take you up on that." Rose fell silent. For the next few minutes Erin focused on driving, moving to the outside lane of the freeway and watching for the exit to Blanco Springs. But she was too curious about Rose's story to let it rest.

"I hope you won't mind one more question," she said. "You say your grandfather was shot by the Prescotts. Who actually shot him? Was it Ferg?"

"It was Ham Prescott, Ferg's father." The strain in Rose's voice revealed the vividness of her memory. "I was there. I saw it with my own eyes. It was cold-blooded murder."

"Was Ham arrested for it?"

"No. That's another long story. But justice caught up with him."

"What happened?" Erin asked.

A moment of silence passed before Rose answered. "I forget how much time passed — several weeks, maybe. Bull and Jasper had taken me in and done their best to protect me, but the night came when I was alone in the house. Ham had learned that I'd witnessed the killing. He showed up with a pistol to silence me. As he got out of his truck and walked toward the house, I grabbed my grandpa's double-barreled shotgun from behind the door, aimed it, and pulled the trigger."

"You killed him?" Erin stifled a gasp as the horror sank in.

"A shotgun blast to the midsection will do that to a man," Rose said. "Ham didn't die easy. But that's a story for another time."

Erin's throat had gone dry, leaving her with no words. Her father had said Rose was tough. She was just beginning to understand how tough.

After an early supper of tamales and beans, prepared by Carmen, the ranch's attractive, middle-aged Latina cook, Rose and Will retired to the front porch to watch the last rays of sunset fade above the caprock. From the dining room, Rose could hear the faint clatter of china and cutlery as Erin cleaned up after the meal. Will's daughter, she sensed, was deliberately leaving them alone so they could relax and talk.

"Your daughter is lovely, Will," Rose said,

40

settling back in her chair.

"Being her dad has been the best thing I ever did." Will popped the tabs on two cold cans of Dos Equis and passed one to Rose. "Tori, my wife, was only able to have one child. Bull never forgave her for not giving him grandsons. But I never minded. We had a perfect daughter."

Rose reached out and laid a hand on his arm. "I'm so sorry about your wife. You must miss her terribly."

"I do. Every minute of every day. But at least I've got Erin. Tori and I tried to talk her into going away to college, but she wanted to stay here and learn to run the ranch. Now I'm glad she made that choice. I don't know what I'd have done without her these past few months. And she's going to make a first-rate rancher."

He fished a half-empty cigarette pack out of his shirt pocket and held it out to her. Rose shook her head. "No thanks. I've never taken to the habit. But you have one. I won't mind."

He took his time, tapping out the cigarette and slipping the pack back into his pocket. His lighter flamed in the shadows.

As he smoked, Rose studied his profile in the fading light. Even as a boy, Will had reminded her of Bull. Now the resemblance

41

was even stronger. But Will had a tender side that Bull had lacked, or at least kept buried. Now, with his wife and his best friend both gone, he was visibly suffering.

"What are you thinking?" she asked after a few moments of silence.

He exhaled, blowing a thin shaft of smoke. "I was thinking how I used to sit out here with Jasper, and the things we talked about. He was the wisest man I've ever known, and the best."

"I know," Rose said. "I miss him, too. I hope he's off somewhere with his Sally."

"Some men only love once," Will said. "It was true of Jasper, and I think it must be true of me, as well."

"Don't count yourself out." Rose sipped her beer, which was already getting warm. "You're a good-looking man, and still young. Don't be surprised when the single women in town start coming around with chicken soup and apple pie — if they aren't doing it already."

"It's too soon." Will sounded almost angry, so Rose changed the subject.

"I'm anxious to see Beau again. How soon will he be getting here?"

"Tomorrow. But don't expect them to stay long. Beau and I . . . we didn't exactly part on good terms."

"And Sky? When do I finally get to meet Bull's other son?"

"He'll be around. I'll introduce you."

"What's he like? What can you tell me about him?"

"What can I tell you about Sky?" Will puffed on his cigarette and watched the smoke drift upward. "He inherited all of Bull's good qualities and none of the bad ones. He's quiet, modest, and a genius with horses. When Bull died, he willed Sky a hundred acres of prime land. Sky lives there, in the house he built for his family."

"I still can't believe he married Garn Prescott's daughter. I hope his wife's better looking than the Prescott men. Garn was certainly no Paul Newman."

Will laughed. "Lauren's a stunner, and smart as a whip. She does the bookkeeping for the ranch. And they've got three of the most beautiful kids you ever saw."

"So there's hope that the ugly gene's been weeded out of the Prescott line for good."

"You're terrible, Rose."

Rose grinned in the darkness. "Yes, I know. But speaking of the Prescotts, I do have one question. I'm aware that Ferg passed away before Bull did. But I've never been told how it happened. It would give me some satisfaction to know."

43

Will flipped his cigarette butt over the porch rail, onto the gravel, where it glowed for a few seconds, then faded in the dark. "I know you're hoping that Ferg got the ending he deserved. You might say he did, but not in the way you'd expect. A few years after you left for Wyoming, Ferg developed early onset Alzheimer's. He went downhill pretty fast. Garn came home, bundled his father off to a nursing home, and put the ranch up for sale. By the time Ferg died, with his mind pretty well gone, the syndicate had taken over, and Garn was using the money to buy himself a seat in Congress.

"That sounds like Garn." Rose shook her head. "And you're right about what happened to Ferg. It wasn't what I expected. Nobody deserves to go that way. Not even a greedy, lying slimeball like Ferg Prescott."

The stars were coming out. Rose leaned back in her chair to sip her beer and watch them appear, one by one, in the deepening sky. She'd meant to mention her land and the condition of her grandpa's grave. But she and Will were both talked out. It might be best to wait until after the funeral. For now, it was good to be back on Rimrock soil. The place was beginning to feel like home again.

■ ■ ■

Hunter Cardwell, manager of the syndicate-owned Prescott Ranch, glared at his son, across the dinner table. "I've noticed that that diamond ring of your grandma's is still in the box," he said. "I expected the Tyler girl to be wearing it by now."

Kyle's gaze dropped to the half-finished beef stroganoff on his plate. "I asked her. But Erin says she needs more time. Don't worry, Dad, I'll ask her again soon. She can't say no forever."

"If you know what's good for you, you won't let her," Hunter said. "Do you think I like working my ass off for wages? Do you think I want the same for my son? That girl is our one chance to get a ranch in the family. She's Will Tyler's only heir, and when he goes —"

"Will Tyler's got a brother, who works for the DEA in Washington."

"Don't you argue with me," Hunter snapped. "I've looked into it. Will Tyler arranged to buy out his brother's share a few years ago. The deal left him cash poor, with a mortgage from the bank, but Will's the sole owner now, and that daughter of his is pure gold. So help me, son, if you screw this up —"

"I won't, Dad. I promise."

"Then why aren't you with her right now? That old-timer the Tylers set so much store by croaked a couple of days ago. The girl's bound to need comforting. The least you could do is be there for her."

"Dad, I talked with Erin on the phone. She doesn't want to see me until after the funeral. That's not till Saturday."

"Damn!" Hunter's fist came down hard on the table, making the dishes and cutlery jump. "You'll never get the girl if you let her push you around like that. Be a man. Go after her. Show her you mean business. Understand?"

"Yes, Dad." Kyle's handsome face wore a sullen look.

"Yes, what?"

"Yes, I understand."

"That's better." Hunter's gaze swung toward his wife. "Vivian, these potatoes are cold. Can't you learn to serve a meal with everything hot at the same time? No, don't get up. Just learn to do it right, unless you're too stupid to learn. If that's the case, we have a problem."

Vivian Cardwell didn't reply. She'd long since learned that meeting her husband's

46

tirades with silence was the only defense available to her. Stand up to him, and she would pay the price for days on end.

She could leave him, she thought. Her mirror told her she was still a pretty woman, with fair skin, green eyes, long, auburn hair, and a nice, voluptuous figure. Some man would want her. Or she could always get a job. But that would mean leaving her home, and leaving her son at the mercy of Hunter's browbeating. Kyle was old enough to strike out on his own. But as long as there was a chance of his marrying Erin Tyler, Hunter would never let him go.

She studied her husband from her place at the foot of the table, nearest the kitchen. Hunter Cardwell was a strikingly handsome man, tall and athletically built, with chiseled features and dark hair that was turning an elegant shade of silver. When he had something to gain by it, he could be charming, especially to women.

As far as Vivian knew, her husband hadn't been unfaithful. He was demanding in bed, but sex tended to be all about him, leaving her feeling more used than loved. Sometimes, like tonight, she almost wished Hunter would have an affair. At least it might improve his disposition — or better yet, give her an excuse to walk away.

When the meal was finished, Hunter retired to his study and the endless record keeping that the syndicate owners demanded. Kyle went up to his room to spend time on his computer course in range management — or at least, that's what he said he'd be doing. Tonight, Vivian didn't care.

After the table was cleared, the kitchen tidied, and the dishwasher loaded, she wandered outside, onto the front porch of the modest, split-level frame house that had come with the manager's job. Standing at the rail, she closed her eyes and let the night breeze dry her sweat-dampened face. Night-flying insects chirped and hummed in the darkness. The jasmine vine she'd planted below the porch and had babied through two years of heat, drought, and cold had finally put out a few timid white blossoms, their fragrance almost drowned by the odors of dust and livestock.

Minutes away, by unpaved back road, lay the neighboring Rimrock Ranch. Its impressive main house, a blend of stone, glass, and timber, was as handsome and rugged as its owner. Vivian had been inside the house just once, when she and Hunter had paid their respects after the funeral of Will Tyler's wife. They'd only stayed a short time, but when

48

Will had taken her hand, the briefest gesture, she'd been struck by his quiet strength and dignity, and by the sheer masculinity of his presence.

Since that day, four months ago, she hadn't been able to stop thinking about him. *How would it feel to be cradled by those powerful arms? To be kissed by him? Loved by him?*

Fantasizing about him was wrong, she knew. Will was mourning his wife. She was married.

But as long as nothing happened, what harm could a little dreaming do? And nothing was going to happen between her and Will Tyler. Not ever.

CHAPTER THREE

"Have you met the new man?" Erin asked her father as they sat down to a breakfast of ham, fried eggs, and toast.

"Not yet. But Sky had good things to say about him. He was up at first light to help with chores — he told Sky he'd been made to understand that he'd be expected to work for his meals."

"That speaks well for him." Erin remembered telling Luke Maddox that if he wanted to eat he'd have to help with chores. He must have taken her at her word. "The question is, how well can he shoe horses?"

"I guess we'll find out. Sky had him set up in the small paddock with the spring foals. He'll be starting on the other horses after the funeral, when there are more hands available to bring the horses in."

"He's doing the foals?" Erin felt a twinge of alarm. "But foals aren't shod. Horses

50

don't need shoes until they're ready to work."

"He'll just be trimming their hooves. Sky insists the man knows what he's doing. That's good enough for me."

"Well, it isn't good enough for me," Erin said. "I want to see for myself what he's doing."

"So what is it you want to see?" Rose, looking fit and rested, walked into the dining room and took a seat at the place that had been set for her.

"Erin wants to check out the new farrier," Will said. "If she can wait till you've had your breakfast, we can go together. All right, Erin?"

"Sure." Erin filled Rose's coffee cup, then refilled her own.

"Erin's our number two horse expert on the ranch," Will said. "Sky's been training her since she was no higher than a horse's belly. He claims she's got a gift. Since she ruled out college to become a horse trainer, all I can say is I hope he's right."

"Erin strikes me as a young lady who knows what she wants and how to get it. I'm sure she'll do fine." Rose added milk to her coffee, then turned to Erin. "I've done a little horse training myself. Maybe I can learn some things from you."

51

"Or we can learn from each other," Erin said. "Wait till I show you my stallion, Tesoro. He's spectacular."

"I'm looking forward to seeing him." Rose downed her coffee and a triangle of buttered toast. "I'm good. Let's go."

The horse paddocks and adjoining pens were a hundred yards from the house, convenient to hay, water, and tack. The brood mares, foals, and stallions were kept here, as well as horses for the family and the regular mounts for the ranch hands. Other horses were corralled at the line camps out on the range, or allowed to graze loose until needed at roundup time.

"What time will Beau be here?" Rose asked as they crossed the ranch yard. "I was fond of him as a boy. I'm looking forward to meeting the man he's become."

"He'll be here with his wife and daughter this afternoon," Will said. "I'm guessing they won't stay much past the funeral tomorrow. He'll be glad to see you, but he's pretty much washed his hands of this ranch — and me."

"I'm right sorry to hear that," Rose said. "It would break Bull's heart to know how things turned out between his two sons."

Will shook his head. "Bull saw it coming. Something tells me he wouldn't even be surprised."

"I'd like to visit Bull's grave," Rose said. "We didn't always see eye to eye, but we parted friends. He was one of a kind."

"He was. Even his enemies would agree to that."

Erin lent half an ear to their conversation, but as they passed the windmill and rounded the barn her attention was fixed on the smallest of three metal-sided pens, where Luke Maddox was working. Walking ahead of Will and Rose, she slowed her steps as she neared the enclosure.

A dozen or so young foals, still ganglylegged, were milling together on the far side of the pen. With his back toward Erin, Luke was bent against the side of a chestnut foal that was tethered to the fence with a soft nylon lariat. One hand gripped the foal's tail, holding it with a twist. When Erin moved farther around the fence, she could see how one small front hoof rested on his knee. He was using a metal rasp to gently trim and smooth the hoof's edge.

By now, Will and Rose had caught up with Erin. Glancing up, Luke gave them a brief nod, then finished the hoof before releasing the foal to scamper back with the others.

Only then did he straighten and turn, taking off the baseball cap he wore and raking back his dark, wavy hair. It was still early, but the day was already hot. The light chambray shirt he wore clung damply to his muscular body. A heavy leather apron, split up the center, circled his waist and covered his legs almost to the ankle. A wooden toolbox, open at the top, sat near his feet.

"Mr. Tyler." He gave Will a nod, ignoring Erin. "Excuse me if I don't shake hands."

"That's fine," Will said. "I'm glad to see you're already working, but I'm not sure I understand what you're doing with these foals. They're not old enough for shoes."

"Let me explain," Luke said. "Or better yet, let me show you."

He walked to the clustered foals and eased one of them away from the others, coaxing it gently as he slipped a lead around its neck. "Now, take a look at his legs. Foals have short necks and long legs, so they get in the habit of spreading their legs to graze, even when they no longer need to. If that isn't corrected, those spread legs will cause problems as they grow. Now watch what we can do about that — it'll only take a few minutes."

Facing toward the rear, with a left-handed grip on the tail, he positioned himself on the foal's right side, reached down, lifted a front leg and placed the hoof on his knee.

54

"Because of the spread legs, the hooves tend to wear away on the inside edge. I'm going to rasp away the outside edge of the hoof so that it will be level. Like this."

With an unbelievably delicate touch, he cleaned the hoof, then used the rough side of the rasp to level off the outside edge. Then, using the finer side of the rasp, he smoothed the surface. The foal showed no sign of pain or distress.

"That's all there is to it. Now we do the other hooves." He moved toward the foal's hindquarters. "These little fellows are so calm, they're easy to handle."

"That's because we imprint them," Erin said. "We handle them as soon as they're born, so they get used to us."

"Good idea." He didn't look up. It took him only a few more minutes to finish all four hooves with a few swipes of the rasp. "There," he said, stepping back. "Take a look."

"I'll be damned!" Will said. "The legs are straight up and down, not spraddled!"

"Keep them that way, and you'll have a stronger animal. You can prevent all kinds of problems just by making sure a horse is standing level on its feet."

"I'll be damned," Will said again.

"I should be done with the foals and

55

yearlings by the end of the day." Wasting no time, Luke chose another foal and led it to the fence. "I know you'll be busy with the funeral tomorrow, but Sky said he'd see that I had plenty of work."

"Sounds like everything's under control," Will said. "Come on, Erin. Let's show Rose your stallion."

They continued on past the barn to the smaller stud barn. The Rimrock had just three stallions. Two of them were retired cutting horses, with the qualities of strength, stamina, and cow sense needed for working a herd. Over the years, they'd passed these qualities on to their offspring, to produce many fine horses for the ranch.

Erin's horse, a magnificent, high-strung palomino, nickered and looked over the stall gate as he heard her voice. She'd been present at his birth, and with him through the seven years of his life. Tesoro, whose name meant "treasure," was a show stopper, commanding handsome stud fees, especially after a few of his foals, out of chestnut mares, were born with shining golden coats like their sire's.

Sky had helped her break and train him, but there was a wild spirit about the stallion. Erin had no trouble handling and riding him, but the men, except for Sky, had

56

learned to leave him alone.

"He's beautiful." Rose raised a cautious hand and stroked the satiny neck. A quiver passed through the stallion's body, but he tolerated her touch.

"He was promised to me before he was born," Erin said. "When we saw that golden coat, we knew we'd want to breed him. My mother was dead set against my having a stallion. She wanted me to choose another foal. But Tesoro was already mine. I wouldn't budge, and my dad supported me."

She glanced at Will. He looked away, as if stung by the memory.

"Rose, I need to go into town and get a few things for the funeral," he said. "You're welcome to come with me. You might enjoy seeing how Blanco Springs has changed in thirty years. We can even get a beer at the Blue Coyote."

"That old bar is still there? I can't believe it!"

"It's passed through a number of hands since you were last here. The man who owns it now is Abner Sweeney, who used to be sheriff. That's a story in itself."

"I can't wait to hear it. Of course I'll come," Rose said. "How about you, Erin?"

"No thanks." Erin excused herself. "I've

57

got plenty to do around here."

Like keep an eye on the hired help?

Erin waited until her father and Rose walked back to the house. Then she turned and headed back around the barn to the pen where Luke Maddox was working with the foals. It wasn't the man she was interested in, she told herself. It was what he was doing and what she could learn from watching him. She wanted to become an all-around horse expert. And this man could be just the one to further her education.

Luke glanced up to see Will Tyler's daughter perched on the metal bars of the fence. She hadn't spoken or made a sound. But her blue eyes seemed to be watching his every move. What was her name? Erin, he remembered now. She was a pretty thing, but he met plenty of pretty things in his trade — ranchers' daughters and even wives, who let him know, sometimes none too subtly, that he might be welcome to do more than shoe horses. He never took them up on their offers. That would be bad for business. If he needed a woman, he'd have no trouble picking up one who knew the score and didn't pull strings.

This little princess, in her tight-ass jeans and cowgirl boots, was strictly off limits.

But she didn't appear to be flirting with him. She seemed more interested in what he was doing.

Luke released the foal he'd finished trimming. When he straightened to ease his back, his gaze met hers.

"Anything I can do for you, miss?" he asked.

"No. I just want to watch you and maybe learn a few things. Is that all right?"

"You're the boss."

"Will it bother you if I ask a few questions?"

"Nope. Ask away." He surveyed the foals a moment, picking out the ones he had yet to work on, and led another to the fence.

"The leg spreading thing. Do you find it in all the foals?"

"Pretty much." He soothed the foal, then picked up a dainty front hoof, braced it, and reached for the cleaning knife.

"What about other problems? Can you fix those as well?"

"You mean like pigeon toes or knock knees?" Luke finished cleaning the hoof and reached for the rasp with his free hand. "Again, most small problems can be kept from turning into big ones with the right trimming. And once isn't enough. It needs to be done every few months. Of course, this is for a healthy foal. If the issue's more serious — say, a leg's bent or twisted — you call in a vet as soon as the foal's born."

Luke shifted to the foal's opposite side. In his work, he'd had hundreds of similar conversations with ranchers and horse trainers. But he'd never had a sweet young thing like Erin ask him these kinds of questions, let alone pay attention to the answers.

Maybe there was a brain behind that pretty face. Or maybe she was just trying to impress him. He was almost thirty, and this little beauty didn't look old enough to order a legal drink. All the more reason to keep things strictly business between them.

He remembered grabbing her last night when she'd almost stepped on that damn fool snake. She'd been in his arms for mere seconds, but the womanly curves of breast and hip against his body had triggered a reaction — one he was better off forgetting.

So why was he thinking about it now?

Damn!

"Have you seen my stallion, Tesoro?" she asked him.

"The palomino? Yes, I looked him over this morning when your foreman showed him to me. He's a beautiful animal — and a lot of horse for a woman."

"I raised him." A note of defiance crept

into her voice. "I broke and trained him, too. No one rides him but me."

Luke kept on working, giving her time to say more.

"I assume you'll be shoeing him," she said. "I was just wondering if you noticed any problems, anything you might correct."

"Not really. Everything seems to line up fine. But before I start on him, I do have a question. I notice he's shod now. Where do you ride him?"

"Wherever I want to. Does it matter?"

"It does. For a stud horse, it's safer for the mares if his front feet don't have shoes. He's less likely to hurt them that way. That's fine if you're riding him in the pastures. But if you're riding him over rough ground, he'll need shoes to protect his feet."

"I never considered that," Erin said. "I'd like to give it some thought before I let you know."

"Fine. There's plenty of time." He glanced up as a dusty-looking SUV pulled into the yard. "Looks like you've got company," he said.

Erin followed the direction of his gaze. "Oh, drat!" she muttered.

Luke expected her to jump off the fence and hurry to meet the newcomer. But she stayed put, as if sending some silent mes-

61

sage, while the big vehicle stopped briefly at the house, then swung around the barn and parked a stone's toss away. The driver's side door opened. The man who climbed out and came around the vehicle was young, tall, nice looking, and neatly dressed in a fresh button-down shirt and jeans. But the expression on his face was sour with disapproval.

"What are you doing out here, Erin?" he demanded. "I thought you'd be in the house."

"And what are *you* doing here, Kyle?" she shot back. "I told you I'd see you after the funeral."

"I know. But I was worried. You must be grieving for that old man. I want to be here for you."

"I *am* grieving. But I'm dealing with it in my own way, and I don't need anybody to help me be sad. Anyway, you scarcely knew him."

"I did so know him. He was always here when I came for you."

"So what was his name?" she challenged him.

"Jasper. See?"

"What was his *last* name?"

He floundered a moment and came up blank.

She gave him a knowing look. "You can go, Kyle. I'll see you when the funeral's done."

He glanced around, as if looking for some excuse to stall. That was when his gaze fell on Luke. "You haven't introduced me to the new hired help," he said.

"I didn't know you expected me to," Erin said. "Luke, this is my friend Kyle Cardwell, whose father manages the syndicate ranch east of here. Kyle, this is Mr. Maddox, the farrier who's going to be working on our horses."

Kyle's eyes narrowed as he looked down at Luke, who was bent over the foal he was trimming. "A farrier, huh? My father might have some work you can do. I'll ask him."

Luke released the foal and straightened to his full height, towering over the young man by three inches and outweighing him by a good thirty or forty pounds. "Right now I'm working full time for the Tylers," he said. "If your father needs me, have him check back later on, in case I have an opening."

"Sure." Kyle turned back to Erin. "Walk me to the car," he said, taking her arm. She seemed to stiffen slightly, but she didn't resist as he escorted her around to the far side of the vehicle. Luke could no longer see them, but without blocking his ears, there was no way to avoid hearing their voices.

"I don't like the idea of your being alone with that man, Erin," Kyle said. "It might not be safe."

"Oh, for heaven's sake, Kyle, I was watching him work and trying to learn from what he was doing. That's all."

"Maybe so. But you're too trusting. I can just imagine what was on that man's mind, with you sitting there on the fence and nobody else around. I don't want you spending time with his kind."

"His kind?" Luke could hear the mounting fury in her voice. "What kind is that?"

"You know. Lower class. Lax morals. You're going to be my wife someday. It's in your best interest, and mine, for me to keep you safe from men like him." There was a pause. "Now come on. Get in the vehicle, and I'll drive you back to the house. We can spend some time and talk."

"No." Erin's voice was flat with tightly controlled anger. "You don't own me, Kyle. And you can't give me orders. Now get in the car and leave before I do something we'll both regret."

"Fine. But only if you kiss me first."

"Just go. I'm not in the mood for —"

Luke heard sounds of muffled protest,

64

then silence. Maybe the lovebirds had settled their differences. In any case, unless he heard screams, whatever was happening on the other side of that SUV was none of his business.

A moment later, he heard a metallic *thump,* like something being shoved against a car door. "What's gotten into you, Kyle? Don't you ever try that again!" Erin's voice crackled with rage. "Now get out of here!"

"All right, for now," Kyle muttered. "But you're mine, Erin. Don't forget that. If any other man lays a hand on you —"

"Damn it, just go!"

A car door opened and slammed shut. An instant later, the SUV roared away. Erin stood in its wake, a cloud of powdery dust settling around her. Her hat was on the ground. Her shirt was pulled partway open to reveal a glimpse of creamy breast and lace-edged white bra. Luke tore his gaze away, aware that he mustn't be caught feasting his eyes on the boss's daughter.

Facing away from him, she buttoned her shirt and tucked it in at the waist before she picked up her hat and turned back toward him. "I'm sorry you had to hear that," she said.

"Hear what?" Luke released the foal he'd been trimming.

"Thank you for your discretion," she said.

Straightening, he faced her. "I don't know if I'd call it that. But in working as many ranches as I've done, there's not much I haven't seen or heard. I've learned to keep my eyes, my ears, and my mouth firmly shut."

"That sounds like a good idea." She walked back to the fence and put a boot on the lower rail to climb up, but the warning look in his eyes stopped her.

"What is it?" she asked.

"Another good idea," he said. "I don't need your jealous boyfriend making trouble for either of us. You're welcome to watch me work, but when you do, you'd better have somebody with you — your dad, the foreman, anybody, so there won't be any questions to ask. Understand?"

Her blue eyes widened. Her booted foot slipped off the rail and struck the ground in a puff of dust. "I can't believe what I just heard!" she said. "You're as bad as Kyle is. What do you think I'm going to do, seduce you and cause you to lose your job? Do you think you're that irresistible, or that I'm that stupid?"

"I know you're not stupid, Erin," he said. "I've just learned it's better to be safe than sorry. Come back when you don't have to

66

come alone."

"Good grief, this is the twenty-first century!" With a huff of indignation, Erin wheeled and stalked back toward the house.

Luke stood watching her walk away. Despite his best intentions, he couldn't help admiring the curve of her waist and the sway of her sweet little rump. Too bad. He'd enjoyed her company. But he could spot trouble coming a mile away, and Erin Tyler was trouble.

With a half-muttered oath, he picked up the soft nylon lariat, looped another foal, and started on its hooves.

Kyle drove the back road with talk radio on full blast and the SUV's big tires kicking up a plume of dust. His stomach roiled with humiliation as he relived the scene with Erin.

Why had he listened to his father? *Don't let her push you around,* Hunter had said. *Be a man. Go after her. Show her you mean business.*

Today, Kyle had done his best to take his father's advice. He'd tried being manly and masterful, but Erin hadn't cooperated. When he'd kissed her and made a grab for her breast — something he'd never done before — she'd shoved him so hard that

67

he'd crashed against the side of the SUV and almost gone down.

Be a man. Hellfire, he'd never felt less manly in his life.

What was wrong with Erin? They'd been dating more than a year. She'd never wanted to move their physical relationship beyond a little front-seat necking, but Kyle had respected that. Erin was a classy girl — a girl who would inherit a ranch one day. Given what was at stake, he could afford to bide his time and find other ways to satisfy his needs.

Still, he'd taken it for granted that she loved him. He'd even proposed, and she hadn't exactly said no. Was she one of those frigid girls who didn't want to be touched? Or had today's reaction had something to do with that new hired man — that farrier?

A dozen yards ahead, a jackrabbit streaked through the dry brush and into the road. Kyle hit the gas, wanting to slake his anger by crushing the animal under his wheels. But the rabbit bounded out of the way, escaping the SUV's oversized tires by a whisker's breadth.

Still in a black mood, he parked in front of the house and stormed inside. His mother was arranging store-bought flowers in a vase on the sideboard. She seemed to spend most of her time fussing, cleaning, and arranging, as if making things look pretty could cover up the ugliness that seemed to hang like a dusty curtain over everything in their boxy, tract-style house, including the family. The only thing that kept him here was the expectation of marrying Erin and moving into that big, fancy home on the Rimrock.

"Back so soon, Kyle?" she asked. "I thought you were going to spend time with Erin."

"Erin was busy."

"Are you going to the funeral tomorrow? I'm sure she'll expect you there."

"Maybe. It's not like I knew the old goat."

"Kyle! You mustn't talk that way about someone who's died." She paused, brightening. "I'll tell you what. Why don't I go to the funeral with you? It would be the neighborly thing to do, paying our respects and all."

Kyle turned away and headed up the stairs, pretending he hadn't heard. Showing up at the funeral with his mother wouldn't just be embarrassing. It would be like having a ball and chain clamped around his ankle, having to escort her around, go where she wanted to go, and leave when she wanted to leave. Maybe he should stay away just to make Erin wonder if he was still mad at her. That might make her think twice about shoving him away the next time.

He'd reached the top of the stairs when she spoke again. "Kyle."

This time her voice was too demanding to ignore. He stopped and turned around.

"Let me know about the funeral," she said. "By the way, how is that computer course coming along?"

"Fine. And I'll let you know about the funeral." He walked into his bedroom, closed the door, and locked it behind him.

If his mother ever saw what he was really viewing on the old desktop computer that was all he could afford, she'd probably have a heart attack. But that wasn't his problem. He was an adult, and what he watched and did for pleasure was his own business.

With a quiver of anticipation, Kyle pulled out the chair, sat down at the desk, and switched on his computer.

CHAPTER FOUR

It was midafternoon on Friday when a white Toyota Camry with rental plates swung into the yard and pulled up below the porch. Rose had been waiting, watching through the front window. She'd kept in contact with Will over the years, but she and Beau had long since lost touch. What would he be like now — the sweet but fiercely independent young boy she remembered so well?

As the Camry came to a stop, she burst through the front door, crossed the porch, and raced down the steps. The sound of light, eager footsteps told her that Erin was close behind her. But Will had remained inside the house.

The driver's side door opened. The man who stepped out, dressed in jeans and sneakers, was tall, with a lean runner's build, light brown hair, and finely drawn features. Only when he smiled did Rose catch a glimpse of the young boy she remembered.

"Rose! I can't believe it." He opened his arms and twirled her off her feet as if she were a little girl, then set her down. "I was hoping you'd be here."

"There was no way I wouldn't have come," Rose said. "We've got a lot of catching up to do."

"And Erin!" He caught her as she flung herself into his arms, then eased her away so he could look at her. "My stars, girl, where did the time go? You're a grown woman!"

"I've missed you," Erin said. "All of you."

A pretty, dark-haired woman, visibly pregnant, was helping a child out of the backseat. "Rose, this is my wife, Natalie, and our daughter, April," Beau said. "Natalie, I've told you about the lady who saved my life, and Will's, when we got kidnapped by the drug cartel. Here she is, in person."

"It's a pleasure to meet you, Rose." Natalie gave Rose her hand. "I've heard so much about you. I wish we had more time to get acquainted, but our flight is leaving early Sunday morning."

"Why so soon?" Rose asked, although she suspected the reason. It was as she'd been made to understand — Beau and Will were barely on speaking terms.

72

"We've both got work commitments," Beau said. "The DEA could only spare me for a couple of days, and Natalie has her veterinary practice."

"But you'll miss the burial," Erin said. "We'll be taking Jasper's body to his old home in the Hill Country. If we leave Saturday, after the funeral, it'll be dark when we get there, so we'll need to take him the next morning — that'll be Sunday."

"I wish I'd known that," Beau said. "But it's too late to change our plans now. We've already booked our flight."

"Well then," Rose said, putting on a cheerful smile. "We'll just have to make the most of the time we have, won't we?"

Will had come out on the porch. He waited there, unsmiling, as Beau and his family climbed the steps, followed by Rose and by Erin with one of the suitcases. Tension, as heavy as water, seemed to thicken the air as the two brothers stood face to face. Then Will held out his hand and spoke.

"We've come together to mourn an old friend. Let's not dishonor his memory with our differences."

"Agreed." Beau accepted the handshake.

"I figured you'd be hungry," Will said. "We'll be eating in an hour. That'll give you time to rest and freshen up. Erin, will you show our guests to their rooms?"

Our guests? Will's words struck Rose as odd. How could Beau be called a guest when he'd grown up in this house?

Rose was tired of second-guessing. When Beau and his family had gone to their rooms, and Erin hadn't returned, she walked into the den, where Will was pouring himself a shot of Jack Daniel's. "Can I get you a glass, Rose? It's good stuff. Takes the edge off whatever's troubling you."

She shook her head. "I've found it doesn't help much," she said, "especially since what's troubling me is you."

He emptied the shot glass and poured another, his silence inviting her to explain.

"The most vivid memory I have of you and Beau," she said, "is the two of you running away from those drug dealers, to your dad. I see your hand, hanging on to your little brother's, so tightly, as if nothing in the world could make you let go."

"That was a long time ago," Will said.

"Erin told me that you'd bought out Beau's share of the ranch," Rose said. "But what happened between the two of you, Will? I need to understand."

Will exhaled. "I guess I owe you that much. But you won't be surprised." He took another sip of whiskey. "Beau never really wanted to take responsibility for his share of the ranch. Oh, he'd come home on and off. He'd make a show of trying to work the ranch with me. But being number two never set well with him. He likes that fancy government job, and the DC lifestyle. I think his wife likes it, too, especially things like having their little girl in that snooty private school."

Will put the glass down on the bar and walked to the window, gazing out at a dust devil whirling across the yard. "Whole damned ranch is blowing away," he muttered.

"So how long ago did Beau leave?" Rose asked.

"Three years. We had a blowup that ended everything. He announced that he had an offer to take his old job back at a higher level and salary. I told him it wasn't fair for him to own half the ranch while I did all the work to run it. He pretty much told me that I could take the ranch and go to hell. He wanted nothing more to do with it, or me.

"As things got even nastier, it became clear that the only way to settle things was for me to get a loan and buy out his share. I didn't want to do it, Rose. I knew it would be a hardship, and that it would put the ranch at risk. But Beau wouldn't back down. When he signed over the deed and I handed him that big check, I told him I wouldn't care if I never saw him again. And I didn't see him — until today."

"I take it you called him about Jasper."

Will nodded. "It was hard. I almost asked Erin to do it. But I figured that would be the coward's way out. And I knew he loved Jasper. We all did."

"At least the ranch is all yours," Rose said.

"Only if I can hang on to it. When I took out that mortgage, the ranch was in good shape. We'd had plenty of rain, plenty of graze, and beef prices were up. Even then it wasn't easy to come up with the payments on the loan. But now . . ." Will's shoulders sagged. "We haven't had a decent rain in a year. The whole damn county is blowing away. And with everybody selling off their cattle early, the prices are down."

Will stared out the window for the space of a long breath. "The way things are going, I won't have enough cash to pay the bank this fall."

"Beau's got money. Can't he help you out?" Rose asked.

Will shook his head. "The money he got for the ranch is tied up in his house and in the clinic he built for his wife's practice.

76

Even if I thought he might help, I'd rather cut off my arm than ask him. That would mean reneging on the deal we made, something I've never done in my life."

"What about Erin? Does she know?"

"Not yet," Will said. "I'm still waiting for the right time to tell her. She needs to be prepared, but it'll break her heart. Chances are, unless some miracle happens, we're going to lose the Rimrock."

Jasper had never been a churchgoing man. But with a crowd expected and no way to hold a funeral outdoors in the dust and heat, the local community church was the only option.

Erin, in the blue dress she'd bought for her high school graduation, sat in the front pew between Will and Beau. She could sense the cold resentment flowing between the brothers, making her feel like some sort of safety barricade, placed there to protect them from sniping at each other.

Her mother's funeral was painfully fresh in her mind, as it would surely be in Will's. Erin remembered the service in the same church, the spring bluebonnets on her mother's casket. She remembered sitting exactly where she was sitting now, clasping her father's hand until her knuckles ached.

77

Beau and his family had been in Europe at the time, so they hadn't been here. In Will's book, Beau's absence had been just one more strike against his brother.

Beau's wife and daughter filled out the pew on his right. April, a sweet, sunny six-year-old, looked like a miniature of her dark-haired mother. She sat with her hands folded in her lap like the little lady she was. Rose occupied the spot on Will's left, with Sky, his wife Lauren, and their three lively youngsters taking up the pew behind them.

The rest of the seats were filled with friends, neighbors, and cowhands who had worked with Jasper. Glancing back, Erin caught sight of Kyle, sitting with his mother. She forced herself to put him out of her mind. Today wasn't about him or their relationship. Today was about honoring the end of a life.

Jasper's casket, a plain pine box adorned with an arrangement of wildflowers, golden chamisa, and sage, spoke of the man who lay inside — honest, brave, wise, funny, and kind to the bone. The pallbearers — Will, Beau, Sky, and three long-time ranch hands — had carried the casket into the church. Now it sat on its stand in front of Erin, so close that she could have reached out and touched it. Jasper had always been there for her, to offer support and unconditional love. It was still sinking in that the man who'd been a vital part of her whole life was gone.

Now, with so many decisions to make and challenges to face, she needed his salty wisdom. What would he say to her about Kyle if he were here? What would he advise her about getting married? But she would never know the answer to those questions. She would never hear Jasper's voice again.

The service was mercifully short. When it was over, Rose walked with Will and Erin to the car for the drive back to the Rimrock. There, a feast of donated casseroles, salads, breads, and desserts would be laid out on the buffet table in the great room for folks who'd come to pay their respects to Jasper's ranch family.

As she waited for Will to climb into the car, she watched people coming out of the church to their vehicles. Not far away, Sky Fletcher was loading his attractive family into their SUV. Rose had yet to be introduced to Sky, but she'd recognized him on sight. Half Comanche and half Bull Tyler, with sharp cheekbones and riveting blue eyes, the foreman of the Rimrock was unmistakable. His wife was, as Will had described her, a stunning woman. Tall and willowy, with cinnamon hair and a model's elegant carriage, she was busy strapping her three young children into the backseat of the vehicle. It was hard to believe she was Garn Prescott's daughter. Maybe they would get a chance to talk at the house.

As Will drove out of the parking lot and swung the car onto the main road out of town, Rose settled back against the seat.

Tomorrow she would make the long, sad drive with Will, Erin, and Sky to the church cemetery in the Hill Country. By the time they arrived, with the casket lovingly cushioned in the bed of Will's truck, the sexton would have dug the grave in the spot Jasper had reserved for himself when he'd buried his sweetheart so many years ago. By the time they got back to the Rimrock, it would be dark.

And then what? Rose asked herself. She hadn't booked a return flight to Wyoming because she hadn't known how long she would be staying here. She still didn't know. But something told her it might be a while. She still had the issue of her neglected property to resolve. But there was more.

Sitting with her in the cab of the truck were two people she'd come to care about — a troubled man and a young woman on the cusp of adult life. Both of them were

80

grieving. Both of them were facing loss. Maybe she needed to be here for them, to lend her support and pass on what little wisdom she'd gained over the years.

Maybe this was where Jasper, her oldest and dearest friend, would have wanted her to be.

Erin had offered to help Carmen with the buffet. As the guests streamed into the great room, she busied herself filling the glass pitchers with iced sweet tea, making sure the casseroles and salads had serving utensils, and checking the supply of paper plates, cups, and napkins.

Kyle and his mother had arrived together. There was no sign of Kyle's father. Not that Erin cared, since she'd never liked the man. Hunter Cardwell struck her as bossy and self-important, and he treated his poor wife as if he owned her.

If she married Kyle, the Cardwells would be her in-laws, she reminded herself. But right now she had other things on her mind. Ignoring Kyle's attempt to catch her eye, she hurried back to the kitchen.

After the first rush of guests, the traffic around the buffet table had slowed. For now, everything appeared to be under control. After telling Carmen she'd return to help clean up, Erin wandered back into the great room.

She could see Will standing next to the tall river-stone fireplace, greeting the guests who came by. Kyle and his mother were talking to him now. Vivian Cardwell was clasping Will's big hand between her palms. Her eyes gazed up at him almost tearfully as she offered her condolences. Kyle was shifting restlessly, looking around the room, probably for her, Erin thought. But after his caveman behavior, she wasn't ready to be with him again — not until she was sure he'd learned his lesson.

"Need a break?" The voice at her shoulder was Beau's.

Erin had been hoping to talk with her uncle while he was here. Grateful for the chance, she gave him a conspiratorial nod. "Out the back," she said.

Like two schoolchildren playing hooky, they cut through the kitchen, slipped out the back door, and headed across the graveled yard to the horse pastures. Beau had always been Erin's favorite relative. She was happy just to be with him. But she also had some serious issues to bring up.

The sun was blazing hot. Erin tugged away the ribbon that tied back her hair, letting the light breeze cool the sweat-dampened roots. Beau had taken off his jacket and slung it over his arm.

"Congratulations on the new little one," she said. "Boy or girl?"

"It's a boy. We just found out. But this trip has worn Natalie out. I talked her into lying down with April for a bit. With luck they'll both get in a nice nap." His eyes followed the flight of a circling hawk. "I never got a chance to tell you how sorry I was about your mother. Tori and I were best friends growing up. And then I couldn't even make it to her funeral."

"It all happened so fast," Erin said. "I understood why you couldn't come, but I can't say that Dad did."

"That's just one more thing he'll hold against me. But I'm worried about Will, Erin. He doesn't look good."

"I'm worried about him, too," Erin said. "Losing Mom almost killed him. And now Jasper. He's reeling under the weight of it all. To make matters worse, he blames himself for Jasper's death."

"That doesn't make sense. The old man was ninety-three. He probably had a stroke or heart attack and ran that ATV into a wash. At least that's what I heard. You could say that he shouldn't have been out there alone in the first place, but nobody ever told

83

Jasper what he couldn't do."

"Maybe so. But Dad's beating himself up because he didn't check on Jasper the night before and send out a search party right away." Erin brushed a lock of windblown hair out of her eyes. "The sheriff took a quick look and ruled Jasper's death an accident. But I'm not satisfied with that. What if somebody killed him, Beau?"

"Crazier things have happened on this ranch."

"After the burial's done, I plan to do some investigating on my own. I owe it to Dad — and to Jasper — to find out what really happened."

"If I were going to be here longer, I'd help you," Beau said. "As it is, feel free to call me about what you find out. At least I might be able to give you some suggestions."

"Thanks, I was hoping you'd say that."

They were passing the windmill when the sharp ring of metal on metal reached their ears. Beau gave Erin a questioning look.

"That's the farrier Dad hired. He claims the work will pay for itself in time saved by the cowboys and in the condition of the horses. I argued against the expense, and I still have my doubts. But at least the man — Maddox is his name — seems to know what he's doing. Come on, I'll introduce you."

The largest pen was covered at one end by an open shed. In its shade, Luke Maddox was shoeing a brown and white gelding with Appaloosa markings. More horses drowsed nearby as Luke, with his back to the fence, shaped a shoe on the anvil he'd set up. Even in the shade, the heat was oppressive. Luke had tossed aside his shirt. Perspiration gleamed like bronze on his muscular torso. As he raised his hammer, a picture from her school days flashed through Erin's memory — the Roman god Vulcan standing over his forge, virile and powerful. *Vulcan in blue jeans* she titled the image in her mind. Luke would probably laugh at her if he knew what she was thinking.

What would it be like, hearing him laugh?

Luke's attention had been focused on the horseshoe he was shaping. As Erin and Beau came to the fence, he glanced up. A questioning look flashed in his eyes. He straightened, lowering the hammer to his side. *What the hell are you doing here?* his expression seemed to say.

"Luke, I'd like you to meet my uncle, Beau Tyler," Erin said, making the introductions. "Beau, I've already told you about Luke Maddox."

85

Beau extended a hand over the fence. Luke held up a work-stained hand and shook his head. "You won't want to shake hands with me, Mr. Tyler. Not unless you want to smell like horse. I never knew Will had a brother."

"I live in DC. I only came for the funeral," Beau said.

"DC? You're a government man?"

"That's right. DEA." Beau's gaze shifted to the horseshoe on the anvil. "I've never seen a farrier work. You don't use a forge?"

Luke shook his head. "Cold shoeing's a lot more common these days. These steel shoes can be bought to size and hammered into the exact shape the horse needs. I have a forge, but I only use it for custom work. On a scorcher like today, that suits me fine." He wiped his brow with the back of his hand. "You're welcome to watch. I don't mind questions as long as I can talk and work at the same time."

"There's plenty of food in the house," Erin said. "Could we bring you a plate?"

"Thanks, but I'll be fine." He inspected the shoe. Then he moved to the horse's side, lifted one front foot and braced it against the leather apron. Positioning the shoe, he hammered two small nails into the outer rim of the hoof, checked again, then hammered two more. The horse stood calmly, in complete trust of this powerful, gentle man.

"I could watch you all day," Beau said. "But I'd better get back and make sure my wife isn't looking for me. Nice to meet you, Maddox."

Luke was snubbing off the nail points where they came up through the hoof. He looked up with a murmured acknowledgment as Beau and Erin turned away.

"Not exactly a warm, fuzzy sort, is he?" Beau said when they were out of Luke's hearing. "How much do you know about the man? Where'd he come from?"

"I have no idea," Erin said. "Dad found him on another ranch and hired him to come here. The only thing I've heard him talk about is work." *Except for when he told me not to come around him without a blasted chaperone.*

"As Jasper would say, the man plays his cards close to his vest."

"Yes, that's what Jasper would say." Erin fought back her welling emotion. "Oh, Beau, we're going to miss him so much. The ranch won't be the same without him."

"I know," Beau said. "And looking around at the drought, I can tell this is a tough time for the Rimrock. I never meant to put Will in such a bind. I thought we were making a fair deal when I asked him to buy me out."

"We'd have been all right if the weather and the market hadn't changed."

Beau sighed. "Will won't even talk to me about the ranch troubles. I feel bad for the bind I've put him in. I'd even be willing to help out with some cash if he'd ask me."

"He won't ask," Erin said. "He's got the Bull Tyler pride."

They were nearing the house. Beau stopped short of the back door. "There's one person you haven't told me about," he said.

"Who's that?" Erin asked.

"It's you. I see you looking after everyone and everything around here. But who's looking after Erin Tyler?"

"I'm nineteen. I don't need looking after."

"Not even by yourself? You're pretty and smart and have your whole life ahead of you. You could be having fun, maybe going to college or seeing the world."

"I could. But how could I leave my dad alone to manage the ranch, especially now? This is where I need to be — where I want to be. It's my home."

"But what about your personal life? Surely you'll want to get married and have a family."

She gave him a frown. "I do have a boyfriend. He's even proposed."

"Did you say yes?" Beau asked.

"I said it was too soon."

"Do you love him, Erin?"

The question shook her. "I'm not even sure I know what love is."

"Well, make sure you do before you say yes."

"I'm not a fool," Erin said.

"No, but you're young and you have a lot to learn. Don't be in a hurry. Call me if you want to talk."

Erin didn't answer. They had reached the back door. Through the screen, she could see people in the kitchen, putting paper plates in the trash. She'd been glad for the chance to talk with Beau. But she couldn't help feeling a vague sense of disloyalty to her father. Beau had invited her to call him. But it wasn't going to happen. Not if it might distress Will.

As she helped herself to leftovers on the buffet table, she looked around for Kyle and his mother. They were nowhere to be seen. A glance out the front window confirmed that their car was gone.

Kyle was probably sore at her for avoiding him after the funeral. Never mind. She'd make it up to him later, after they'd both had some time to cool down.

Do you love him, Erin?

Beau's question lingered in her mind. She'd replied that she didn't even know what love was. But that wasn't quite true. Love was what she'd observed between her mother and father, between Sky and Lauren, between Beau and Natalie — and what she'd heard in Jasper's voice when he'd spoken of his beloved Sally. She had second-hand knowledge of what love was. But as far as she could tell, she'd never experienced it, not even when Kyle was kissing her.

She wanted a husband and family in the future. But what if something was missing in her? What would she do if love never happened?

CHAPTER FIVE

By the time Luke had shod his sixteenth horse for the day and turned it out to graze, the sun was sinking behind the escarpment. Even at day's end, its searing fire blazed like a brand against the pitiless blue sky. Heat waves shimmered over the gravel in the ranch yard. Blown by a stray breeze, a dust devil swirled across the pasture and vanished behind a clump of mesquite.

Dripping with sweat and aching in every muscle, Luke stowed the anvil and his tools in the trailer he'd parked alongside the barn. That done, he picked up an empty bucket, filled it with cold water from the pump, and tipped it over his head. The cold water flowed through his hair, trickled over his face, and streamed down his chest and back. He shuddered as the icy cascade gave his senses a welcome shock. The shed's corrugated metal roof had lent some shade, but working in the space below had been

91

like standing under a broiler.

Recovering, he sluiced the water off his chest and arms, slicked back his hair, and reached for the chambray work shirt he'd tossed over a fence rail. By the time he made it to the bunkhouse kitchen, his body would be dry enough to slip the shirt on.

Shadows lengthened as he crossed the yard. The warm evening breeze carried the aromas of simmering ham and beans and fresh biscuits. Luke hadn't eaten since breakfast and his empty belly rumbled with a working man's hunger. He had no complaints about the meals here. The food was nothing fancy, but it was good, and there was plenty of it.

Other men would be coming in, too. The cowhands who shared the bunkhouse seemed friendly enough, but Luke, by habit, kept to himself. He seldom stayed long enough in any one place to make close friends. If things worked out, he'd be with the Rimrock through the fall roundup. Then, with winter weather coming on and no more horses to shoe, he'd likely head south to the big ranches that ran cattle year round. There were bosses down there who knew him and would have need of his skill.

Or he could go home to Oklahoma, where he'd been raised, and spend time with the elderly grandmother whose nursing home care he paid for. It cost a lot to keep her in a good place, but she had taken him in when he had nowhere to go. Aside from the half brother he'd lost touch with years ago, she was his only living relative. Almost ninety, she was too hard of hearing to use a phone, but he sent her monthly letters, which the caregivers read to her. And he kept the staff informed of his whereabouts — something he'd need to do again in the next few days.

Most of the time, he avoided thinking about his half brother Bart. Thoughts of Bart only triggered the nightmarish memory that had plagued him for years.

Eleven years his senior, Bart had reluctantly taken in twelve-year-old Luke. Life with Bart and his Comanche wife, sleeping on the sofa in their one-bedroom apartment and holding his ears against the noise coming through the bedroom door, had been no picnic. Neither had washing his clothes in the bathroom sink and going to school hungry most days. But at least he'd had a roof over his head, and he could look forward to the day when he'd be old enough to leave and get a job.

Then one night, everything had changed. Luke had been jarred out of sleep by the sounds of a drunken fight. He'd rushed into the kitchen to find a nightmare scene.

Brandishing a butcher knife, Bart had backed his wife into a corner. As Luke watched in horror, he'd slashed her face from her temple to the corner of her mouth. Amid the bleeding and screaming, Luke had thrown the woman a towel, ordered his drunken brother out of sight, and called 911 for an ambulance. That was the last he'd seen of her.

The police had never been called, but Bart had paid the price for what he'd done. His wife's brothers had caught him alone and beaten him up so badly that he'd suffered head injuries and been forced to go on permanent disability. A few months later, when Bart had been arrested for stealing to support his drug habit, Luke's widowed grandmother, who owned a small farm, had taken in the traumatized boy and given him the love and support he'd needed. Paying for her care now was the least Luke could do.

The call of a whip-poor-will brought Luke's thoughts back to the present. In the big house, a single light had come on. Except for visiting family, the funeral guests had gone. Only the white Camry with rental plates remained parked among the family vehicles.

He remembered the sight of Erin in her simple blue dress, her loose-blowing hair catching the sunlight. His memory lingered for a moment on the way the sleeveless top had clung to the firm peaks of her breasts and narrowed around her tiny waist. The first sight of her had stopped his breath. Then he'd noticed the tall, handsome man with her and wondered if she'd picked up an older boyfriend. Luke's relief, when she'd introduced the stranger as her uncle, had caught him by surprise. Why the hell should it matter? For all he cared, the man could be her sugar daddy.

All he wanted from the Rimrock Ranch was a season of steady work and enough money to pay for a few months of his grandmother's care, with cash left over to get him to wherever he was going next. The last thing he needed was the distraction of Will Tyler's sexy little princess daughter.

Forcing her image from his mind, he slipped on his shirt, buttoned it, and lengthened his stride toward the bunkhouse.

Erin took Kyle's phone call in the kitchen, where she'd been cleaning up after an informal supper. He was sweetly repentant, apologizing for his earlier behavior and for

95

being forced to escort his mother to the funeral.

"Mom was so emotional," he said. "I didn't know that she'd ever even met the old man. But when she took your dad's hand, I thought she was going to cry. I wanted to come and find you, but she wouldn't leave my side."

"Don't worry about it," Erin said. "I was busy the whole time."

"I know you'll be going to the Hill Country for the burial tomorrow," he said. "But I'm hoping we can spend some time together next week. Maybe we could even drive into Lubbock for a movie and dinner. We've gotten into a rut with the Burger Shack. It's time we had a real date. How does that sound?"

"Not bad," she hedged. "Let me check Dad's schedule and see when he can spare me."

"You're not still mad at me, are you?"

"Of course not." Erin could almost picture his puppy dog expression. "I'll call you on Monday. We can make plans then."

She ended the call, wondering why she wasn't more eager for an evening in the city. It wasn't as if she was still angry with Kyle. It was more like she didn't care — as if her attitude had undergone a subtle shift.

96

Maybe it had something to do with Beau's advice to take her time until she was sure of her feelings.

Drying her hands on a dish towel, she walked into the den, where Will and Rose were watching a newscast on the big screen TV. Beau's family had gone into town for pizza, probably to avoid any chance of an ugly confrontation over the evening meal.

"Here you are," her father said, using the remote to switch off the TV. "Sit down. I have a big favor to ask of you."

Erin sank onto a footstool, knowing that, coming from her dad, any request for a favor would be more like an order.

"You may not like it," he said.

Erin braced herself and waited for him to continue.

"Tomorrow, when we take Jasper to the Hill Country, I'll need somebody to stay behind and supervise the ranch work," he said. "The best person available for that job is you."

Erin stifled a murmur of disappointment. She'd wanted to make the drive and see Jasper laid to rest. But she was old enough to know that ranch duties had to come first. "I thought Pete Waxman was going to do that," she said. "He's been here long enough to handle things."

97

"Pete's had a family emergency. He'll be gone most of next week. And since Sky will be going with us tomorrow, we'll need somebody in charge who knows the horses and can make sure Maddox has enough work."

Maddox. Something that felt like a coiled spring tightened in Erin's stomach. The surly farrier wasn't going to like her bossing him. But that was his problem.

"As long as you're staying here," Will continued, "you may as well clean out Jasper's side of the duplex. Throw away the junk, box his clothes and things for donation, and save anything that looks important. I know that might be hard on you, Erin, but somebody's got to do the job. Strip the bed and put out clean sheets for Maddox. You can leave the dishes and some coffee, too."

"Maddox?" It was more of a protest than a question. "But Jasper lived in that duplex for years. It was his home."

"Well, it's not like he's coming back," Will said. "Maddox is a tradesman, not a cowhand. He deserves better quarters than the bunkhouse. You can tell him it was my decision."

Erin sighed and nodded. On the Rimrock, even for her, Will's word was law. But she wasn't looking forward to the next day.

98

As if sensing some tension, Rose broached a different subject. "Erin, I met your young man and his mother at the luncheon today," she said.

"My young man?" Erin didn't recall having told Rose about Kyle.

"That's how his mother introduced him to me," Rose said. "Not as your young man — I suppose that's an old-fashioned term these days — but as your boyfriend. He seemed very nice and polite — and handsome, too. Of course, it'll take more than a pretty face and good manners to make the kind of husband you'll want to stand by your side and help you run this ranch someday."

Erin had learned that Rose tended to speak her mind. But even she was startled by the older woman's frankness.

"Kyle's young," Will said. "He's got a lot to learn. But his father manages the old Prescott Ranch for the syndicate. He's a capable man. I'm guessing that given time, his son will be the same."

Erin had to stop her jaw from dropping. She'd guessed that her father approved of her dating Kyle. But she'd never expected Will to defend him, let alone talk as if he might have plans for their future.

Arguments sprang into her mind. She was

only nineteen. She hadn't made up her mind about Kyle. She wasn't even sure she was in love. But Erin kept her silence. Her dad had been through an emotional three days. He deserved some peace. They could talk later. Right now, there was only one thing to do.

Rising from her seat, she said a subdued good night and walked out of the room.

The long day had drained her. But it was too early to go to bed, and she was too restless to settle somewhere and read the novel she'd started. After the luncheon, she'd shed her dress and sandals and changed into jeans, sneakers, and a plain black tank top. Now she wandered out the front door and onto the porch.

The night was warm, the breeze no more than a whisper. She inhaled the parched air, yearning for the fresh scent of rain. But there was nothing to smell but dust, blended with the odors of horses and cattle and the lingering aromas of ham and beans that drifted from the bunkhouse kitchen. A mosquito whined around her ears. She brushed it away. The pesky insects had never plagued her like they did some people. They'd never bothered Will, either. Maybe there was something in Tyler blood that drove them away.

Needing to move, she headed down the front steps. Her father had never liked her wandering the ranch alone after dark, but she wasn't a child anymore, and she didn't plan to be gone long.

The security light clicked on as she reached the bottom of the steps and moved out into the yard. Her shadow stretched behind her, elongated by the angle of the light. With each step, gravel crunched under her sneakers. She'd hoped that walking might help clear her thoughts, but her father's words kept replaying in her mind. His support of Kyle had caught her by surprise. What had he been thinking?

Maybe Jasper's death had made Will more aware of his own mortality. Maybe he wanted to see her safely settled. Or maybe he was hoping for grandchildren to carry on his line. Erin loved her father, but marrying anyone just to please him could turn out to be the biggest mistake of her life.

Pausing, she scanned the yard for any sign of Henry. But if the big bull snake was out of his den, he was evidently hunting somewhere else. A smile teased Erin's lips as she remembered how Luke Maddox had grabbed her in a panic to keep her from stepping on the scary but nonvenomous snake. She'd glimpsed the vulnerable, human side of the farrier that night.

But she certainly hadn't seen that side of him since. The word *prickly* didn't do the man's disposition justice. She didn't look forward to working with him tomorrow.

She passed the windmill, its vanes barely moving in the listless breeze. Now she could hear the mares and foals in the paddock. Their peaceful blowing and nickering told her all was well with them. Being with horses always calmed her spirit. That was just one of the reasons why Erin had dedicated her life to breeding, raising, and training them.

Her horses were like her children. The thought of selling them off to keep the ranch afloat through the drought was enough to break her heart. But she was a Tyler — Will's daughter and Bull's granddaughter. The long-range future of the Rimrock was in her hands. She would do what had to be done.

The moon was rising to the east, a thin sliver above the distant hills. Beyond the pens, Erin could see the mares moving in the shadows, keeping their foals close. The paddock was large, about the size of a rodeo arena. The near side faced the barn and the pens. The far side bordered on open land that sloped up to the foothills of the escarpment. It was a safe place as long as the horses stayed together, but a straying foal, alone at night, could become prey for a roving pack of coyotes or feral dogs. The mares seemed to know this. They stayed alert for any danger — which made it strange that they hadn't warned Erin about the dark shape of a man standing by the paddock fence.

Her pulse lurched when she saw him. She paused, about to back away and make a silent retreat, when the man turned his head and saw her. The faint glow of the security light fell on his face. It was Luke Maddox.

His relaxed posture sent an unspoken message that he wasn't going anywhere. "Does your daddy know you're wandering out here at night, young lady?" His voice dripped irony. "Don't you know there could be some unsavory characters hanging around the place with mischief on their minds?"

"That's my problem," she retorted. "And this is my ranch. I'm the one who should be asking the questions."

"So, ask away."

The man's insolent undertone made her want to lash out at him. But something told her that if she did, he'd only laugh at her. "I'll start by asking what you're doing out here," she said. "Shouldn't you be in the bunkhouse?"

"I thought you were running a ranch, not a prison camp. Is it against the rules to go outside — especially when that damned bunkhouse is noisier than a riot in a Tijuana cathouse? I came out here for some peace and quiet."

"Well, then, I've got some good news for you." Erin claimed her own spot against the fence. They stood a few feet apart, looking out over the paddock. "My father asked me to clear out one side of the duplex for you tomorrow. You can take your meals in the bunkhouse, but you'll have your own quarters."

"Now that's right nice. Tell your father I said thank you." He actually sounded sincere.

"You can thank the man they'll be burying tomorrow. It was his place for years. Boxing up his things won't be easy for me. Jasper Platt was loved and respected by everyone on this ranch. He'll be missed — terribly."

"I'll keep that in mind when I move in. If you need help packing, let me know."

"You'll be too busy shoeing horses to help," Erin said. "That's another thing. Tomorrow Sky and my father are taking Jas-

104

per's body to the Hill Country for burial. I'm being left in charge."

"So you'll be my boss for the day. That should be interesting."

Erin bristled. "My father's been training me to run this ranch for years. And Sky's been teaching me to manage horses most of my life. I'm as capable as any man on the Rimrock. I can take anything you throw at me, and don't you forget it. Oh — and I'll be alone, without a *dueña*. Sorry about your precious reputation."

A slow grin sidled across his face. His laughter was a bone-deep chuckle. "Remind me not to throw anything at you," he said. "But as long as you're going to be around tomorrow, I'll plan to have a look at your stallions. Those boys tend to be unpredictable, and I'd just as soon not have any sur—"

He broke off, suddenly tense. The mares were stirring, snorting their wariness, calling their foals closer.

"What is it?" Erin asked.

"Shhh," he whispered. "Along the back fence line, beyond the horses. That moving shadow. Do you see it?"

Erin peered across the paddock, into the darkness beyond the reach of the security light. She shook her head. "I don't see anything. Maybe it's a coyote, or just the breeze blowing some brush."

"No. I only caught a glimpse of it, but it moved like a man. And listen to the horses. Something's spooking them. Stay here. I'm going to check it out." Keeping low, he slipped between the fence rails.

"But you don't even have a gun," Erin whispered. "You can't just —"

"Stay here and be quiet. If you hear a ruckus, go for help." Without another word, he vanished into the shadows.

Keeping to the darkness, Luke moved along the fence toward the far side of the paddock. The tall, shadowy figure he'd glimpsed could almost have been a trick of light and shadow, or a product of his imagination. But the wariness of the mares had told him otherwise. Somebody was out there. And he'd bet good money that whoever it was, they were up to no good.

Too bad he hadn't brought the .38 he kept under the seat of his truck, Luke reflected. If the intruder had a weapon, Luke would be at a disadvantage. As it was, the best he could hope for would be to get a look at him, or at least scare the bastard off.

A stand of mesquite grew shoulder high near the back corner of the paddock. Using it as a screen, Luke scanned the length of the stout barbed wire fence that separated the grassy pasture from the brushy foothills that rose to the west. Clumps of sage, chamisa, and mesquite grew outside the fence, offering plenty of cover. Only when the strange figure moved did Luke catch a glimpse of long, bony limbs and straight, black hair. As he moved closer for a better look, a flock of quail, bedded in the mesquite, exploded almost under his feet. The burst of calling, fluttering birds sent the alarmed intruder sprinting off to vanish into the darkness.

Swearing, Luke straightened to his full height. There was no way he could catch up with the strange figure. For now, there was nothing to do but go back to where he'd left Erin.

There was no need to be stealthy now. He fished a small LED flashlight out of his pocket and switched it on to illuminate his path over the bumpy ground. He was halfway across the paddock when he saw Erin coming to meet him. "I told you to stay put," he said.

"No need for that now, is there? Do you always carry a flashlight?"

"Only when there's a chance I might run into Henry."

She laughed — not a tinkly, little girl laugh, but a full-bodied woman's laugh that surprised Luke with its innocent sensuality. He forced himself to focus on the danger that lurked in the darkness beyond the paddock.

"You shouldn't be here," he said. "I saw a man outside the fence, tall and thin, with long hair. When those birds flew up, he ran. I don't know who he was or what he was up to. But people with good intentions don't go sneaking around in the dark."

Luke was hoping she'd be sensibly frightened. Instead she was excited. "You've got a flashlight. Let's go look for tracks. That way, if we see them again, we'll recognize them."

"I'll look — *after* I've seen you safely to your front porch."

"No, I need to see them, too, so I'll recognize them in case they show up again. Come on."

Even against his better judgment, Luke couldn't argue with her logic. "All right," he said. "But stay close behind me. There's no way to know who's out there in the dark, or what they want, or whether they have a gun." He moved ahead of her. "I mean it. Don't do anything stupid."

Erin slipped between the rails and followed

108

Luke up the slight slope, toward the fence at the rear of the paddock. He'd turned the flashlight off. The thin crescent moon lent enough light for them to see their way.

Don't do anything stupid. His words rankled her, as if he viewed her as a brainless little doll. Maybe she ought to tell him what had happened to her six years ago, when Stella Rawlins, the woman who'd owned the Blue Coyote and run a smuggling ring on the side, had kidnapped her, knocked her out with chloroform, and headed for Mexico with her in the trunk. Not only had Erin managed to get loose, but when her father caught up with them, she'd managed to stop Stella from killing him.

Stella was in prison now, serving a life sentence for kidnapping Erin and murdering a county prosecutor. Erin's testimony at her trial had been the key to putting her away.

Don't do anything stupid.

Luke Maddox would never have said that if he'd known whom he was dealing with.

They had reached the mesquite clump where Luke had startled the quail earlier. The mares and foals had settled back into their grazing, a sign that the intruder had probably left. But there was no way to be sure.

109

"Get down and stay put," Luke whispered. "I want to check around before we look for tracks."

Keeping low, he covered the last few yards to the barbed wire fence that bordered the west side of the paddock. Hunkered in the shadow of the mesquite, Erin watched as he picked up a rock from the ground and flung it over the fence. It crashed into the heavy underbrush beyond, startling an owl into flight. The mares raised their heads and pricked their ears. When nothing happened they lowered their heads to graze again. If an intruder were close by, they would be nervous and alert.

Without waiting for a signal from Luke, Erin made her way up to where he crouched by the fence, directing the beam of his flashlight low on the other side. "There," he said. "Take a look."

Clumps of yellow grass and ragweed grew outside the fence line, with taller scrub farther back. In the circle of light, Erin could see where the dry vegetation had been recently crushed. Here and there were spots of open ground where the dust lay fine as talcum powder. On one of these, the beam of light found one perfect track — the print of a cowboy boot with an underslung heel and long, pointed toe, a style known as a cockroach kicker.

Erin studied the print, trying to brand the image in her memory. Had she ever seen it before? Surely if she had, she'd remember.

"Does anybody you know wear boots like that?" Luke asked her.

"Not that I've noticed. And nobody who works on the Rimrock matches the description of the person you saw."

"Well, until you know who it is and what they want, be careful. Don't be alone out here. And you may want to put a guard on the stock, in case your visitor is a thief. For now, you need to get back to the house before your father sends out a search party. Come on."

He walked slightly ahead of her, using his flashlight on the uneven ground. "Are you going to tell your father?" he asked.

"Not yet. He's got enough worries on his mind. I may tell Sky if I need to. But I hope you'll keep this quiet for now. We don't need a bunch of crazy rumors flying around the ranch."

"Fine with me." He paused suddenly, turning back to face the way they'd come. "Listen," he whispered. "Tell me what you hear."

Erin stood perfectly still, ears straining to hear beyond the buzz of night-flying insects and the rustle of wind in the scrub. It took a moment, but when she caught the sound, a shiver passed through her body.

It was the faint but unmistakable rumble of a departing motorcycle.

CHAPTER SIX

Erin listened as the motorcycle's distant thrum faded into silence. "Whoever that was, I hope they're gone for good."

Luke listened a few seconds longer, then nodded. "With luck, we scared them off. Come on, you need to get back to the house before your boyfriend gets word that you've been sneaking around in the dark with the hired help."

She spun around to face him. "Stop it! What is it with you, Luke Maddox? This isn't the eighteen hundreds. I'm nineteen years old, a grown woman and, technically, your boss. Why do you have to be so damned" — she searched for the right word — "so damned *proper*?"

His expression was unreadable in the dark. But Erin sensed that she might have pushed him too far. Taking a half step backward, she stumbled into a low spot on the uneven ground. The slight drop threw her off-balance. Too late to save herself, she went down hard on her rump.

Not hurt but stunned, she glared up at Luke. "Go ahead and laugh," she muttered.

"I wouldn't dare."

She took the hand he offered, feeling its rock-hard power as he pulled her up. He held on long enough to help her regain her balance, then let her go. "Are you all right?" he asked.

Standing, she felt her left ankle twinge when she put weight on it, but that would pass. "I'll be fine," she said. "Let's go."

She moved out ahead of him, but her ankle was still hurting. She forced herself to look calm, trying not to show the pain that shot up her leg with each step. But she couldn't hide her injury from Luke. After a moment, he stopped her. "Don't be a martyr," he said. "Here. Just until we get out of this pasture."

In a single, deft move, he swept her off her feet, lifting her as if she were no heavier than a child. His chest was a solid wall of muscle, his breathing effortless. This was a man who worked with heavy iron tools, hammering steel shoes into shape and nailing them onto the hooves of massive animals that could easily crush him. Carrying a woman would be nothing for him.

As he strode down the slope toward the east fence, he seemed unaffected by her closeness. But where her head rested against his thin shirt, she could hear the galloping cadence of his heart. The awareness of his powerful body, its heat, its pungent, masculine aroma, flowed through her like a current of delicious little sparks. When she breathed, she inhaled him into her body, a sensation that she found strangely intoxicating.

Was he aware of what she was feeling? He said nothing, but Erin was aware of a building tension in him, as if he could hardly wait to put her down.

They were two-thirds of the way to the fence when he cleared his throat and spoke into the stillness.

"About that question you asked," he said.

"What question?" She'd all but forgotten.

"The one about my being so *proper,* as you put it. I'd like to answer it."

She waited, her silence implying consent.

"Proper isn't the word I'd use," he said. "It's more like being cautious, like an animal that's been burned is cautious of fire. I'm older than you are, and I've been around long enough to know that work and women don't mix. A couple of years ago I lost a good job and almost got myself arrested because a rancher's sixteen-year-old daughter wanted to get too friendly. After I told her to go play with her dolls, she told her dad some lies about me. I managed to talk my way out of her accusations, but it made me more cautious than ever. If a client thinks I'm coming on to his daughter, or, God forbid, his wife, I may do an excellent job with the horses, but I'll never work for him or his friends again."

"I hear you," Erin said. "But I'm not just my father's daughter. The horses on the Rimrock are my responsibility. I'm your *client*. Tomorrow I'll be working as your boss. If I don't want to bother with a chaperone, that's *my* decision. But I can promise you one thing — whatever takes place between you and me will be strictly business. Understand?"

"Got it." They had reached the fence. Lifting her over, he set her down on the other side, then ducked through the rails. When she put weight on her ankle, it hurt, but it felt better than earlier. A minor sprain, Erin decided. She'd be all right.

The security light had turned off. It came on again as a white Camry swung into the yard. That would be Beau's family, returning from their pizza night in town.

"I can make it to the house," Erin said.

116

"No need to help me."

"You're sure? It's a long way to walk when you're hurting," Luke said. "I can at least offer you an arm."

"But then we'd have to explain ourselves, wouldn't we?" Erin said. "Don't worry, I'll be fine."

Steeling herself against the pain, Erin set out toward the house. She didn't look back, but her instincts told her that Luke was watching, and that he wouldn't turn and go until she'd reached the safety of the porch. She didn't know the man well, but she was already sure of that much.

Beau had parked the car below the porch and was helping his wife and daughter up the steps. For a moment Erin weighed the idea of telling Beau about the mysterious intruder and the boot print she'd seen. Beau was a lawman. He might be able to give her some advice. But no, she decided. Her story would involve too much explaining. And the last thing she wanted to do was lay more worry on her father's overburdened shoulders. For now, she would keep the incident between herself and Luke.

By the time she reached the porch, Beau's family had gone into the house without noticing her. Her ankle was throbbing, but she'd had her share of injuries before. She

117

would wrap it with an elastic bandage and be all right in the morning.

Pausing on the top step, she turned in the direction of the paddock and waved her hand in an okay sign. From the darkness by the corral, beyond the reach of the security light, she caught the answering blink of a flashlight.

Beau and his family left before dawn the next morning, leaving no trace of their visit except the beds they'd slept in. Will and Erin were there to see them off, but Erin couldn't help noticing a distinct coldness between the brothers.

At five thirty, Erin joined Will, Rose, and Sky for breakfast at the kitchen table. They'd be leaving for the Hill Country as soon as the meal was over. Rose was alert and animated, the men subdued, as if they were still waking up over their coffee.

"Any questions before we go, Erin?" Will asked. "Are you squared away to take over for the day?"

"I'll be fine. I know what needs to be done." Erin's ankle was tightly wrapped beneath her boot. It still pained her but it was well braced. She knew better than to mention the injury to her father.

"Maddox will be checking the brood

mares and stallions and starting on the remuda," Will said. "That should be enough to keep him busy. If he needs help controlling a horse, call somebody. The rest of the boys know their jobs. Unless something unexpected comes up, they should do fine. Just make sure they know you're watching, so they don't slack off. You should have plenty of time to clean out Jasper's side of the duplex."

His voice broke slightly when he spoke of his lifetime friend. Although Bull Tyler had loved his sons, Jasper had been the patient, nurturing father figure who'd made up for Bull's harshness, especially in Bull's later life.

Will turned to Rose. "You'll have a new neighbor when you get back here," he said. "We'll be moving Maddox, the farrier, into Jasper's old quarters."

Rose smiled. "Well, I won't complain about having a handsome, young neighbor. But I'll miss the long talks Jasper and I had on that porch, sitting in those old chairs and watching the moon come up."

"I miss them, too," Sky said. "I lived in the other side of the duplex for years before I got married. Those talks with Jasper gave me enough wisdom to last the rest of my life." He put down his coffee cup with an ironic twist of a smile. "Almost enough wisdom to keep me from making a fool of myself."

"I don't believe that, Sky," Erin said. "You would never make a fool of yourself."

"Clearly, you haven't asked my wife about that." He rose from his place. "I'll bring the truck around."

The cost of having the hearse transport Jasper's body to the Hill Country would have been more than the ranch could afford. Will had made long-distance arrangements for the grave to be dug in the cemetery next to the country church where Jasper and his Sally would have been wed. The grave would be waiting when the casket arrived in the covered bed of Will's pickup, where it was resting now, wrapped in blankets and cushioned for the long, sometimes rough drive.

Jasper would have approved, Erin thought as she watched the truck drive away and vanish down the graveled lane that led to the main highway. He'd never been one for fancy trappings.

The ranch hands were already at their morning chores — feeding the stock, filling the water troughs, cleaning the pens and barns, and putting fresh straw in the stalls. Luke would be pitching in until breakfast

120

time. After that, he would set up his equipment in the shed and begin his real workday. Sky had left instructions, but it would be up to Erin to make doubly sure that Luke had horses available and any other help he might need.

For now, it might be a good idea to show up around the ranch yard, let the men know she was in charge, and alert herself to any problems that might have come up, such as a sick animal or a damaged fence. It would mean a lot of walking on her sore ankle, but it wasn't like a Tyler to show pain, she reminded herself. Trying not to limp, she set out across the yard.

The hands knew her — and they were decent men. Will didn't knowingly hire any other kind. They greeted her cheerfully. A few of the old cowboys joked about her being the new boss, but it was all in fun. She had no reason to expect trouble from any of them.

Except, maybe, the kind of trouble that played havoc with her pulse when she was with Luke Maddox.

She found Luke in the stallion barn, forking hay from a wheelbarrow into the feeders. For a few moments she stood in the entrance, watching his smooth, sure movements. She'd noticed earlier how horses

121

tended to stay calm around him. Something in the man's demeanor inspired their trust. Even the high-strung stallions barely raised their elegant heads as he opened their roomy box stalls, refilled their feeders and water buckets, and took time to look them over, running his hand down their legs and nudging them to lift each hoof for inspection. It was as if he spoke a silent language that only he and the horses understood.

Sky had trained the animals to lift their feet so they could be easily shod. He had passed his methods on to Erin, who, he claimed, also had a natural ability with horses. But what she saw in Luke was not just skill born of experience. It was a pure instinct that bordered on magic.

Coming out of a stall, he caught sight of her. His dark eyes met hers, triggering a flash of memory — his strong arms cradling her across the paddock, the warm fragrance of his skin, his heart pounding next to her ear.

"Good morning, *boss*," he said, giving the word a sardonic twist. "Any orders?"

Erin made sure her "business" mask was in place. "Sky told me you were set for the day. The brood mares are in the pen, waiting for you."

"And their foals?" In the shadows, his

122

deep-set eyes were the color of black coffee.

"The foals are with them," Erin said. "Sky told me you didn't want the mares separated from their babies."

"Right. The mares will be calmer with their young ones close by." Luke was all business, as they'd agreed he would be. It was as if last night had never happened. "I noticed that the mares were shod. If their hooves are in good shape, I'll leave the shoes on them for now — unless you want them off in the rear. I'd recommend that if you're going to breed them again soon. One good kick from a mare's shod hoof can put a stallion out of business, sometimes for good."

"Most of them are already pregnant, so let's leave the shoes on for now. I'm sure Sky would agree with me." Erin walked down the row of stalls to where Tesoro was kept. Hearing her voice, the stallion raised his head and nickered. She reached over the gate of the stall and stroked the golden arch of his neck, tangling her fingers in his creamy mane. Luke came up to stand beside her, studying the horse. When his shoulder brushed hers, Erin felt the contact as a spark of heat passing between them. She willed herself not to notice, but it was hard to forget that they were alone in the stable. If she were to turn toward him or reach out

123

with her hand . . .

But nothing was going to happen. She stepped to one side, giving him more room.

"One more thing," she said. "Remember to make sure I'm there when you work on Tesoro."

"Not a problem. But I'll need to know what you've decided about leaving his front hooves shod."

"I thought about that. If it were early spring and Tesoro had a long breeding season ahead of him, I'd say take the shoes off. But by now, that's mostly done. This fall, I'll be riding him more, sometimes in rough country. So let's leave him shod. The same goes for the other two stallions. They'll be used as spares in the roundup. For that they'll need shoes. Does that make sense?"

"Perfect sense," he said. "One more question — earlier I noticed that Tesoro's hooves had overgrown the shoes. I could trim the edges back, maybe replace the shoes with a better fit. You can decide when you get a better look at him outside. We can do him first if you want. Then you'll be free for the day."

"Thanks. For now I'll be starting on the duplex. Let me know when you're set up and ready." She turned and walked away from him, toward the square of daylight at

124

the end of the barn. She'd kept her word, she congratulated herself. She'd let the man know that she could be all business, like any other client.

"Erin."

His voice stopped her short of the door. She turned back with a questioning look.

"You're limping," he said. "How's the ankle?"

"Not bad. I've got it wrapped."

"You should take it easy. You'll only make it worse."

"I'll be fine, and I can't take it easy today. I've got a job to do." She lifted a hand and swept her hair off the back of her neck. "See you after breakfast."

Luke muttered a curse as he watched her walk away, favoring the injured ankle. They'd agreed to keep things strictly business between them. But business had been the last thing on his mind as he'd stood next to her, watching her stroke her horse. Being alone with her, in the intimate space of the barn, it had been all he could do to keep from touching her — if only to lay a hand on her shoulder or brush his fingertips across the small of her back. Even that would have been a breach of conduct. Worse, it would have left him wanting more of what he mustn't have.

Then there was that little hair toss as she walked away. He'd seen that flirting gesture more times than he could count. It was something women did, an unspoken invitation that said, *Come and get me, cowboy.* In Erin's case, he could only believe that she'd done it unconsciously. But what if she hadn't? What if she was playing games with him?

Forget it, Luke told himself. She was the boss's daughter. She was barely out of high school, and she had a boyfriend who struck him as an entitled brat. He'd be crazy to give her so much as a wink.

He would shoe her horses, answer her questions, and treat her like the client she was. And he would do his best to forget the way she'd felt in his arms, or how his body had responded when he'd carried her out of the paddock last night.

That, as Luke had long since learned, was the only safe way to play it.

Clearing Jasper's things out of the duplex turned out to be an easy but heart-wrenching task. Jasper Platt had been a man of simple tastes and few needs. In the alcove that served as a bedroom, his bed was neatly made with clean sheets already on it. His clothes were neatly laid in the dresser drawers or hung in the closet, where his good boots stood like soldiers at attention. Even looking at the possessions her lifelong friend would never touch again caused tears to well in Erin's eyes.

Questions swirled and clashed. If it had been his time to die, why couldn't it have been in peaceful sleep, or with his ranch family at his bedside? Why had he been taken alone in the rough land beyond the heart of the ranch? Had he been aware and afraid, or had life simply stopped for him?

And then there were the most tormenting questions of all — had another person been involved in Jasper's death? Could Will, or anyone else, have saved him if they'd found him in time?

Jasper's mahogany gun rack, a gift from Bull, was bolted to the wall next to the door. Erin was so familiar with his four guns that she could picture them with her eyes closed. There was the lightweight .22 he'd owned since his boyhood. Erin had happy memories of Jasper teaching her to shoot with that little gun, using it to plink at bottles and tin cans. There was the Remington .30-06 rifle he used for hunting deer, coyotes, javelinas, and other game, and for the times he had to put a cow or horse out of its misery. His favorite gun was the single-barrel 12 gauge, loaded with bird shot, that he used for hunting doves, quail, wild turkey, and the occasional duck or goose.

Jasper's fourth gun was a Smith and Wesson .38 revolver that he sometimes carried with him, in a holster buckled onto the ATV, when he went out on the range. The pistol came in handy for unexpected emergencies, such as an aggressive animal or human. Jasper had been a dead shot with that pistol, and he was as tough as he was kind. Years ago, when Erin had asked him whether he'd ever shot anybody, he had deftly changed the subject.

Two of the guns — the .22 and the heavy rifle, were still in the gun rack, locked into place with a crossbar. After Jasper's death, the sheriff had come by with a box of his personal things — his clothes and boots, his hat, his spectacles, his keys, his cigarettes and lighter, his watch, and the bird gun. The pistol hadn't been among the returned items, but it had been easy enough to assume that Jasper hadn't taken it with him.

The duplex had been locked with Jasper's key. Nobody had checked inside to make sure the pistol was there.

Until now.

If Jasper hadn't taken the pistol, it would

have been locked to the rack. He would never have left it lying around. Since the gun was missing, one of two things was possible. Either it had flown off the ATV and landed out of sight, or someone had picked it up and taken it — maybe the strange intruder she and Luke had seen last night.

A fly buzzed in the silence of the stuffy room. Erin's mouth had gone dry. She took a moment to deliberate. She could call the sheriff now and tell him what she'd discovered. Or she could check out the accident scene herself, look for the gun or any other evidence that might have been missed, and take what she'd learned to the sheriff in person tomorrow.

If she wanted the sheriff to pay attention, the second choice made more sense. But she couldn't go now. Luke would be working on Tesoro soon and she wanted to be there to make sure her stallion was all right. Maybe, if she finished clearing out the duplex and no one needed her, she could go this afternoon. But right now, she had work to do.

A plastic laundry basket was half full of dirty clothes. The familiar odor of tobacco smoke that rose from them brought tears to Erin's eyes. The small fridge was stocked with Mexican beer and stale sandwich makings. This simple space had been Jasper's home for years. He had left with no idea that he wouldn't be coming back.

She was putting the perishable fridge contents into a trash bag when her cell phone jangled. When she saw that the number was Kyle's, she almost didn't pick up. She already had too many distractions. But if she failed to answer, he would only call again, or come over. She might as well talk to him now. Shifting her attention, she answered.

"Hi," she said.

"Hello, you." Kyle's voice was cheerful. "Have I caught you on your way to the Hill Country?"

Erin was tempted to lie. But she knew that a lie might come back to bite her. "No. My dad needed me to stay home and work. I'm the boss for the day."

"Boss, huh? That sounds sexy. Does it have anything to do with whips and chains?"

Erin groaned. "That's not funny, Kyle, at least not today. What is it you want?"

"You said you'd call to let me know about our dinner date in the city."

"Oh, that's right. But didn't I say I'd call you on Monday?"

"You did. But I might need to make reservations, so I thought I'd check with you now."

"Sorry, I've been so busy with the funeral and all, I haven't had time to think about it. Right now I'm boxing up Jasper's things and clearing out the duplex. I didn't expect the job to be so . . . so emotional."

"You do sound a little ragged around the edges," he said. "An evening out might be just what you need. If you want to go tonight, we can do it. A lot of places are open on Sunday."

Erin sighed. Kyle really had been patient with her. He deserved an answer. "Tonight I'll need to be here when my dad gets home," she said. "Besides, I'll be worn out. But how about tomorrow? Would that work for you?"

"Sure. I'll pick you up about six-thirty. There's a new steak house I've been wanting to try. I'll call and make reservations."

"Thanks. Got to go. I'll see you then."

"Dress up and look your prettiest," he said. "Are you sure you don't want me to come over and help you clear out that duplex?"

"You don't want to be with me right now. I'm a wreck. I need to do this alone."

"Okay, then. I'll see you tomorrow."

Erin ended the call and went back to organizing Jasper's things — what to keep, what to donate, and what to throw away. Her thoughts drifted back to the phone call. She could tell that Kyle wanted to make the evening special. In the likely event that he was planning to propose again, she'd be wise to have an answer ready. She'd given it some thought, but the only good reply she could come up with was the truth. She liked him. She even had to admit that he was good husband material. But she wasn't sure she loved him. And with her father needing her help, she wouldn't be ready to make marriage plans for at least a year, maybe longer. If he didn't want to wait that long, she would understand and wish him well.

Refocusing on her task, she looked around for what to do next. The single bookshelf held a well-thumbed Bible, a few classic hardbound books like *Huckleberry Finn* and *The Yearling,* and a dozen or so paperback novels by authors like Zane Grey, Bret Harte, and Louis L'Amour. The paperbacks could be donated or recycled. But Will might want to keep the hardcover novels. She ruffled through the pages of each book to make sure nothing important, like a photograph, had been left inside. All she found was a pressed four-leaf clover and a couple torn strips of newspaper that had been used as bookmarks.

The Bible, at least, would be worth saving. Erin pulled it off the shelf and opened the weathered cover. On the first page was a record of Jasper's family back through his grandparents — the births, marriages, and deaths.

The last date recorded, in a slightly unsteady hand, was the death of Jasper's widowed sister, Bernice, who'd served as cook and housekeeper to the Tylers, and as surrogate mother to young Will and Beau after their mother died. Bernice, who'd retired and gone to live with a daughter, had passed away two years ago. The daughter, who'd moved back home to the Hill Country, would be at the cemetery when Jasper was laid to rest.

By right, Bernice's daughter should have the family Bible, Erin reasoned. Too bad it hadn't been discovered before the truck left with Jasper's body. But never mind, she could mail it the next time she went to town.

As Erin was laying the Bible aside, something dropped from between the pages and fluttered to the floor. She picked it up. It was a small, colored photograph, probably a high school yearbook picture. The young woman in the photo had auburn curls, a freckled nose, and a dimpled smile. She wasn't a striking beauty, but her eyes, the

133

deep azure of Texas bluebonnets, seemed to radiate kindness and good nature.

Erin turned the picture over. Written on the back, in faded blue ink, was the name *Sally*, along with a blurred date.

Tears flooded Erin's eyes. Jasper had never shown her this picture. But its edges, worn thin from handling, told her he'd spent a lot of time looking at it.

What would it be like to love someone so much — to love them your whole life, even though they were gone?

Erin slipped the photograph back into the Bible. As she closed the book and set it aside, she realized she was weeping. Tears streamed down her cheeks. Her shoulders quivered with silent sobs. When her mother had died, she hadn't allowed herself to cry. She'd been making too much of an effort to be strong for her father and shoulder all that had to be done. Now, in a shattering release of grief, the tears came; and there was nothing she could do but bury her face in Jasper's pillow and let the flood sweep her away.

CHAPTER SEVEN

"Erin, are you all right?"

At the sound of Luke's voice, Erin raised her head. Through a blur of tears she could see him standing in the open doorway of the duplex with the morning sun at his back.

"Yes. A little emotional, but I'll be fine," she said, conscious of her swollen eyes and tear-streaked face. Some girls cried prettily. Erin wasn't one of them.

His eyes took her in. "I'm sorry. The door was ajar. I knocked, but you must not have heard me. Is there anything I can do to help?"

Erin stood and stepped away from the bed. She couldn't help wishing she could put a bag over her head. But she wouldn't apologize for crying. Jasper had earned her tears.

"There's nothing anybody can do," she said. "It's just this place. The old man who lived here for years was like a grandfather

135

to me. Everything here reminds me of him. But I need to do this, even if it's hard."

"You don't have to do it today," he said. "I can survive in the bunkhouse."

"You were complaining about it last night. You said it was as noisy as —"

"I know. But I've slept through worse. At the end of a long day, shoeing horses in the heat, I could probably sleep through a tornado."

"I'll get it done. I promised my dad. It won't get any easier if I wait."

"Well, I'll appreciate the effort. And I'll consider it an honor to sleep in a good man's bed. If there's any way I can help —"

"A stranger wouldn't know what was worth saving. I have to do this myself. It's just knowing that I'll never see him again, and . . . *Oh, blast!*" The tears were back, trickling down her cheeks in salty streams. Erin pressed her hands to her face. "Ignore me. I'll be fine in a minute."

He crossed the space between them and took a clean, folded bandanna out of his pocket. Easing her hands away, he lifted her face with a thumb under her chin and began blotting away the tears. "It's all right," he said. "Sometimes the only thing you can do is cry."

His face was so close that his breath

mingled with hers. It was as if she could look into the depths of his eyes and see the reflection of her own raw need. Erin's desire to be in his arms and to feel the sensual power of his kisses, sweeping away the sting of her tears, was like an unanswered cry. If she were to stretch upward by an inch, he would know. . . .

And she would be in serious trouble.

"Here, give me that," she said, stepping back and snatching the bandanna from his hand. Wadding it in her fist, she dabbed furiously at the tears that were already drying on her face. "I'll wash this and give it back to you," she said, stuffing it into her pocket. "Are you ready to work on my stallion?"

"That's why I'm here. But it can wait."

"No, let's do it now," she said. "Just give me a minute."

In the bathroom, she splashed her face to wash away the salty tear trails. Her eyes avoided the mirror. She didn't have to see her reflection to know that she looked a red-eyed mess. But why should it matter? Luke Maddox was her employee — that was all. He'd already seen her at her worst.

She led the way to the barns, her head high, her stride determined, as if defying anyone to notice that she'd been crying. Luke walked a step behind her, feeling strangely protective. He'd dismissed Erin as a spoiled princess. But in the past two days she'd proven herself to be strong, courageous, proud, and now, vulnerable in a way that touched his heart. Back in the duplex, when he'd found her in tears, it had been all he could do to keep from taking her in his arms. He could have rationalized that he was giving her comfort. But he'd long since learned not to lie to himself. He *wanted* her — wanted her in a way guaranteed to get him horse-whipped and run out of town.

Erin's palomino stallion, a registered quarter horse, was big for his breed, powerful, and beautifully proportioned. An ideal stud. One of the cowhands had mentioned that, in this year of drought, it was Tesoro's stud fees that had kept the Rimrock from going under. Even the foals that lacked his golden coat were superb. All the more reason to keep the horse in prime condition.

Erin led Tesoro out of his stall to the shed where Luke had set up his anvil and tools. Luke had already spent time around the stallion, talking to him, stroking him, and checking his legs. He didn't expect trouble. But Tesoro was high-spirited and definitely a one-woman horse. Having Erin there to keep him calm would make the process of trimming and shoeing safer.

"Come and take a look." Wearing his heavy leather apron, Luke positioned himself against Tesoro's side. At a touch, the well-trained stallion raised a front hoof for inspection. Erin moved in closer as Luke pointed out the edge of the hoof. "See how it's grown past the shoe. If he's to be ridden much, it'll wear and give him trouble. All four hooves need to be trimmed around the edge and fitted with shoes that won't let this happen again. Make sense?"

"It does. Go ahead." She watched him, soothing her horse as Luke pried off the shoe and began cleaning and trimming the hoof. "I had no idea there was so much involved in shoeing a horse," she said. "Where did you learn all this?"

"I spent my teens on my grandmother's farm in Oklahoma," he said. "Her neighbor was a farrier. When he saw that I was interested, he took me on as an apprentice and trained me. Later on, I went to school and learned more."

"That's interesting," she said. "You say you spent your teens on a farm. What about before that? What about your family?"

"That's not a story I enjoy telling."

"Please," she said.

He shrugged. "You might say I grew up rough. I never knew my father. My mother and her boyfriend died in a motorcycle crash when I was eleven. After that I went to live with my half brother in Oklahoma City. That didn't turn out so well either. That was when my grandma took me in. I'd probably be in prison now if it hadn't been for her."

"You were one of the lucky ones. Is your grandmother still alive?"

"Yup. She couldn't keep the farm, but she's still in Oklahoma, in a retirement home."

"Sky's from Oklahoma, too," she said. "His mother's people were Comanche. But Sky's father was my grandfather, Bull Tyler. That makes him my uncle. It's a complicated story."

"I'm impressed with your foreman. He's a good man."

"Sky's the best. He taught me everything I know about horses." Her smile was like the sun coming out. Even with her face bare of makeup and her eyes still showing traces of tears, she was beautiful.

For the next forty minutes, she watched him clean, trim, and shoe each hoof while she soothed the restless stallion and asked questions about the work in a manner that was as businesslike as she'd promised.

"All done. Good boy." He patted Tesoro's shoulder, then turned to Erin. "I wouldn't mind seeing you ride him. That way, I could check his gait and make sure the balance is perfect."

"Would you like to ride with me later today?" she asked. "I want to visit the spot where Jasper had his so-called accident and see if there's anything the sheriff and his deputy missed. I have my suspicions about what happened, but without proof, there's nothing I can do. It's not very far, only about a mile from here."

"That sounds intriguing," he said. "Of course, I'll go with you. After what we saw last night, there's no way I'd feel good about your riding out there alone. I'll trim and shoe the other stallions and ride one of them."

"They're both easy to handle. Unless you need my help, I'll put Tesoro away and finish cleaning out the duplex. When I'm all done, I'll check back with you."

Luke watched as she led her horse back to the barn. Spending so much time with Erin wasn't a good idea, he told himself. Forbidden lust aside, he enjoyed her. She was smart, funny, and totally natural. But the

141

voice of caution was telling him to back off. Spending time with her, especially alone, was flirting with trouble. Whether he liked it or not, he was beginning to care for her. If he didn't put a stop to it, the time would come when caring for her wouldn't be enough.

Later today, he'd be riding with her to where her old friend had wrecked his ATV. He'd be fighting temptation all the way, but he couldn't let Erin go alone. One man had died in the scrub land beyond the heart of the ranch. A subtle sixth sense warned Luke that the danger could still be out there, waiting.

Jasper had been laid to rest in the old country churchyard, his grave decorated with wildflowers and blessed with prayers. Now, with Will at the wheel, Rose in the passenger seat, and Sky dozing in the rear, the pickup was headed for home.

This, Rose decided, would be as good a time as any to broach the subject of her land. She cleared her throat. "I didn't want to bring this up until after the burial, but we need to talk about that parcel on the creek."

The subtle tightening of Will's mouth told her he wasn't surprised.

"That land still belongs to me," she said. "When I married Tanner and went off to Wyoming, Bull promised to take care of it. I haven't seen the place, but going by what Erin told me, I'd guess that promise hasn't been kept."

Will's chest rose and fell in a deep sigh. "I'm sorry, Rose. My father's been gone a long time. And there've been some rough years between then and now. I never meant to let the place go to seed like it has, especially your grandpa's grave. But the truth is, I've had more pressing things to worry about, like keeping the cattle alive and the ranch solvent — and watching cancer take my wife."

Rose laid a hand on his arm, remembering what a serious, responsible young boy he'd been. In her eyes, he hadn't changed that much. "I understand, Will," she said. "I'm not trying to cast blame. The situation is what it is. But I've been doing some serious thinking — and I've concluded that it's time for me to take my property back."

"What the — ?" Will flinched, causing the truck to swerve slightly. "Damn it, Rose, we've got to have that creek water. The ranch can't survive without it."

"I know. I signed an agreement with Bull that the Rimrock would always have access

143

to the water. But you can fill your tank from the creek without running cattle all over my property. All you need to do is bury the pipe and install a couple of valves, so you can turn it on at the tank. It shouldn't take a genius to figure that out. That piece of land was beautiful once. I want to make it beautiful again."

Will was silent. Rose could almost feel him weighing her words, letting them sink in before he spoke.

"Are you saying what I think you're saying? That you want to live on your land?"

"Why not? Because it didn't work out the first time? Things have changed, Will. I'm not running from the cartel. The Prescotts are gone. And I'll have access to money now. Tanner built us a nice home in Wyoming. His brother has married children coming back to the ranch. He's asked me about selling the house to him for cash. I can pay to have a pretty little cabin built, with a place for a garden and animals, and a good, stout fence to keep out your cattle."

Will didn't reply. Rose studied his stubborn profile as he drove. She should have known that he wouldn't have an easy time accepting her news. His first reaction would be to see it as a threat to the Rimrock.

"Be happy for me, Will," she said. "Living

on my grandpa's land was my dream once. Now I can make it come true. And you won't be losing anything. The land was never yours. You'll still have the water — and we'll be neighbors."

"Not if I lose the Rimrock, which is going to happen if I can't make that bank payment. The syndicate would buy the place in a minute, like they did the old Prescott property. But that's not what I want. My grandfather, the man I'm named for, literally gave his life to keep this land for his descendants."

"I know," Rose said. "Jasper told me the story, how he chose to die of cancer rather than sell the Rimrock to pay for treatment that could have saved his life."

"And Bull? Lord, my father would rise out of his grave and haunt me if I lost this place."

"Having known Bull, I'd almost believe he could do that. But, Will, if you're that desperate, I'd be happy to loan you —"

"Oh, no! No! Rose, I wouldn't think of taking your money. That's not who I am."

"Then what about Beau? I know how things are between the two of you, but he's not heartless. He never meant for this to happen."

"I wouldn't ask Beau for a damned nickel.

145

All I can do is sell off most of the cattle while they're still in decent shape, and as many of the horses as we can spare, although that'll break Erin's heart. She's raised and trained so many of them."

"Surely you wouldn't sell her stallion."

"No, not Tesoro or the breeding stock. We'll still need enough cow ponies to run the ranch. But any extras will have to go. That's why I hired the farrier. If I want to get top dollar for the horses, they'll need to be in good condition."

"How much of this have you told Erin?" Rose asked.

Will slowed to pass a sheep that was nibbling grass alongside the two-lane road. "Erin knows we're struggling," he said. "But I haven't told her the worst. I want her to enjoy her life while she can. Maybe she'll even marry that boyfriend of hers. At least that way, if anything were to happen to me, she'd have some security."

Rose felt a chill. "Will, you're scaring me. Is something wrong with you?"

"As far as I know, I'm sound as a dollar. But losing Tori and Jasper within a few months of each other has got me thinking about my own mortality. You've heard that deaths tend to run in groups of three. After what I've seen over the years, I'm inclined to believe it."

"Superstitious nonsense, that's all it is!" Rose shook her head. "You can't set any store by it. Let's talk about something else. Tell me about that young man of Erin's. How long have they been dating?"

Will took a moment to think. "A little over a year, I guess, since Erin graduated from high school and Kyle came home from junior college. His dad manages the syndicate ranch that used to belong to the Prescotts. A good man, and his wife seems friendly. Kyle has an associate degree in ranch management. Experience will teach him the rest of what he needs to know. Earlier you asked whether he was the right man to help Erin run the Rimrock someday. If that's the way things turn out, he'll certainly be qualified."

"So you approve of the match?"

"I wouldn't object to it. But only if it makes Erin happy."

But will he *make her happy*? Rose kept that question to herself, knowing that Will would have no way to answer it. She had met Kyle Cardwell at the luncheon following the funeral. The young man had been polite and charming, and he was certainly handsome. But Rose had sensed something hidden below the surface — a weakness, perhaps, like a flaw in a good-looking horse. There'd been no word for it — no proof that it was even there. But she'd walked away feeling that Erin deserved better.

"I'd like to see my land tomorrow," she said. "If you don't have time to take me, could I borrow a vehicle?"

"I'll be glad to take you. That's the least I can do." Will swung the truck onto the freeway ramp and hit the gas. "But you won't like what you see."

"That's all right. We'll take a look at what's wrong and figure out how to fix it." Rose settled back in the seat. She was worn out from the long drive, and the ranch was hours away. But she wasn't sorry to be here. Years had passed since she'd felt useful to anyone but herself. But some inner voice whispered that in the time ahead, her help would be needed.

The midday sun beat down on the scrubby foothills below the escarpment. Under its searing rays, the landscape seemed stripped of anything that moved. Even the basking lizards were gone from rocks that were hot to the touch. Heat waves swam above the parched ground. Out on the flatland, the white alkali patch that had been a bitter playa lake before the drought glittered like diamond dust.

Birds, snakes, mice, rabbits, and coyotes, even spiders and scorpions, had taken refuge in the shade or under the ground. Only the vultures, riding the updrafts on outstretched wings, seemed to thrive in the heat.

Mounted on Tesoro, Erin tilted the water canteen to her lips and passed it to Luke. Beneath her broad-brimmed hat, her hair was soaked with perspiration. The distance to the dry wash where Jasper's life had ended wasn't much more than a mile from the heart of the ranch. But the going was slow, because she and Luke were taking the stallions at a walk to spare them in the heat.

"Are you sure you know where you're going?" Luke, mounted on a bay stallion named Ranger, took a long gulp of water and passed the canteen back to her. "Every place out here looks the same to me."

"I'm sure," Erin said. "I grew up riding out here, and going bird hunting with Jasper. When the sheriff described the place where they found him, I knew exactly the spot he meant. Jasper and I could always find quail and doves in that wash. I'd flush them out and Jasper would bring them down with his shotgun. They make good eating if you've got the patience to dress

149

them." Her throat tightened at the mention of her old friend.

"I know about quail and doves. My grandmother was the devil with a shotgun. I used to dress the ones she bagged on the farm. It took about a dozen of them to make a meal for us." Luke scanned the horizon.

Erin had told him about the circumstances of Jasper's death and the missing pistol they'd be looking for. She still wasn't sure whether he took her suspicions seriously or if he'd only come along to make sure she was safe. Either way, it was reassuring to have him with her, especially since he was wearing a gun belt with a Smith and Wesson .38 in the holster.

"Over there, about fifty yards." She indicated the direction with a nod. "See that crooked bush? That's the spot."

"I see it. Let's find some shade for the horses. We're more likely to see something useful if we go on foot from here."

"Maybe — providing the sheriff's men left anything for us to see. I can imagine their big clumsy boots stomping out any evidence that might've been left behind."

They tethered the stallions in the lacy shade of a mesquite. Erin felt a painful twinge as she put her weight into the left stirrup and swung out of the saddle. Tightening her jaw, she willed herself to ignore it.

They walked carefully toward the edge of the wash, looking down. "I see plenty of tire tracks," Luke said.

"That would be the sheriff's Jeep." Erin walked a little farther, trying not to limp. "See, right here is where they got out, the sheriff on this side, and his deputy, Roy Porter, on the driver's side. I went through school a year behind Roy. I'm hoping he'll be willing to talk to me about what they found here."

"I don't see anything else yet, do you?"

"Just the tracks that Roy and the sheriff left. At least we know what they look like." Erin paused, scanning the ground ahead. "There's a trail that goes along the edge of the wash. There — those tire tracks are from Jasper's ATV. See where they swing and go right off the edge? Careful where you step. If anybody else was here, this is where they would have been."

"I don't see anything but those damned big boot prints. They're all over the place. If there were any other tracks here, they've been covered."

"Let's keep going," Erin said. "Farther up the trail there's a place where we can climb down into the wash."

They followed the ATV tracks up the trail,

151

finding nothing else. "Maybe I was wrong after all," Erin said as they made the rocky descent into the wash. "Maybe Jasper just had a stroke or heart attack and went over the edge."

"Wouldn't the medical examiner have discovered that?"

"The medical examiner for this county is just a general practitioner. He made an educated guess, with Jasper's age as a factor. According to the sheriff, the only marks on Jasper were from the wreck. If we find that missing pistol where it would have fallen, there'll be less reason to suspect that someone else was there when he died."

Moving down the wash, they could see the wrecked ATV ahead, still waiting to be pulled out and hauled away. It had gone over sideways, crushing a deep-rooted clump of sagebrush where it had landed top-down. The bed of the wash was covered with rocks, gravel, and small boulders, carried down from the escarpment by untold years of flash flooding. No tracks were visible here, even though the sheriff and his deputy would've taken plenty of steps, recovering Jasper's body and searching around the ATV for any evidence.

But had they looked under the wreck? Glancing at Luke, Erin met his eyes and realized they both had the same idea.

The four-wheeler was lying at a slant, its wheels in the air. One corner was propped up by the partly crushed branches of the sagebrush plant.

"If the pistol's anywhere, it would be under here." Erin dropped to her knees. As she leaned forward for a better look, Luke stopped her with a hand on her shoulder.

"Don't try to go down there until we get it braced," he said. "And no reaching under with your hand. You never know what might've crawled in there to get out of the sun. Stay put while I look for a rock to shore up that corner."

He moved down the wash, searching among the rubble for a boulder substantial enough to stabilize the ATV but not too heavy to carry. Erin watched his easy stride, admiring the way his perspiration-soaked shirt clung to his muscular arms and shoulders. He looked like a man who could handle anything — a man who would keep her safe.

When she'd first thought of coming here, she'd planned on coming by herself. Now she realized what a foolish idea that had been. This was a dangerous place, where it would be all too easy to lose her balance on the rocks, to be crushed by a slip of the

ATV, or even bitten by a rattlesnake. A man had died here under suspicious circumstances. If anyone was involved in Jasper's death, they might not like her snooping around. Alone, she would be almost helpless.

Still searching, Luke moved beyond her sight. A shiver of apprehension crept up Erin's spine. Even knowing that he was minutes away, she felt vulnerable without him.

The seconds ticked by, only to be broken by the sudden, loud report of a gunshot. Acting on reflex, Erin ducked low, her heart slamming. "Luke!" she called. "Are you all right?"

"Fine. But I can't say the same for the rattler." He strode into sight, one hand holstering his pistol, the other hand carrying a hefty rock. "Blasted critter almost got me when I reached for this rock. That'll teach me to keep a better lookout."

Kneeling, he shoved the rock under the corner of the ATV, where it would catch the weight if the vehicle shifted.

"One more thing." Picking up a broken branch, he thrust it under the overturned chassis of the ATV and moved it around to check for anything hiding in the shade. "Nothing there, as far as I can tell," he said.

"Want me to take a look?"

"You don't know what to look for. I do." Erin took off her hat and got down on her belly. There was an eight-inch space between the chassis, which had no roll bar, and the ground. She crawled close enough to peer into it. As her eyes became accustomed to the dim light, she could make out what would have been the top side of the ATV — the seats, the steering mechanism, the brake, and the holster where Jasper would have put his pistol. But there was no pistol, not on the vehicle or on the ground beneath.

She sat up. "I couldn't see a gun, or anything else that might be a clue to what happened."

Luke took her hand and pulled her to her feet. Her ankle had become so tender that she could barely put weight on it. "I've looked all around for the pistol," he said. "If you didn't find it, I think it's safe to say that it isn't here. Now let's get you back to the ranch before somebody thinks you've run off with the hired help."

Erin laughed because she knew he was joking — although she had to admit the idea had some appeal. Being with Luke was intoxicating, and the forbidden element lent an extra spark to every meeting of their eyes, and every accidental touch.

155

But she was a sensible young woman. Luke wasn't interested in her. And even if he wcre, such a reckless choice on her part would break her father's heart.

To climb out of the wash, they would need to go back up the narrow, rocky trail where they'd come down. Luke walked slightly behind her, lending his arm for support as they climbed toward the rim. Erin's ankle was throbbing, but she knew better than to expect him to carry her as he had last night. On the treacherous ground, unable to see where he was stepping, he could lose his footing and send them both tumbling.

"Stop! Look at this!" He caught her arm to steady her as she turned back. Erin went cold as she saw what he'd found.

On the right-hand side of the trail was a spot where sand had washed down and filled a space between the rocks, leaving a smooth patch that glittered in the blazing sun. There on the sand, faint but unmistakable, was the shallow print of a boot sole — a narrow cockroach kicker with a long, pointed toe.

From her hiding place in the rocks above the wash, Marie Fletcher watched the man and the slender young woman walk back toward the place where they'd left their horses. Spitting her chew on the ground, she uttered a string of curses that would have made a drunken sailor blush. Seven years in the hell of Gatesville Women's Prison, where she'd served time for armed robbery, had done wonders for her vocabulary.

Now she was out on parole, planning to slip across the border and start a new life in Mexico. But for that she was going to need money — and getting that money, along with the right business connections, depended on her carrying out a mission of revenge.

Marie had nothing personal against Erin Tyler. But Stella Rawlins did. And Stella held the key to everything Marie wanted.

Stella and Marie had a long history. In Blanco Springs, back when Stella had owned the Blue Coyote, they'd gone from being partners in crime to bitter enemies. When they'd reconnected in Gatesville, where Stella had been sentenced for kidnapping and murder, they'd circled each other like a couple of hissing cats before deciding to join forces once more. It had been a good idea. Together, they'd become powerful and feared in the complex social structure of prison life.

Stella would never leave Gatesville. She

was serving a life sentence with no parole. She also suffered from emphysema and diabetes. Wheezing and overweight, she would almost certainly die in prison. But there was one thing Stella wanted — revenge on the young kidnapping victim whose testimony had put her behind bars.

Even now, remembering what Stella had said, Marie could almost hear her rasping voice. "If it wasn't for that little Tyler bitch, I'd be free and living high. When you get out, Marie, I want you to find her and make her pay. I don't care how you kill her. Just do it, so I can die happy."

"So, what's in it for me?" Marie had asked.

Stella had smiled, showing a missing front tooth. "Don't worry, I've got that covered. When I left Blanco Springs, I left a stash of heroin — solid bricks, at least a half million dollars' worth — as a sort of insurance policy. Nobody knows where it is but me. Bring me proof that the girl's dead, and I'll tell you where that stash is. Not only that, I'll tell you how to contact my friend Don Ramón, in Mexico. He can shelter you and set you up fine."

Agreeing to kill the girl had been an easy decision. Marie had killed before. She killed coldly and efficiently, without a twinge of regret. Killing the girl would be no problem.

But the last thing she wanted was to end up back in prison for murder. However the young Miss Tyler was to die, it couldn't be traced back to Marie. Ideally it would look like an accident.

Much like the real accident that had killed the old man.

His death hadn't been part of Marie's plan. In fact it hadn't even been her fault. She'd encountered the old man on the trail by pure chance. His startled expression told her he'd recognized her from years ago, which meant she'd be smart to kill him. But before she could act, he'd gone rigid and run the ATV off the rim of the wash. When she'd climbed down there, she'd found him dead.

Since there was nothing she could have done, even if she'd wanted to, she'd picked up his loaded pistol from the ground, picked his pockets with a handkerchief covering her fingers, and left the scene.

She examined the .38 now, hefting its weight and checking the cylinder. She'd needed a gun, and this one had almost fallen into her lap. She could use the $360 cash she'd found in his wallet, too. Sometimes she got lucky. Too bad she hadn't had better luck with the girl.

If Erin Tyler had ventured out here alone

today, arranging an "accident" for her would have been easy. Unfortunately, she'd brought along that dangerous-looking man. But never mind. With patience and careful planning, sooner or later, another chance would come.

As the pair mounted up and rode away, Marie settled back into the shade to think. Her fingertip stroked the ugly scar on the left side of her face. Running from her temple to the corner of her mouth, it was a lasting souvenir from the abusive husband she'd left years ago, back in Oklahoma. If she could kill the girl and sell Stella's drug stash, she should be able to pay for plastic surgery in Mexico. That would be a dream come true.

But to do this right, she would need to know more about Erin Tyler — where she liked to go, what vehicle she drove, where and when she was most likely to be alone. Once she knew those things, she could make a plan and set her trap.

Stella would have her revenge, and Marie would be free.

CHAPTER EIGHT

After a twenty-minute ride, Luke and Erin came within sight of the ranch yard. Even in the blazing heat, Luke could see that Erin was shivering beneath her perspiration-soaked shirt. Someone was stalking the ranch — a sinister stranger who had no good reason to be here. And she was too proud to admit that she was scared.

"You should tell your father about this," Luke said.

"Not yet." Luke could sense her resistance as she answered. "It would just add to the strain he's under."

"And Sky? Maybe he could help."

"Sky works for my dad. He'd feel obligated to tell him. For now I can handle this by myself. Nobody else knows about it but you — and you promised not to tell, right?"

"Right." Luke was beginning to regret that promise, but if nothing else, he was a man of his word.

161

"At least I've got a photo of the boot print on my phone," she said. "I'll take it to the sheriff's office tomorrow. When I tell them about the missing gun, they'll have to listen to me. I'll even take that box of his personal effects, in case the sheriff needs to dust them for prints."

She eyed him, cocking her head. "Why are you looking at me like that? Do you think I've been watching too many crime shows on TV?"

"No. But I think you're being foolish. This isn't a game, Erin. We know somebody's out there. If that person killed your friend, you could be in danger, too, especially if you get too close. Don't do this alone. Bring in the troops — that includes Sky and your father. The whole ranch needs to be on alert."

"Not until I've talked to the sheriff. Otherwise, who's going to believe me?"

"I believe you." He hesitated, deciding to be honest. "At least I believe what we saw."

"See?" Her chin came up in a defiant thrust. "Even you have your doubts. You think I'm just a silly girl, overreacting from grief. Fine. Think what you want to."

She nudged her palomino to a gallop that carried her well ahead of him, toward the barns. Luke muttered a curse. The stallion would be all right. The barns weren't far, and they'd both been careful not to exert the horses in the heat. But Erin's headstrong recklessness made him want to grip her shoulders and shake some sense into her.

Not a wise train of thought — especially since what he really wanted had nothing to do with shaking her.

Back off. She's not your problem. Let her go her own way. Until last night he could have done just that. But now he was concerned. Whether he liked it or not, he cared what happened to her — cared deeply. But anything beyond caring would have to stop right now. He was already treading a thin line. To step over it would mean trouble, not only for him but for Erin.

Erin slowed the stallion to a walk as they entered the ranch yard. Tearing toward the barn as if in a panic could draw unwanted attention and raise questions she wasn't ready to answer.

At least Luke hadn't come after her. A glance over her shoulder confirmed that he'd stayed back and was barely in sight. Maybe he was thinking of her reputation and his own. It was just as well that they hadn't ridden in together. Even that might have been enough to cause some damaging talk.

163

She'd be smart to stay away from Luke, she told herself as she rode into the shadow of the stallion barn. The man was a stickler for propriety. But what she found herself wanting from him was anything but proper. She remembered how, after they'd left the wash and returned to mount their horses, pain had stabbed her swollen ankle when she'd tried to put her weight in the stirrup. Without a word, he'd clasped her waist with his big, hard hands, hoisting her high enough to grab the saddle horn and swing her right leg over the cantle.

The pressure of his hands and the brief contact with his body, her breasts skimming his face as he lifted her, had sent a shock of sheer pleasure rocketing through her senses. The feeling had been so intense that she'd swallowed a gasp. Never in her life had she felt anything like it — certainly not with Kyle, not even when he kissed her.

But kissing Kyle was safe. It came packaged with the idea that this was how things would be, maybe for the rest of their lives. Being with Luke held the lure of the forbidden, heightened by a spark of danger.

Even touching him made her blood race.

What would kissing him be like?

But that was only a fantasy. She was a sensible young woman, raised to make the right choices. And Luke was older, a man of experience. He probably saw her as a willful child who'd gone riding off in a huff when he hadn't told her what she wanted to hear. What she was imagining was out of the question.

She had to stop thinking about it.

Luke held the bay stallion to a walk, cutting around the periphery of the yard to enter from the back road to the syndicate property. By the time he arrived at the barn, Erin had unsaddled Tesoro and was in his stall, rubbing him down. Leaving her alone for now, he unsaddled the bay stallion, gave him a quick rubdown, checked his food and water, and put him away. When he came out of the stall, Erin was there, her damp hair clinging around her face where her hatband had covered it. Her blazing blue eyes and the set of her jaw told him she still had a score to settle.

"Did you happen to notice whether the new shoes worked for Tesoro?" Her voice was chilly.

"Actually, I did. His gait looked fine. So did Ranger's."

"And you have plenty of work for the rest of the day?"

"I do. If I finish early, I'll have one of the

men bring me a few more horses. You won't have to worry about me, boss."

He hadn't meant the last word to sound sarcastic, but the sharp rise of her eyebrows told him that was how she'd taken it. Fine. Let her walk away mad. That would be safer for them both. Here, in the dark, intimate space of the barn it was hard not to imagine taking her in his arms and devouring that sweet, plum-ripe mouth of hers. That, and more — more than enough to get him in serious trouble.

Walk away, girl. Walk away while I still have a hold on myself.

Luke didn't say the words. He could only hope she was intuitive enough to understand.

She turned to go, then paused and turned back. "Oh — one more thing." She reached into the hip pocket of her jeans and took out a brass key on a leather thong. "The duplex is ready for you. You can still eat at the bunkhouse, but you won't have to sleep there anymore."

"Thanks. And thanks for clearing the place out. I owe you."

He held out his hand. She dropped the key into it. The metal still held the warmth of her body. He closed his fist around it, then dropped it into his shirt pocket.

166

Erin hadn't moved. Her deep blue eyes seemed to hold him suspended, as if he could lose his grip and spiral into their depths. If she didn't leave now . . .

Without a word, she reached with her right hand and caught the back of his neck. Stretching on tiptoe, she brought her lips up to his.

Erin felt his resistance, unyielding as stone. Would he thrust her angrily away from him? But no — a groan of surrender rose in his throat. His mouth molded to her kiss, deepening the intimate contact, taking possession. Erin's pulse exploded. The spark she'd felt earlier, when he'd lifted her into the saddle, became wildfire, racing through her veins to pool its heat in the depths of her body. She reveled in glorious new sensations. Her senses feasted on the warm, salty taste of his mouth, the velvety scrape of his stubble against her face, and the heady aroma of his skin, a blend of sun, sage, and horses.

Erin had experienced the usual necking with high school boys and with Kyle. But the burning need she felt now was unlike anything she'd ever known. She ached for more — to be touched by him, held by him; but his arms remained at his sides, as if

167

some part of him were still determined to resist her. She could almost feel his inner struggle. Where she stood against him, his body was as rigid as steel — warm steel with a pounding heart beneath its surface.

He ended the kiss and pushed her away, not angrily but firmly. He was breathing hard, his lips still moist from their kiss, but his expression had frozen over like winter ice.

"This never happened, Erin." His voice was a low rasp. "And it mustn't ever happen again. Do you understand?"

She willed herself to ignore the sting of his words. Luke's reaction was exactly what she should have expected — and probably what she deserved. But she wasn't sorry.

Her own voice emerged as a whisper. "I understand. It won't happen again. But if you're waiting for an apology, you're going to have to wait for a long time."

With that, she lifted her head, squared her shoulders, and strode out of the barn.

Compared to the noisy, crowded bunkhouse, the duplex was a four-star hotel. There was a kitchenette with stove and fridge, a coffeemaker, and a small microwave. An old but working TV faced a worn, overstuffed chair with a side table. There was even an efficiency-sized washer-dryer combo off the bathroom.

At the end of the day, Luke had moved his things into the new quarters, taken a quick shower, put on clean clothes, and gone back to the bunkhouse dining room for meat loaf and fried potatoes. He'd finished supper in time to return to the duplex, take a cold beer out of the fridge, and settle himself in the lawn chair on the front porch to watch the sun set over the Caprock Escarpment.

The weight of the key in his pocket reminded him of the extra effort that Erin had put into making the place comfortable — the fresh towels, the beer, the well-made bed, and the supplies for the coffeemaker.

He would have thanked her, but after storming out of the barn, with that soul-searing kiss still burning on his lips, she'd kept her distance. Given the way they'd parted, he wouldn't be surprised if she never spoke to him again. But that was just as well. He wanted her. And if she showed up again, he would have a struggle keeping his hands off her.

Erin's kiss had caught him by surprise. But when those soft young lips had pressed his, no amount of self-control could have kept him from responding. Even then, he'd held himself back. He'd known that if he let his hands roam free, he'd be in danger of going too far.

He would never have asked Erin if she was a virgin. But he'd sensed her innocence in the tender way she'd kissed him. This girl had grown up on a ranch. She would have seen countless animals perform the act of mating. But she was still exploring her own sensuality. To spoil that slow-flowering discovery would be the cruelest thing he could do to her.

Now twilight was falling over the Rimrock. With the sun gone and the heat fading, the growing darkness came alive with the chirps, flutters, and scurrying sounds of small creatures.

The lights were on in the big house. The pickup that had taken the old man's casket to the Hill Country had returned a couple of hours ago. Sky Fletcher had taken his blue truck and gone home to his family. Will would probably be with Erin. Luke couldn't help wondering how much she'd told her father about the day's events.

"May I join you?" Rose, the petite, silver-haired woman Luke had met earlier, stepped out onto the porch that spanned both sides of the duplex. She was wearing a navy blue track suit, her hair braided in pigtails like a

170

little girl's.

Luke lowered his boots from the porch rail, meaning to stand up and get her a chair, but she stopped him with the brush of a hand on his shoulder. "No, don't get up. There's a chair by my door. I'll just pull it over, next to you."

"I can get you a beer," Luke offered as she took her seat beside him.

"No need." She gazed across the ranch yard to where the dark outline of the escarpment jutted against the sky. "Forgive the intrusion. It's such a beautiful evening. I'd hoped it might be a good time to get acquainted with my neighbor."

"You're not intruding at all," Luke said. "As my grandmother used to say, there's no bad time for good company."

Rose chuckled. "I'll have to remember that one. So how are you finding the Rimrock so far?"

"Fine. Everybody's been friendly and easy to work with. When you see Erin, could you thank her for me? She did a great job of cleaning out this place and getting it ready."

Rose studied him a moment. "Why not thank her yourself?"

Had he revealed too much to this perceptive woman? Luke shrugged. "Let's just say

171

that she might not be too happy with me now."

"I see." Rose's dark eyes narrowed. "I've only known Erin a short time, but if she's anything like the rest of the Tylers, I'm guessing she's extremely strong-willed."

"That sounds about right," Luke said.

"You should know a few things about her," Rose said. "Erin is Will's only child. If he can hold on to the Rimrock in these hard times, it'll be all hers someday. To do that, she'll need to be extremely tough. A few months ago, she lost her mother. Now she's lost a man she depended on for wisdom and support. To add to that, her father is so grief-stricken that she's had to shoulder extra burdens for him. So if she's a little short-tempered with you —"

"I understand. It's making more sense now," Luke said. Rose hadn't quite hit the target but she'd come close enough. He was about to say more when the headlights of a familiar black SUV swung into the yard. The duplex was set back from the main house but it was angled enough that it was possible from where Luke sat to get a side view of the front porch. The long-legged figure climbing out of the vehicle and mounting the porch was unmistakably Erin's boyfriend, Kyle Cardwell.

172

Luke tried to ignore the gnawing in his gut. He had no right to be jealous. Erin wasn't his and never would be. But when Cardwell came out a minute later, holding her hand and leading her to his vehicle, the gnawing chewed deeper. If Rose hadn't been with him, he would have cursed and gone inside to drink another beer and watch some mind-numbing show on TV until he felt sleepy enough to go to bed.

As the SUV's red taillights disappeared down the lane, Luke turned to find Rose watching him, a knowing expression on her face. Those sharp eyes of hers didn't seem to miss a thing.

"So, do you think those two will get married?" Luke forced himself to ask.

Rose sighed. "Will seems in favor of it. But having met the young man . . ." She sighed again. "I remember how things were with Tanner, my husband. Heavens, we were on fire! We would have died for each other — in fact, we almost did. He was my world, and I was his. I don't sense that with Erin, or with Kyle. I worry about her missing out on what real love can be."

"It sounds like you must've had a wonderful marriage."

"Oh, I did. I miss him terribly now that he's gone. But it helps to know I had the very best there was." She gave Luke a wistful smile. "You remind me of him — the same kind of quiet strength. You even look a little like him. He was tall and dark, like you."

"If that's a compliment, I'll take it." Unaccustomed to praise, Luke changed the subject. "What's your connection to the Tyler family, Rose? I get the impression that it goes way back."

"Oh, indeed it does! It's a long story, some of it so fantastic that you'd think I was making it up. If you're not in a hurry to go inside, I'd enjoy telling it to you."

"I'd enjoy hearing it, and I'm not going anywhere." Luke was grateful for the needed distraction.

"Very well." Rose slid her chair forward and propped her sneakers on the rail next to Luke's boots. "It all started when I was fourteen years old, and Bull Tyler saved my life. . . ."

The SUV rumbled along the graveled lane, headed for the junction with the paved road to town. Erin had rolled down the side window. The night breeze fluttered her hair and cooled her face.

Kyle had phoned her after dinner. Tomorrow's date night in the city would have to be canceled because his father had insisted on taking him to a cattle auction in Lubbock, and they'd be staying for dinner that evening. Erin hadn't minded. She'd been ambivalent about their plans, dreading another proposal that she would turn down.

With her emotions in turmoil after that burning kiss with Luke, this was hardly a good time for a romantic evening. But when Kyle had asked to see her tonight, just long enough for a drive, she'd seen no reason to refuse.

"Thanks again for coming with me tonight," he said. "And thanks for not being mad about canceling our big date."

"We can go another time," Erin said. "I know your dad wants you to learn the business."

"I wish I had the nerve to tell him that I don't give a shit about the business," he said. "Why should I want to be like him, working for wages on a ranch he doesn't own — not even the house — and making everybody miserable in the process? He's a nobody. He knows it and he hates it. Maybe if I had a ranch of my own, and I was building something for the future, to pass on to my children and to their children . . ." He gave Erin a meaningful glance.

There was no way she could have missed

his intent. This wasn't a proposal in so many words. But Kyle had laid his cards on the table. At least he was being honest. Maybe there was nothing wrong with that. Any man she married would be tied to the Rimrock. And the way he'd expressed it, *building something for the future, to pass on to my children* — wasn't that what she wanted to hear?

A flying insect smashed against the windshield, its body splattering on the glass. Erin tore her gaze away from the mess. Steeling her resolve, she touched Kyle's arm. "Pull over," she said.

He pulled off the road, the engine still idling. Crickets chirped and rustled in the long, dry grass. "What is it, Erin?" he asked. "Is something wrong?"

She turned toward him in the seat. "Kiss me, Kyle," she said. "I mean *really* kiss me!"

For an instant, he looked startled. Then his smile gleamed in the lights of the dashboard. He switched off the ignition and reached for her. She went to him willingly, his embrace pulling her awkwardly over the console. She shut her eyes as his soft, moist mouth closed on hers, pressing harder, deepening the kiss. His tongue, tasting of spearmint, invaded her mouth. She responded with enthusiasm, returning the playful thrusts, wanting to feel the magic, that hot racing of her blood that had happened when she'd kissed Luke. If it happened, that would simplify everything.

But she felt next to nothing.

She tried harder, arms twining his neck, fingers raking his hair. Even when his hand closed on her breast, she didn't push him away as she had the last time he'd done it. He squeezed her through her blouse. She bit back a whimper of pain, allowing him to fondle her until he began to fumble with her buttons. Only then did she pull away.

He grinned, leaning back in the seat. "Was that a yes, Erin?"

"Not yet." Erin wiped a hand across her mouth. "Just drive, okay?"

"Sometimes I can't figure you out. But I'm not complaining." He started the engine and swung the SUV back onto the road. "Kiss me like that, and I'll have a hard time waiting much longer to marry you."

Erin didn't reply. She leaned toward the open window to let the night breeze cool her face. What was wrong with her? She certainly didn't love Luke. She barely knew him. But the ecstatic rush she'd felt with that single kiss was something she craved to feel again. And she wasn't feeling it with Kyle.

Marrying Kyle would please her father. Kyle was decent and responsible, and he clearly wanted a life with her. But could a lifetime love, the kind of passionate love she'd seen between her parents, grow and flourish without that vital spark?

Now that she knew what she was missing, there could only be one answer to that question.

Not that the answer was Luke. He'd made it clear he didn't want her. She could only hope that later on she would find the magic with someone else — maybe someone she had yet to meet.

"We could go into town and get ice cream at the Burger Shack," Kyle said. "I've got time, if you have."

Erin almost said no. But she needed to unwind before she went home. If she walked through the door in her present emotional state, her father would ask her what was wrong, and she wouldn't know what to tell him. The Burger Shack was usually crowded at this hour. They might even meet some friends. It would be a good place for them both to cool down. Maybe that was the reason Kyle had suggested it. He wasn't a bad person, Erin reminded herself. He could be sweet and thoughtful. Maybe that was why it was going to hurt when she gave him her final answer.

Inside the Burger Shack, they found a birthday party for a middle schooler going on. Surrounded by noise, they ordered root beer floats and drank them at the bar. Kyle leaned close to Erin's ear. "When you have your twenty-first birthday, we're going to celebrate with Coronas at the Blue Coyote. No more damned kid parties."

Erin smiled and nodded, wondering where she'd really be and with whom when she turned twenty-one. She wasn't looking forward to the ride home. It would be all too easy to put Kyle off, but in the end, it would only be cruel.

The distance from Blanco Springs to the Rimrock was a little less than twenty miles. The ride home wouldn't be a long one. As Kyle drove out of the parking lot, onto Main Street, Erin steeled herself and cleared her throat.

"I have my answer to your proposal," she said.

He glanced at her with an expectant grin. "After that kiss, it had better be yes," he said.

"I'm afraid it isn't. Kyle, I'm still growing up. Right now, I don't even know who I am. I'm not ready to get engaged, let alone get married. And I don't want you to wait for

179

me. My final answer is no."

Kyle didn't reply, but the stomp of his foot on the gas pedal spoke for him. The SUV shot down Main Street, breaking speed limits and running a red light. Luckily, the evening traffic was sparse, and the local sheriff was busy elsewhere.

Kyle didn't speak until they'd turned onto the highway. "I thought you loved me," he said. "That kiss —"

"That kiss was a test, to make sure. And now I know. I'm fond of you, Kyle. You're a good man. But I'm not in love with you."

"So I take it you didn't hear bells or see shooting stars. Is that so important? We're good together. We want the same things. That's what matters."

When Erin didn't answer, he gripped the wheel tighter and pressed down on the gas. The speedometer needle swung up to seventy miles an hour, a dangerous speed on the narrow, two-lane highway where farm rigs and wandering animals could appear out of nowhere.

Erin touched his arm. "Slow down. You're scaring me."

Kyle ignored her plea. "Is there somebody else, Erin?" he demanded. "Is that what's changed your mind?"

"Of course not. I just realized I wasn't ready."

"What about that hired man you were with when I came over the other day? I saw the way he was looking at you. If that bastard has laid a hand on you —"

"Don't be ridiculous. He's not even — *Look out!*"

Erin screamed as a cow lunged out of the grassy bar ditch. Its face flashed stark white in the SUV's headlights. Kyle wrenched the wheel hard left. Brakes screeched as the vehicle shot across the road and jumped the ditch on the far side. The airbags deployed with an explosive hiss as the SUV crashed into the post of a barbed wire fence.

As the shock wore off, Erin's anxious gaze found Kyle. He was moving and appeared to be all right. Cautiously she tested her limbs, flexing her hands and feet, shifting her back and shoulders. Except for some soreness from the air bag and a painful bruise where the shoulder strap had pulled across her chest, she seemed unhurt.

"Are you all right?" she asked Kyle in a shaky voice.

"I think so." He gazed through the windshield at the vehicle's crumpled hood. "Wow, that was close! My dad's going to kill me when he sees the car."

Relief swept over her, swiftly followed by a tide of white-hot anger. "You're worried about the car? We could have been killed, Kyle! You were driving like a crazy man!"

"Well, you made me crazy. If I thought you'd meant it when you said you wouldn't marry me, I'd have been even crazier. This wreck is as much your fault as mine." He turned the key in the ignition. The engine caught and started on the first try. "If the wheels aren't stuck, I should be able to get us out of here." Shifting into reverse, he backed away from the fence. The wheels made a grinding sound, but by backing and filling, he was able to make progress. The ranch was more than ten miles away. If Erin hadn't left her cell phone at home, she might have called her father to come and get her. As it was, she had little choice except to stay.

Luckily, the damage to the vehicle's front end didn't affect its operation. After several tries and some choice curses, Kyle was able to pull back onto the road. There was no sign of the cow. Erin could only hope the animal had made a safe escape.

"Don't worry, Erin." Kyle reached over and patted her knee. "You'll feel differently about all this in the morning."

"Don't touch me. Don't even talk."

Erin sat in stony silence as Kyle drove her back to the Rimrock. She'd assumed that she knew him. But tonight he'd shown her a different side of himself — angry and reckless, with no regard for her safety or even for his own.

What if they'd been married, with their children in the car? He could have killed them all.

If she'd had any doubts about not marrying Kyle, those doubts were gone.

Now the question was, would Kyle accept her decision?

From her vantage point in the outcrop above the horse paddock, Marie had a clear view of the Rimrock's main house. Aided by the security light, her sharp eyes could see that the black SUV pulling up next to the porch was damaged in front. And the figure climbing out of the passenger side, slamming the door behind her before she raced up the steps, was Erin Tyler.

Marie couldn't see the driver of the departing SUV, but the situation appeared to be a date gone bad. Maybe that had something to do with the wrecked car.

If the accident had just happened, Marie mused, it was a shame she hadn't been there. She could've taken out the girl and her boyfriend, done some skilled re-arranging, and nobody would have suspected the truth. As it was, the girl wouldn't be going anywhere until tomorrow. Time to call it a night and go back to the deserted line shack where she'd made her camp.

Marie cursed as she wound her way among the rocks, taking care not to leave a trail. She was losing patience. She'd already missed the appointment with her parole officer. If it took her much longer to complete Stella's job, pick up the drugs, unload them for cash, and beat it out of the country, the cops would be on her tail. Or worse, she'd have to run before the job was done, and she'd be stuck with no money, a crappy motorbike that barely ran, and no place to go.

From higher up, she could see the distant lights of a smaller ranch. She'd checked it out earlier. Sky Fletcher, her cousin, had done well for himself — a fine house, a high-class wife, and plenty of livestock. Marie and Sky had grown up together after his mother died and her family took him in. As children, they'd been like brother and sister. But those days were over. The first time she'd shown up here, Sky had tried to help her. But he'd washed his hands of her after she'd tried to murder his fiancée, by ramming her car. If she were to show her face now, or give any other sign that she was here, Sky would be the first one to call the police.

Her motorbike was waiting on the far side of a rocky hill. Marie avoided riding the noisy piece of junk within hearing of the central ranch. She was getting tired of that, too. Her cockroach kicker boots, relics from before her arrest, weren't made for walking. Tonight her feet were screaming. It was a relief to climb on the bike and roar off to her vermin-infested hideout.

She'd spent the better part of a week watching the ranch, waiting for a chance to move in on the little Tyler princess. That chance hadn't come, and Marie was running out of time. She needed a more aggressive plan. If that plan entailed more risk, so be it. Her whole future depended on her killing Erin Tyler.

CHAPTER NINE

The next morning, after her father had left the house, Erin prepared to go into town and present her evidence to the sheriff. Except for the bird gun, which Will had locked in his gun cabinet, the box of personal things found with Jasper's body had been left in the ranch office. The box had been opened, but no one had felt the need, or the desire, to go through the contents in any detail. So much the better, Erin told herself as she lifted the box out of the corner and set it on the desk. Jasper's simple possessions could hold clues, maybe even fingerprints.

Or maybe nothing. She had to be prepared for that.

She'd put on rubber gloves from the kitchen and was about to lift off the lid of the cardboard box when her cell phone rang. She pulled it out of her pocket and glanced at the caller ID. Kyle. It appeared he hadn't given up. She let the phone ring until voice mail came on.

"Erin, I hope you're listening. I was a fool last night. Can you ever forgive me? I'll be with my dad today, but I'll call you when I get home. I love you."

She deleted the voice mail. Kyle's behavior last night had been the final straw. She was finished with him. Why couldn't he just give up and move on?

Dropping the phone back into her pocket, she opened the box. Jasper's dusty old Stetson covered everything beneath it. Erin blinked back tears as she set the hat aside. She wasn't just looking for what was *in* the box, she reminded herself. What she really needed was to discover what was missing.

Jasper's clothes and boots had been bagged by the medical examiner. The things in the box were smaller, more personal items. Her gloved fingers touched each one — the red bandanna Jasper had worn against the dust, his khaki shooting vest with shotgun shells stuck into the cotton loops, his cheap Timex watch, his belt, a few coins, a bottle of nitroglycerin pills for occasional heart pain, his empty water canteen, a pack of Wrigley's gum, and his beat-up leather wallet.

There would be no cell phone. Jasper had

187

refused to own one of the contraptions, as he'd called them. The same went for credit cards. Jasper hadn't believed in them. He'd always carried cash, sometimes as much as several hundred dollars.

The pistol wasn't in the box. And it wasn't in the gun cabinet where Will would have put it. But the wallet would be worth checking.

She picked it up carefully. Jasper's driver's license and Medicare card were in the slots where he kept them. But in the compartment that held bills . . . Erin's heart slammed. There was nothing there but a single dollar bill, which appeared to have been left behind as a joke.

So far the pistol and the cash — the first items that a thief would take — were missing. Was there anything else? It appeared not. But Erin had to be sure.

Jasper's cigarettes and lighter weren't here, but Erin had found them when she'd cleaned the duplex. What about his keys? The key to the ATV had been in the ignition, but Jasper also had his own keys to the ranch truck, the duplex, the barns and sheds, and the main house, which he kept together on a ring with a leather fob. If someone had taken those keys, every lock would have to be changed.

188

Panic building, she rummaged through the items one last time. Relief weakened her knees as she found the key ring, deep in the pocket of Jasper's shooting vest with a handful of extra shells. One worry out of the way, at least.

Erin took a few minutes to box and address the old Bible for Jasper's niece in the Hill Country. It was almost eight o'clock when she carried the two boxes outside to the station wagon. From the direction of the horse pens came the ring of Luke's hammer as he shaped a steel shoe on his anvil. She resisted the urge to cross the yard and tell him what she'd discovered. Before she'd kissed him, that might have been an easy thing to do. But that impulsive kiss had destroyed the chance of an easy relationship between them. They'd agreed to forget it had happened. But Erin hadn't forgotten it. Something told her that Luke hadn't forgotten it either.

The morning was already warm, and the AC was going out on the old station wagon. As she drove to town, she opened the side windows to let the air blow through. The breeze was better than nothing, but she could feel the dust in the air like grit on her teeth.

She passed the spot where Kyle had

189

swerved to avoid the cow the night before. She could see the black, curving skid mark on the road, the crushed weeds, and the smashed barbed wire fence. But there was no sign that an animal had been struck. At least she could be relieved for the cow.

The sheriff's office was in a wing of the county building, adjacent to the courthouse. Sheriff Harger hadn't come in yet, but his young deputy, Roy Porter, was at his desk. The sight of him raised Erin's hopes for a sympathetic hearing. She and Roy had gone through school a year apart. With luck, he'd be more inclined to listen than the crusty, older sheriff.

He stood and motioned Erin to a seat opposite the desk. She remembered him as quiet and smart, but not the kind of boy who stood out. Looking at him now, she surmised that he hadn't changed much. In his tan lawman's uniform, with his ginger hair buzzed short, he looked like a bright-eyed, apple-cheeked Boy Scout.

Erin took her seat, setting the box on the floor next to her chair. "I have some concerns about Jasper Platt's death," she said, wasting no time.

"What kind of concerns?" Roy's demeanor was all business.

"I've found evidence that Jasper wasn't

alone when he died. There was someone else at the scene — someone who may have murdered him."

Roy looked skeptical. "I know what our investigation found. But go ahead. I'm listening."

She told him about the missing gun and the almost empty wallet. And she showed him the photo she'd taken of the boot print in the sand. "We found another print, like this one, above the paddock, by the fence. And the night we found it, we saw somebody moving and heard the sound of a motorcycle going away."

"We?"

Erin gave herself a mental slap. She should have known better than to imply she hadn't been alone. "One of the ranch hands was with me."

"His name, for the record?"

"Luke Maddox. He's the new farrier we hired." Why did giving out Luke's name strike Erin as a bad idea? She certainly didn't suspect him of anything criminal.

Roy jotted down some notes, then leaned back in his chair. "Here's what we're looking at," he said. "What you've told me sounds credible as far as it goes. But the only marks on Mr. Platt's body were those that could be attributed to the accident.

191

Even without an autopsy, there was no sign that foul play was involved in his death."

"But what about the evidence?" Erin argued. "Somebody was there. Otherwise you'd have found Jasper's pistol. And I know for a fact that Jasper always carried cash in his wallet."

"I believe you," Roy said. "But it's easy enough to explain. That wash is a known hangout for illegals and smugglers. Before the old man was found, somebody came along and helped himself to whatever was worth taking. If you saw that track again on the ranch, the same lowlife was probably looking for something else to steal. Case closed. If you'd like to file a report on the theft of the gun and the money —"

"No. Whoever the thief was, I'm sure they're long gone."

"Fine." Roy stood and offered his hand. "Let us know if there's any more trouble."

With sagging spirits, Erin mailed the Bible at the post office, picked up some groceries at the supermarket, and headed back to the ranch. She'd set out to prove that Will had not been at fault in Jasper's death. But she'd proven nothing. There was no way of knowing whether Jasper could have been found in time to save his life. As for the so-called evidence, Roy's argument made perfect sense. There had been no murder, only theft.

At least she hadn't voiced her suspicions to Will. Now they could be put to rest and forgotten. Her father already had enough worries on his mind.

As she parked by the house and climbed out of the car, she could hear the distant metallic ring of Luke's hammer blows. For a moment she considered walking down to the pens and telling him what she'd learned in town. But their encounter was bound to be awkward. The news could wait. If he was curious, he could find her and ask.

She was getting the groceries out of the wagon when Rose hailed her from the front porch. "Here, let me help you." She hurried down the steps to take one of the bags.

"Thanks. You just saved me a second trip," Erin said.

"You're very welcome." Rose mounted the steps beside her. "There aren't many ways for an old woman to make herself useful around here. The house is spotless, and your cook already shooed me out of the kitchen. But I do want to do my share while I'm with you, and I've never been one to sit around and read or knit."

"Dad mentioned last night that he was going to take you to see your land," Erin said as they set the grocery bags on the counter.

"He did, but something must've come up. Poor Will, I know how burdened he is. I hate bothering him about it."

"Why don't I take you?" Erin had seen Will's truck headed for the pastures on the upper range, where the men would be rounding up cattle for early sale. "We could go now, if this is a good time. I'll even throw some gloves and shovels and rakes in the back of the wagon. We can spend a little time cleaning up your grandpa's grave."

"Oh, thank you!" Rose's face lit with pleasure. "Just let me get a hat. And I brought my own work gloves. I thought they might come in handy."

"I'll load the tools," Erin said. "Come around to the car when you're ready."

Luke watched the station wagon head north along the back road, with Erin at the wheel and Rose beside her. Wherever they were going, he couldn't help worrying about them. With a stranger prowling around the ranch, anything could happen.

But maybe his concern was old-fashioned. This was the twenty-first century. Women were tough and independent, especially those two. Erin was young, but she was

194

quick and smart. As for Rose . . . He'd been stunned to learn that the petite woman had killed three men, the first one when she was just fourteen. But after hearing her story last night, he couldn't doubt the truth of it.

Still . . . Luke worried as he watched the station wagon vanish in a cloud of dust. He worried too damned much, he told himself as he chose another horse to trim and shoe. Last night, after Rose had gone inside, he'd seen the black SUV pull up to the house with a crumpled front end. He'd watched Erin climb out, slam the door, and storm into the house. At least he knew she was all right. But she'd given him no chance to ask her what had happened. She hadn't even come to tell him about her visit to the sheriff in town.

He understood the reason. She didn't want to face him after that kiss — the kiss that had left him with a lingering ache. Luke had told himself it didn't matter. She'd only been flirting with him, or trying out her charms on an unsuspecting male just to see what would happen. But he couldn't look at her, or even think about her, without wanting to crush her in his arms and pick up where they'd left off before he pushed her away.

Maybe he should just quit this job, pack

up, and leave. There was always work to be had, especially before and during roundup season. But he had an ideal situation here — plenty of steady work, good people, decent quarters and food, and animals that were healthy and well cared for. He'd be a fool to leave because of an impulsive beauty who was too young to know her own mind.

I worry about her missing out on what real love can be.

Rose's words came back to him as he watched the dust settle in the empty distance. He hoped to heaven Erin didn't marry that entitled brat of a boyfriend. But if the kid was her choice, there was nothing more to be said.

One thing was certain, Luke told himself. He was no fit match for her tender young heart. If he were to give in to temptation, he might offer her a few thrills. But in the end, given their age difference, his rootless lifestyle, and his troubled past, he would only end up leaving her wounded and angry.

For now, the best he could do was keep his distance, control his urges, and struggle against the memory of that kiss.

But what if he was falling in love with her?

After arranging for the wrecked SUV to be picked up and repaired, Hunter Cardwell,

Kyle's father, had taken one of the ranch pickups to drive to the cattle auction in Lubbock. He drove most of the way in silence, his lips pressed into a grim line. For Kyle, seated beside him in the cab, it was like waiting for a ticking bomb to explode.

Kyle had learned the hard way not to hide the truth from his father. By now, Hunter knew how the wreck had happened. He also knew that Erin had turned down his son's proposal. He had taken the news with surprising calm. Even the sight of the damaged SUV hadn't set him off.

For Kyle, his father's icy demeanor was even more ominous than a burst of anger. He knew that the blowup would come, and when it did, the consequences would be devastating. Meanwhile, all he could do was wait in slow, excruciating torment.

Vivian sat in the porch swing, drinking her second glass of iced coffee and savoring the prospect of a day to herself. It was amazing how the knots of tension inside her loosened when her husband and son were out of the house. When they were here, it was as if she were constantly pulled between pleasing her husband and protecting her son — and failing at both. Only when she was alone did she feel free to breathe and to think her own thoughts.

What would she do with her time? With the SUV in the shop, she couldn't go to town. And even after years as a ranch manager's wife, she'd never learned to ride a horse. It was too hot and dusty for any kind of walk. But here in the house, she could do whatever she liked.

Sunlight slanted through the trees, its rays turning the dust motes in the air to flecks of gold along the rutted back road. Vivian's gaze traced the road to where it curved out of sight, ending at the Rimrock Ranch. She imagined herself, maybe with a pie or a batch of homemade cookies, knocking on the door of the ranch house and finding Will at home alone. He would invite her in, and the two of them would talk. He would reach out to her, touch her, and whisper, *You don't know how much I've needed you, Vivian. . . .*

But that was only a fantasy. It was too hot to bake anything. If she were to walk to the Rimrock, she would arrive a sweaty, dusty mess. And Will would probably be off working somewhere. Even if he happened to be home, Will's daughter, the cook, and that older woman who was visiting would probably be there, too.

But there was no law against a little daydreaming.

Maybe she should try writing a romance novel. She had lots of ideas. She could start by writing down some of her fantasies, or better yet, maybe a make-believe letter to Will. It wouldn't be a real letter, of course, and she wouldn't dream of sending it. But Vivian found the idea of writing down her erotic thoughts strangely exciting.

Going inside, she found a pad of good quality notepaper and a pen in Hunter's desk. She wouldn't use the computer. A machine would be too impersonal. And there was always the chance that Hunter or Kyle would find the file. They would probably laugh at her. That, or she'd have a lot of explaining to do.

Feeling vaguely naughty, she sat down at the kitchen table and thought for a moment. The words came slowly at first, then, as she wrote, they began to flow.

My darling Will . . . Last night in your arms, I became a woman all over again. . . . Until our bodies became one, I never knew how love-making could bring two souls together. . . .

Rose's parcel was a twenty-minute drive north from the heart of the Rimrock. The dirt road was rutted and dusty, the landscape open and dotted with scrub. Red and white Hereford cattle, most of them wearing the Rimrock's rocking-R brand, grazed among mesquite thickets and scraggly clumps of sage.

The cattle looked poor, Rose thought. Clearly the dried grass and weeds weren't giving them the nourishment they needed. No wonder Will was worried. But here, at least, with the creek filling the tank, the animals would have water.

As the station wagon, with Erin at the wheel, neared the thirty-acre strip of land, Rose felt the tug of memories. So many memories. She pictured her grandfather's little cabin, where he'd moved after his retirement from the university and the death of his wife. He'd taken Rose in when she'd fled an abusive foster home, sheltering her and giving her the best education a young girl could want. She remembered his tragic murder, with Bull and Jasper snatching her to safety before the cabin went up in flames.

After eleven years in Mexico, where Bull had taken her after Ham Prescott's death, she'd come back, reclaimed the land, and tried to make a life here. Once again, violence had caught up with her. But one happy memory remained. Here, she had met Tanner. Here, they had fallen in love.

"This is it," Erin said, stopping the vehicle.

"There's the tank. Do you want to get out here?"

"Might as well." Rose opened the door and climbed out, mindful of the small, loaded pistol she wore in a belt holster at her hip.

Erin had been surprised to see Rose show up with a gun. "I can't imagine you'll need that," she'd said.

"Bear with me, sweetheart," Rose had replied. "If you had my memories of the place, you'd probably be packing a gun, too."

The tank was galvanized metal, built up around the rim with earth. A hose connected to a heavy PVC pipe ran between the tank and the creek. There were a few trees growing near the water, mostly cottonwood and elder. But the grasses and wildflowers were gone, eaten or trampled away. Only the sound of the creek, so sweet and pure that Rose had never forgotten it, remained unchanged.

Erin opened the back of the wagon and pulled out two rakes and a shovel, along with a pair of leather work gloves. "Let's go," she said. "If there's something special you want done, just let me know."

With a nod, Rose followed her to the littered grave beneath the old fallen tree. The condition of the place made her want to weep. But everything would be all right, she told herself. Her land was beneath her feet, and today she was starting work on her new home.

Screened by a patch of mesquite, Marie watched the two women carry the tools toward the creek. After seeing the station wagon leave the ranch, she had cut through the foothills on her bike. It had been easy enough to guess that the women were coming here. They were driving north on the road that was more of a trail, and this place was where it ended.

By the time the wagon had stopped, Marie was in her hiding place, close enough to watch, but too far away to get a good shot with the pistol she'd taken off the old man. When she was ready to fire, she would need to move in closer. That might mean showing herself, but if she killed both women, which she would have to do, it wouldn't matter if they saw her.

She could see them through the trees, moving in and out of sight. They appeared to be raking and digging at a spot near the creek, talking as they worked. It would be easy enough to get closer, but difficult to get a clear shot without hitting a tree. It might be better to wait until they came back to the car.

Marie sighed in frustration. She knew how to make a simple bomb and wire it to the ignition of a car. But she had no way to make one here. Too bad. For this situation, it would have been perfect.

She was about to move in closer when the smaller, older woman turned to one side. That was when Marie saw the holstered pistol at her hip. A woman wearing a gun in that fashion would know how to use it. If she happened to be a fast draw and a good shot, the risk of being hit was greater than Marie was willing to take.

Moving soundlessly, she backed away. By the time the two women returned to the station wagon, Marie was back in the foothills, waiting for them to leave so she could start her bike.

Maybe it was time to do some creative thinking.

Erin loaded the tools into the back of the station wagon and closed the hatch. It had taken a little less than an hour to clean off the grave and erect a protective barrier of sticks and branches around it.

"I can't thank you enough for your help." Rose brushed the dust off her jeans before climbing into the passenger seat. "My grandpa was a wonderful man. He taught me everything I know about science, math, and history, and he died protecting me from the Prescotts. His resting place deserves to be honored, not trampled by cows."

"It was an honor to help." Erin settled into the driver's seat and started the vehicle. "We might have some leftover fencing materials in the shed. If I can find what we need, we can come again and put up a real fence around the grave."

"You'd do that for me? Thank you. That would make me feel so much better about the place."

"What are your plans?" Erin turned the wagon around and headed back toward the heart of the ranch. "I know you've talked to my dad, but he hasn't told me much."

"I'm still making plans," Rose said. "What I hope to do is sell my Wyoming house to Tanner's brother and use the money to build my own little home here, on my property, with chickens and goats and maybe a dog or two."

"Then we'd be neighbors. I'd love that."

"So would I. But I'm still getting a grip on how much work it's going to involve. Just burying that ugly water pipe and fencing off the boundary will take some doing. I

204

only hope your father will go along with my plans." Rose took a moment to lower her side window. "And what about your plans, Erin? Will tells me you want to stay on the ranch. But what about the rest? Are you going to marry that young man of yours?"

"He's not my young man, and I'm not going to marry him. We broke up last night. For good."

"Oh." Rose sounded almost pleased. "I could say I was sorry, but it would be a lie. You can do better than that boy."

"I hope my father agrees with you. I haven't told him yet."

"Will loves you. All he really wants is for you to be happy."

"I know. But his idea of happy is for me to be married to a suitable man who'll stay on the ranch and breed a new generation of little Tylers, or whatever their names will be."

"So, what's your idea of happy?" Rose asked.

"I'm still figuring that out. What my father wants for me is fine, I guess. But it's not enough. I want to be in love — truly in love, like my parents were. Right now, I'm not even sure what that feels like. I only know I didn't feel it with Kyle."

"You're still young," Rose said. "Give it

some time. I was twenty-six when I fell in love with Tanner. It took me that long to find the right man, but the wait was worth it — not that I was waiting. I wasn't even looking for love. He just happened along, and I knew."

"But how did you know? Was it like a sky full of fireworks going off the first time he kissed you?"

Rose gave Erin a knowing look, as if she'd already guessed about Luke and that wild, forbidden kiss. "It can start like that," she said, smiling. "But the real thing goes much deeper. When his happiness comes to matter more than your own, when you'd risk any danger or hardship to be with him . . ." She paused, perhaps remembering. "When it feels like that, you're on your way."

"So you think I was right to turn down Kyle's proposal?"

"Only you can be the judge of that, dear. But if you want my advice, I can offer you three things that life has taught me — wait for as long as it takes, don't settle for less than real love, and when it comes to you, don't close the door."

They had reached the ranch yard. Erin let Rose off at the duplex and drove around to the shed to unload the tools. From the far side of the yard, she could hear Luke's intermittent hammering.

Sooner or later she would have to talk to him, if only about the horses. The longer she waited, the more uncomfortable the silence between them would become. He would want to know what she'd learned in town. She would have questions about his work. It was time she ended the awkward standoff between them.

She put the tools on the rack, closed the shed, and parked the station wagon next to the house. Climbing out, she hesitated a moment. He could still be angry with her. He could rebuff her with cutting words, as he had the young girl who'd been told to go play with her dolls. Or he could simply turn his powerful back and ignore her.

But he was her father's employee, and hers, Erin reminded herself. She was the one in charge — although being in charge of Luke was like being in charge of a wild stallion.

Taking a moment, she went inside the house, hung the car keys on their hook by the door, and found a bottle of Corona in the fridge.

With her pulse racing, and the ice cold bottle dripping condensation, she set off across the yard.

CHAPTER TEN

Erin found Luke under the open shed, shoeing a young gray gelding. She stood by the fence watching, waiting for him to look up and notice her.

He'd taken off his chambray work shirt and tossed it over the fence. Perspiration beaded his face and streamed down his arms and torso. His skin gleamed like polished bronze, the light casting every muscle into sculpted relief. He was beautiful, Erin thought, if that word could be applied to a gruff, masculine loner like Luke. Maybe *rugged* would be more appropriate, or even *majestic*.

For a few minutes he seemed totally intent on his work. Only when he shifted his position from the gelding's front hoof to the back did he glance up and see her. "Hi," he said.

"Hi." Heart pounding, Erin held up the beer. "I brought you a peace offering."

He grinned, showing a slightly chipped tooth in front. "Hang on to it while I finish shoeing this pretty boy. He won't take kindly to standing still while I drink it."

"Fine, but I can't promise it'll be cold." Erin felt the tension easing between them. Maybe they could even be friends again.

"That's okay, as long as it's wet."

"Take your time — I've got an idea." An empty metal pail stood next to the gate. Erin carried it to the outside tap by the barn, filled it with cold water, and lowered the bottle of Corona into it. When he finished shoeing the horse, the beer would still be cold.

"So, how did your visit to the sheriff go?" he asked, talking while he worked.

"Not great. The deputy pretty much convinced me that Jasper was robbed by somebody who came along after the so-called accident."

"You say *pretty much*?" He used a small hammer to nail the shoe to the outer layer of the hoof, keeping clear of the sensitive inner part. "Does that mean you still have your doubts?"

"Some, I guess. But there's not much I can do about it."

"You can be careful. Trust your instincts. If you sense danger out there, assume you could be right." He finished clipping the nail points on the last hoof and released the gelding with a gentle slap on its haunch. "Time for a break. I'll take that beer now."

He came out of the pen, closed the gate behind him, and reached for the beer in her hand. After popping open the lid, he took a long, slow drink. When he lowered it, the bottle was half empty. With his free hand, he picked up the pail by the handle. "Just what I need, a nice, cold shower. Want to do the honors?"

"What? You want me to dump it on you?"

Laughter glinted in his dark eyes. "That, or hold the beer while I do it myself."

"Here." Erin took the pail from his hand, raised it as high as she could, and upended it over his head.

He laughed, shivering as the cold water cascaded down his body. Droplets clung to the mat of black hair on his chest, the sun turning them to tiny rainbows. His nipples had shrunk to hard nubs. Looking at him, Erin felt a subtle clench, like a tightening fist, deep in her body. Her close-up experience with men was limited, but her instincts told her she was on the path to trouble.

He raked back his dripping hair, finished the beer, and dropped the bottle into the pail, which Erin had set on the ground.

"Thanks, I feel like a new man," he said.

"You're welcome. I was afraid you were mad at me." As soon as the words came out, Erin wanted to bite them back. She sounded like a fool.

"Mad at you?" One dark eyebrow slid upward. "What for?"

"For . . . what didn't happen." She was digging herself deeper and deeper.

"Oh, that!" He chuckled. "Believe me, the one thing I wasn't was mad. Crazy, maybe. But not mad. So shall we pretend to forget about it?"

"Yes. That's a good idea." Ignoring her blazing face, she changed the subject. "How's my stallion doing?"

"He was fine early this morning. But he was a little stand-offish with me. I can tell he's a one-woman horse. Maybe you should go and say hello to him."

"I'll do that." Erin thought she might have been dismissed, but when she turned away and headed for the stallion barn, Luke walked with her.

"So, are you going to tell your father about our visitor?" he asked her. "For the record, I think you should."

Erin shook her head. "There's no point in it now. My dad has enough worries on his mind. The same goes for Sky. Whoever came

211

around and left those tracks, they've probably moved on."

Shadows deepened around them as they walked into the stallion barn. The horses nickered and stirred, wanting attention. Erin stopped by Tesoro's box. At the sound of her voice, the palomino thrust his elegant head over the gate. Erin stroked his satiny golden neck, whispering little words of praise as her fingers freed a tangle in his mane. In a moment, she moved to greet the other two stallions. As she stroked and talked to them, she sensed Luke's eyes on her. The awareness rippled over her skin, like a breeze over quiet water.

"Horses always make me feel peaceful," she said as they turned to go back the way they'd come. "Do they make you feel that way, too?"

"I never gave much thought to that," Luke said. "I like horses. But I spend so much time with them, they're just part of my work." He slowed his step, allowing her to keep pace with him. "You're not limping. Your ankle must be better."

"It is, as long as I don't overdo."

"Have you told anyone else about our visitor? Maybe your boyfriend?"

Her calm mood evaporated. "No. And he's not my boyfriend. We broke up last night, for good this time."

"I wondered when I saw you get out of that smashed-up SUV. Not that it's any of my business, but I hope the breakup didn't have anything to do with his seeing you and me together."

"Of course it didn't. I was the one who broke up with him. I didn't love him and I wasn't ready to get married. And when I told him that, he started driving like a maniac. If he'd hit that cow on the road, he could've gotten us both —" She broke off as the realization struck her. "You saw me come home? What were you doing, waiting up for me?"

He looked at her as if she were five years old. "I'm not your babysitter, Erin. I was having trouble falling asleep, so I went outside and sat on the porch. That's it. I was hired to shoe horses, not be your nanny."

Go play with your dolls! The words were different, but the meaning was the same and stung just as deeply. She might be his boss's daughter, but to Luke, she was nothing but a bothersome teenager.

"Fine. Maybe it's time you got back to work. And I don't need a babysitter or a nanny. I don't need anybody looking out for me, especially *you*!"

213

She spun away from him and stalked toward the rectangle of sunlight at the far end of the barn. This man had opened her to a world of new sensations and emotions. But Luke Maddox was more than just exciting. He was also responsible, caring, and gentle, a man who could calm a frightened horse with a word and a touch. He was a man she could even love.

But he'd made it clear that he didn't want her around. And why should he? As far as Luke was concerned, she was nothing but a privileged brat, no different from other ranchers' daughters he'd met and brushed off.

She bit back a whimper as she stumbled over an uneven spot in the floor. A dart of pain shot into her ankle. Chin up, she kept moving toward the door.

"Erin."

The hunger in his voice stopped her as surely as if he had reached out and seized her arm. She turned to see him standing where she'd left him, his hands at his sides, open in a gesture of surrender.

"Come here."

Nothing, not even common sense, could have stopped her. She ran to him and flung herself into his arms. He caught her hard against him, lifting her off her feet as his

214

lips found hers. His kiss ignited heat waves that spread through her body, as if every part of her had been touched with glowing flame.

His bare skin was cool and damp from the water. Her hands ranged like wild things over his body — the muscular planes of his shoulders, the crisp mat of hair that trailed down his chest to narrow and vanish under his jeans. As he deepened the kiss, she arched against him, aching to feel the full length of his body touching hers.

Her damp shirt clung to her breasts. She gasped as his hand brushed a sensitive nipple through the thin fabric. The light contact triggered shimmers of need in the depths of her body. She moaned, reveling in the new sensations. Never in her young years had she felt more alive.

Drunk on her own daring, she let her roaming hand move downward to the hard ridge that rose beneath his jeans. As she pressed it, he groaned, then suddenly thrust her away from him.

"My God, Erin, are you trying to get yourself raped?"

Shocked into silence, she stared up at him.

He sighed and gathered her close, holding her with a gentleness that no woman could misunderstand.

215

"A man has his limits, girl," he murmured against her hair. "I wouldn't harm you for the world. But you have the power to drive me crazy and consign my soul to hell. Do you understand?"

She nodded, feeling his stubbled jaw against the skin of her forehead.

"I've wanted you from the first time I saw you," he said. "And after I got to know you — your courage, your passion — I wanted you even more. I thought I had it all under control, but when you walked away, I knew I couldn't let you go."

She wrapped her arms around him, holding him tight. "You make me feel things I couldn't have imagined until now," she whispered. "If this happens again — and I want it to happen —"

"*Will* it happen again? Is this what you really want? Hiding out in the barn like a couple of fool kids, probably getting caught? I like this as much as you do. But you deserve better than a roll in the hay, Erin. I want to treat you right — without having anything to hide."

"What about my father?" She looked up at him.

"I don't expect he'll approve. He wants to see you with a proper boyfriend, like the one you just dumped."

"I wouldn't go back to Kyle for a million dollars," Erin said.

"And I won't stand for making you a girl who sneaks around with the hired help. I've got my pride, Erin. And part of that pride is seeing myself as an honorable man. Either I speak to your father about spending time with you, or —"

"Fine, but you don't know my father. Let me bring it up to him first."

"All right." He brushed a kiss along her damp hairline. "But I meant what I said. If we have feelings for each other, I want to know where those feelings will take us. But not this way."

They broke apart at the sound of voices outside. Two of the cowboys were passing the barn. "We can't let them see us together. You go. I'll stay here," Luke said. "Will you talk to your father?"

"I will. Tonight if I can." Erin walked out of the barn, trying to look casual to anyone who might be watching. The sooner she spoke to Will the better. She could only hope to catch him in a good mood, but there wasn't much chance of that. Not these days.

Having an ally in her corner might make things easier. And she knew just the person to ask.

217

The cattle auction in Lubbock had taken most of a very long day. Kyle had endured the boredom, swatting away flies as his father watched the animals trot around the ring to the blaring patter of the auctioneer's voice. In the end, Hunter had bought nothing, claiming that he'd only wanted to see what was available and get a feel for the prices before he put his own stock up for sale.

Kyle suspected his father had other motives for bringing him along — like maybe showing him more of the cattle business, or, more likely, keeping him in suspense, waiting for the ax to fall. Between the wreck and Kyle's failure to put a ring on Erin's finger, his father had plenty of cause to be angry. So far Hunter had held his volcanic temper in check. But for Kyle, who knew the explosion was coming, the slow torment of waiting was its own kind of hell.

As they walked out to the truck, after a tension-filled dinner in a noisy, crowded steak house, Kyle braced himself for what was to come. The hour-long drive home was the only time left for Hunter to vent his temper.

It started as they drove out of the restaurant — beginning on a low key, as Hunter's tirades usually did. "Well, Kyle," he said in a conversational tone with a slight edge. "What do you have to say for yourself?"

"Not much, I guess," Kyle said. "I know you're mad about the car."

"Cars can be fixed," Hunter said. "But a million dollars won't fix stupidity. And that's what wrecked the car — your damned stupidity. So the girl says she isn't ready to marry you, and you react by punching the gas and almost getting both of you killed. Hell, that cow in the road had more brains than you. No wonder the girl doesn't want you. Sometimes I wonder if your mother was fooling around before you were born. You sure as hell don't act like any son of mine."

Kyle slumped in his seat, taking the abuse. He'd heard most of it before, including the part about his mother. But that was just thrown in for meanness. His mother was too naive to fool around, and he looked too much like Hunter to be anybody else's offspring.

"So what've you got to say for yourself now?" Hunter demanded.

"I don't suppose *sorry* would cut it," Kyle said.

219

Hunter lit a cigarette and rolled down the window, driving one-handed while he smoked. "Listen to me, you little shithead. Wrecking the car's bad enough. But if you let that Tyler girl get away, your whole future — and your family's — is in the dumper. If she doesn't want you now, you're going to have to change your tactics. Whatever you have to do to get her back, you do it. Hear?"

"I hear. But have you got any ideas? Erin is so mad she won't even talk to me. I can't exactly break down her door and drag her home by the hair, can I?"

Hunter swore and flipped his cigarette out the window. "You do whatever the hell it takes. For starters, since I knew you wouldn't think of it, I ordered flowers delivered to her, in your name, with a note. That should at least buy you an opening. But this has got to be up to you. If you're too dense to figure things out . . . ." The words trailed off, diminishing to a growl. "If you can get the right kind of woman into bed, you can get her to the altar. But I don't think you have a clue."

"Are you saying what I think you're saying?" Kyle asked.

"Do I have to spell it out for you? Seduce her. Knock her up if you have to — that is, if you know how to do more than get it off looking at those damn porn sites."

"What the hell —"

"I've been in your room. I've seen what's on your computer."

"You've got no business going into my room!"

"In my house I can go where I want to. So tell me — have you ever done it for real?"

Kyle stared down at his knees. "I fooled around some in junior college." And he had, though none of the girls had let him go all the way. He'd never understood why. Maybe he'd said the wrong things or come on too strong. Maybe he'd scared them.

Hunter snorted with disgust. "That's what I thought. That's why I've arranged to do you a big favor."

Kyle hadn't paid much attention to where his father was driving. Now he realized they were in a part of town he'd never seen before. The streets were lined with bars and cheap hotels. Neon lights flickered on and off. In their glow, scantily clad women strolled the sidewalks. Hunter parked the pickup, climbed out, and slipped a bill to a man who stepped up — evidently to keep the vehicle from being stolen.

They'd parked next to a bar with a naked lightbulb over the door. "Come on." Hunter

221

beckoned to Kyle. "Don't drag your feet and make a fool of yourself."

Kyle followed his father inside. The lights were low, but he could make out tables and a bar with stools in front and shelves behind. The few male customers, playing cards or drinking at the bar, paid them no attention.

Maybe they were going to have drinks, Kyle thought. But that notion faded as a young woman greeted them from the foot of a stairway. She wasn't bad looking, Kyle thought. But she would have been prettier without the heavy makeup and garishly bleached blond hair. Never mind — she looked like what she was, and Kyle knew enough to realize why his father had brought him here. He made an effort to look cool, but his pulse was galloping and his mouth had gone dry. He could smell the nervous sweat that soaked his armpits.

"Kyle, this is Destiny," Hunter said. "I'm going to have a drink in the bar while she gives you a few lessons in being a man. Take your time, and don't worry about money, it's all taken care of."

Hunter sauntered over to the bar while Destiny took Kyle's hand and led him up the stairs. Only as he was coming down again, forty minutes later, infinitely wiser, did he pause to ask himself why his father seemed to know this place so well.

After a long day of cutting cattle in the high pasture, Will was tired, saddle sore, and as cranky as a bear with mange. He'd weighed the idea of showering before dinner. But he was too hungry to take the time. He would fill his belly first, then wash the dust and sweat from his body and fall into bed. And Lord help anybody who got in his way.

He parked the pickup, slapped the worst of the dust off his clothes, and splashed his hands and face at the outdoor tap, then dragged himself up the porch steps. Above the escarpment, the last streaks of sunset were fading to the deeper hues of evening. A pair of ravens flapped off the roof of the barn, and Will stood on the porch, watching until they became black specks against the barren sky. Hellfire, what he wouldn't give for rain. This drought was sucking the life out of everything but the ravens and vultures and flies.

Stomping the dust off his boots, he opened the front door. The aromas of beef stew and fresh bread wafted out to greet him. His belly growled in response as he crossed to the dining room. There, a new sight struck his eyes.

"What the hell?" he muttered. "Did somebody die?"

A lavish bouquet of pink carnations, daisies, ferns, and baby's breath stood in a vase on the dining room table. Will stared at it, shaking his head.

Carmen stood in the open doorway to the kitchen. "A van delivered those flowers a couple of hours ago," she said. "The envelope has Erin's name on it. Of course I didn't peek inside. You'd better not peek either, if you know what's good for you."

"But there's not even a florist in Blanco Springs. Where would they come from?" Will sank onto a chair.

"The van had the name and address of a florist in Lubbock," Carmen said. "That's a long way to deliver flowers."

"Has Erin seen these?"

"She told me she'd be training a colt all afternoon. But she should be coming in soon. Do you want to eat now or wait for her?"

"I'd wait, but I'm starved. Go ahead and dish me up some food. Keep the rest warm. Where's Rose?"

As if in answer to his question, he heard the back door open and close. Rose walked in through the kitchen. "Oh, my goodness," she said, gazing at the flowers. "Aren't they lovely? What's the occasion?"

"Don't ask me," Will grumbled. "They're for Erin."

"Oh?" Rose took a seat at the place that had been set for her. "Do you know who sent them?"

"I guess that's for Erin to find out." Will looked up with a nod of thanks as Carmen set a bowl and some bread in front of him. The savory stew and warm, buttered bread smelled like heaven, but he paused long enough to ask Rose whether she wanted to be served now.

She shook her head. "Go ahead and eat. I'll keep you company while I wait for Erin."

Will forked a steaming morsel of stew and blew on it before taking a bite. It tasted as good as it smelled, and he was ravenous. When he glanced up, Rose was watching him. She had the look of a woman with something on her mind.

"What is it, Rose?" he asked. "Have I done something wrong?"

"Nothing like that," Rose said. "I was just thinking what a shame it is that you haven't spent time with our new farrier. We got to know each other last night. He's a remarkable man. So intelligent and responsible."

"So? If I'd thought he was stupid and careless, I wouldn't have hired him." Will

225

broke off a piece of bread and dipped it in the stew.

"Oh, I understand that," Rose said. "But maybe you should keep him around permanently. A man who's that good with horses could be a real asset to the ranch."

"An expensive asset. I can't afford to keep him on past the roundup. Sky and Erin are plenty good with horses. And this ranch is a cattle operation. The horses have always been a sideline. Unless we want to start shoeing the damned cows, I can't justify —"

"Oh, no, what's this?" Erin had come in from the kitchen. She was staring at the flowers.

"We were wondering the same thing," Will said. "Maybe you've got a secret admirer. Why don't you open the envelope and find out."

Erin pulled the envelope from the plastic clip that held it in place. Her pretty face fell as she opened it and read the message on the card inside. She groaned and shook her head. "Wouldn't you know? It's from Kyle."

"Well, what does it say?" Will demanded.

"Read it yourself." Erin tossed the card on the table, within Will's reach, before she sat down.

Will picked up the card. Mostly for Rose's benefit, he read the message aloud. *"I am so sorry. Please give me another chance. I love you too much to let you go.*" He looked up at his daughter. "Well?"

"Well, what, Dad? You already know what happened. I told Kyle I wouldn't marry him and he was so upset that he wrecked the SUV. We could have been killed." Erin dished up some stew from the tureen Carmen had set on the table. She handed a bowl to Rose and filled another for herself.

"I remember your story," Will said. "But you never told me why you didn't want to marry the boy. It looks to me like he's really trying to redeem himself."

Erin and Rose exchanged glances. Will sensed a conspiracy. But he was the head of this family. Whatever was going on, he wasn't about to be manipulated.

"Dad, why are you so set on my being with Kyle?" Erin asked in a civil tone.

Will sighed. He was tired to the bone, and this wasn't going well. "Because I know who Kyle is," he said. "He's polite and well-spoken. He's from a good family — a family in the ranching business. If you were to marry him, you'd be close by — not running off to some other part of the country like Beau did. Kyle is safe, and he seems to care for you. How many men would send you flowers like these? Does that answer your question?"

"But what if I don't love him? What if I want to spend time with other people?"

"Other people?" Suddenly this was beginning to make sense. "Do you have somebody in mind?"

Erin's expression reminded Will of the way she'd looked as a little girl, about to jump off the high dive at the pool.

"I've been working with Luke Maddox," she said. "We enjoy each other's company, and we want to spend more time together. But he insists on being open about it. He doesn't want me seeing him behind your back."

"And *would* you see him behind my back?" He cast her a stern look across the table.

"I'm not a child," Erin said.

Will shook his head, feeling as if he'd been gut punched. "Erin, this is wrong in so many ways. You're not even twenty-one yet. Maddox, I'm guessing, is at least ten years older than you are. Apart from his being good at his job, we don't know anything about him. He could be a criminal. He could have a wife and family somewhere. Or maybe he's a fortune hunter, with his eye on the heiress to a ranch."

Erin seemed to flinch as each point of his

228

argument hit home. Everything he'd said was true, and she had to know it. But he could tell that he hadn't convinced her.

"Luke is a good man," she said. "Even Rose knows it."

"Leave Rose out of this!" Will snapped, his temper rising. "You've always had a good head on your shoulders, Erin. I've never had to forbid you anything. But I'm forbidding you now. Aside from work, in the open with other people around, you're not to spend any time with this man. I know I can't control you every minute. But if I find out you've been sneaking around behind my back, so help me, I'll fire him on the spot. Do you understand?"

"I'm not hungry," Erin said, pushing out her chair and standing. "I'm going to my . . . room." Her voice broke as she turned away and fled toward the hallway.

"Really, Will —" Rose began, but he cut her off.

"Stay out of this, Rose. Don't encourage either of them. You'll only cause trouble. Do I make myself clear?"

Rose sighed and nodded. "You do. But I need to say something. You inherited the traits that made Bull Tyler great. But you also got his stubborn, controlling nature, and that's what's coming out now. If you don't rein yourself in and learn to bend, Will, you'll lose your daughter, just as your father lost Beau."

CHAPTER ELEVEN

Luke had risen at dawn to help with morning chores. He was working in the stallion barn, forking fresh hay from a wheelbarrow into the feeders, when Will Tyler appeared in the open doorway.

Luke hadn't seen much of the boss since his arrival on the Rimrock. But Will had struck him as a fair man, who trusted him to put in an honest day's work. So far, their relationship had been distant but cordial. However, it was a very different Will who strode toward him now.

No words were needed. Will's narrow-eyed gaze and the determined set of his jaw signaled trouble. And Luke was pretty sure what kind of trouble it was.

Luke laid the pitchfork across the wheelbarrow, straightened, and turned to face his employer. "What can I do for you, Mr. Tyler?" he asked, already knowing what the answer would be.

"You can leave my daughter the hell alone!" Will's face was florid with rage. "She told me what was going on. You've got no business putting your filthy hands on her, or even talking to her."

Luke chose to ignore the insult. "I would never hurt Erin, or bring her down in any way," he said calmly. "I care about her, and she feels the same way about me."

"Don't you tell me how she feels!" Will's voice was getting louder. "She's an innocent girl! She has no idea what a man like you might be thinking. Turn her head with pretty words, and the next thing you know, you'll have her down in the hay! Or maybe you think she's got money, and you want to get your hands on the ranch. Whatever your game is, I won't allow you to ruin her reputation and her life!"

At the far end of the barn, a couple of cowboys were standing in the open doorway, probably getting an earful. Either Will couldn't see them or he didn't care.

"Nothing you say can change the way I feel about her," Luke said. "But you're her father, and I respect that. If you want me to go, just say so. I'll be out of here today."

Will cursed and shook his head. "This is a warning. I'm not firing you, but if I hear you've so much as laid a finger on my daughter, or tried to talk to her alone, you'll be run off the place with a shotgun, and I'll see that you never work in this county again! Hear?"

Before Luke could reply, Will seemed to realize that he had an audience. Rage exploding, he swung his attention toward the two cowboys in the doorway. "What the hell do you two galoots think you're doing?" he yelled at them. "Get back to work!"

As the cowboys beat a fast retreat, Will stalked out of the barn. Luke watched him go. He'd hoped for a different response from Erin's father, but this was pretty much what he'd expected. At least he hadn't been fired. But defying Will's warning would only get both him and Erin in trouble.

He knew what would come next — seeing Erin from afar, aching to hold her, or even just to ask her if she was all right — and knowing that her father, if he chose to do so, had the power to separate them forever. What the hell, maybe he should just leave. Staying would only stir up trouble. Erin could do better than a rootless man with a clouded past and nothing of his own but his truck and trailer, his gear, and the skill in his hands. She could move on with her life, find someone who was right for her.

He'd seen her drive away with Rose and

233

guessed, from the direction they were headed, that they'd be working on Rose's property again. If he truly cared about what was best for Erin, he would pack up and leave now, without even saying good-bye.

He would do it, Luke decided. He would finish the morning chores, have some breakfast, then pack his clothes and gear in the trailer, leave an address where his pay could be sent, and go. His leaving would be best for all concerned.

As the memory of Erin in his arms, her passion, her sweet, young body pressing against his, flashed through his mind, Luke's lips moved in a silent curse.

This was a hell of a time to realize that he loved her.

Will's day had begun on an annoying note, and it wasn't getting any better. When he'd gone out to confront Luke Maddox, he'd been spoiling to inflict some damage. But the man's quiet dignity and his refusal to engage in any kind of verbal shouting match, which would have given Will an excuse to fire him, had taken the wind out of Will's sails, leaving his anger still unvented.

It hadn't helped Will's mood to hear that a valuable heifer had broken her leg in the night and had been finished off by a pack of coyotes, or to check yesterday's mail and find, enclosed with his bank statement, a reminder that the payment on his loan would be due the first day of October, along with the annual property tax a month later. The thought of how much money he'd have to come up with, and the consequences if he couldn't pay, almost made him physically ill. But one thing was certain. He'd spent enough time wringing his hands and worrying. Whatever it took, he couldn't give up. He had to save the ranch.

It was time he talked to the bank again. If they wouldn't redo the note or give him an extension — which they'd so far refused to do — he would need to pull himself together and come up with a realistic plan. Not just vague ideas, but solid numbers and projections on paper. How many cattle would he have to sell? How many horses? What about the land? Would the syndicate buy a parcel to expand the old Prescott Ranch? How much would they pay for what they wanted?

He would talk to people, make phone calls, get it all down in black and white. And he would need to involve Erin. If anything were to happen to him, the responsibility for saving the Rimrock would fall to her.

Last night, when he'd forbidden her to

see Luke Maddox, she'd declared that she wasn't a child. Fine. He'd allowed her to be a child long enough. It was time she stepped out of her girlish, romantic world and took on her duties as the future head of the Rimrock family.

Will hadn't seen Erin since last night. When she hadn't joined him for breakfast, he'd looked outside and noticed the missing station wagon. A brief panic had struck him. What if she'd run away? But then Carmen had told him that Erin and Rose had eaten early and gone to work on Rose's property.

Will had masked his relief with a shrug. At least his daughter wasn't with Maddox. But it was damned annoying that Rose had taken Erin's side against him. Now he had two stubborn women to contend with.

He'd hoped to take Erin to town with him, so that she could see and hear for herself where they stood with the bank. Maybe then she'd be more interested in the ranch and less interested in her own love life. But never mind, Will told himself as he went out to his pickup truck. He wanted to confront the bank president now, while he had a head of steam worked up. Otherwise, he'd be liable to put it off, letting other urgent matters interfere. Now, while he could still maneuver, was the time to get a solid plan in place.

He was climbing into his truck when, from inside the house, he heard the shrill ringing of the landline phone in his office. He was tempted to rush back inside and pick up the call. But no, Carmen could answer the phone. She knew where he was going, and she could take a message.

With the phone still ringing, he climbed into the cab, started the motor, and headed for town.

Erin had found some leftover posts and chicken wire in one of the sheds. Now she and Rose were working to fence off the grave of Rose's grandfather, Professor Cletus McAdoo. It was hard work. The metal posts were designed to be hammered into the ground, but pounding the points into the hard earth had proven to be more than the two women could do. Instead they were forced to dig a hole for each post.

"I'm glad we got an early start on this," Erin said. "We've barely begun, and the day's already getting warm."

Rose thrust her shovel into the dirt. Again, today, she'd strapped on her pistol. "Thanks again for helping me. I could never have managed this on my own. And I'm sorry I wasn't more help with your dad last night. I tried to soften him up before you came in, but it wasn't enough."

"It's all right. I should've known what he'd say when I told him I wanted to be with Luke. Why does he have to be so judgmental?"

"Your father loves you," Rose said. "He only wants to keep you safe."

"Oh, I know." Erin tossed a shovelful of dirt out of the post hole she was digging. "Ever since I was thirteen and got kidnapped by that awful woman, he hasn't let me out of his sight. But I'm not thirteen anymore. Why can't he see that?"

"He can see it, dear. And it scares him to death."

"But Luke's a good man. Why else would he insist on letting my father know we were seeing each other?"

"I agree with you," Rose said. "But your father's being cautious. Now that your mother's gone, you're all he has — you and the ranch. You can't blame him for wanting to protect you and keep you close." Rose straightened, massaging the small of her back with one hand. "For now, I hope you'll do as he says and keep your distance from Luke. If the two of you are meant to be together, love will find a way."

But what if Rose was wrong? Erin thought.

238

What would she do if she came back to the ranch to find that Luke had already been fired, packed his things, and left?

Or what if she found him leaving? Would he take her with him? Would she go?

She picked up a post and stood it upright in the hole she'd dug. "Can you steady this while I fill in the dirt?"

Rose put down her shovel and moved to hold the post, keeping it centered in the hole. "What about the flowers?" she asked. "Are you going to see Kyle again?"

"I don't want to. It would only encourage him." Erin shoveled the loose earth around the post and packed it down. It wouldn't hold securely, but once the fence was done, it should be enough to discourage wandering cattle until Rose could enclose her entire yard.

"In that case, I hope you can have a friendly parting," Rose said. "But Kyle strikes me as a young man who doesn't like taking no for an answer."

"Then maybe it's time he learned. I wouldn't mind staying friends with him, but after the last time I turned him down, I don't know if that's possible. I just hope he doesn't make trouble for Luke."

"Then don't give Kyle any reason to make trouble. Until things get better around here, you and Luke will be walking a fine line. Try not to cross it."

"Thanks. That's good advice." Erin paced off the hole for the second of four fence posts and started digging. The morning sun cast lacy patterns through the trees. Blackbirds called in the willows that grew along the creek. Water gurgled and splashed over the stones.

The morning was as cheerful and pleasant as anyone could wish. Given such a fine beginning to the day, it was hard to believe that anything could go wrong. So why, as she worked beside Rose, did Erin sense a vague darkness pressing down on her, like a whispered warning that everything she cherished was at risk?

Will had spent nearly an hour in the bank — all but the last fifteen minutes of it waiting to see the president, Sim Bartlett. He needn't have bothered. Bartlett's answer was the same as before. The payment was due as scheduled. If it wasn't made by October 1, along with two years' back taxes a month later, the Rimrock would be in foreclosure.

As if he needed more bad news, Bartlett had let it slip that an agent for the syndicate that owned the Prescott place had been asking about the Rimrock and the status of the loan. That could only mean one thing. The syndicate people were waiting for the Rimrock to go into foreclosure so they could buy it at a bargain price. There was no way they would buy land or livestock from Will. Not when the bastards were waiting like vultures for him to default on the loan. And Sim Bartlett was probably getting a fat piece of the action.

So scratch that option. Never mind. Somehow he'd find another way. But right now he needed a cold beer.

The Blue Coyote had just opened. Will parked in the meager patch of shade on the north side. Since the AC had gone out on his truck, any measure to keep the blistering sun off the cab was worth the trouble.

The look of the old bar hadn't changed much over the years. The blue neon coyote on the sign out front had been a fixture for at least fifty years. But when former sheriff Abner Sweeney had taken the place over from Stella Rawlins, he'd kicked out the drug dealers and closed the upstairs room where the waitresses had carried on a side business.

Portly, bald, and easygoing, Abner was better at bartending than he'd ever been at

241

enforcing the law. "Your usual, Will?" he asked.

Will nodded and laid a bill on the bar. Abner gave him change, whipped a bottle of Corona out of the cooler, and opened it. Will muttered his thanks and settled into a quiet corner booth. He hoped Abner wouldn't try to start a conversation. He didn't feel like talking. Hell, he didn't even feel like breathing, but he had to keep doing it.

A couple of regulars came in and sat at the bar. Will knew them, but he kept quiet, nursing his beer and pondering his choices.

One thing was clear — he was wasting time when he needed to be acting. He would finish the beer, go home, and call a meeting with Erin, Sky, and maybe Rose, who wasn't directly involved, but might have some good ideas. They would assess the ranch's resources and somehow come up with a workable plan to save the Rimrock. No plan could succeed without hard and bitter sacrifices. But they would do whatever it took to save the Tyler legacy.

Still lost in thought, Will left the bar and crossed the parking lot to his truck. His biggest worry was for Erin. She loved the Rimrock — the land, the cattle and horses, and the rhythm of daily life, from morning chores to watching the sun set over the caprock. She'd been raised on the ranch, and she'd never wanted to be anywhere else. His failure could take all that away from her, leaving her with nothing but a broken heart.

With the windows down, he drove north on Main Street and took the main highway out of town. By now it was late morning. Heat waves rose from the asphalt. A farm truck passed him headed toward town. Otherwise there was no traffic. People who had errands would be apt to run them earlier, before the stifling midday heat set in.

He passed the black skid marks and smashed fence where Kyle Cardwell had swerved off the road to avoid hitting the cow. Erin had told him that Kyle had been driving seventy miles an hour when the crash happened. Maybe she'd been right to break up with him. Flowers or no flowers, a man who'd put her life at risk in a fit of temper wouldn't be great husband material.

By the time Will turned off the highway onto the long, gravel lane leading to his ranch, his thoughts had moved on to other matters. It was a shame he'd never bothered to buy life insurance. At least, if something were to happen to him, Erin would be provided for. As it was —

What the hell?

He slammed on the brakes, swearing as the truck screeched to a stop. A large tractor tire was lying across the lane, almost as if some idiot had left it there on purpose. He could have gotten around it by driving with two wheels in the bar ditch, but he couldn't leave it there to cause an accident for somebody else. The least he could do was drag it out of the way.

Will opened the door of the cab and stepped out. At that instant he glimpsed a movement in the brush beyond the bar ditch. In the next instant, the explosion that roared inside his head ended everything.

By the time Erin and Rose finished the makeshift fence and returned to the ranch, it was almost one o'clock. Carmen met them at the front door, a concerned look on her usually cheerful face.

"Is everything all right, Carmen?" Erin asked.

"I'm not sure," Carmen said. "Mr. Maddox, the farrier, has gone."

Erin's heart dropped. Surely she'd misunderstood. Maybe Luke had just gone to town. "Gone where?" she asked.

Carmen shrugged. "Just gone, with his

244

trailer and all his gear. He gave me a note for your father, with his hours and a forwarding address. I left it in the office. And he said he left a note for you in the duplex."

"But when did he go?" Erin's pulse was skittering. "How long ago?"

"Two or three hours, maybe. I was busy and didn't pay attention to the time. You must be hungry. Would you like some lunch?"

"Not now, thanks. Where's my father?"

"He went to town. He should be back soon."

Rose put a hand on Erin's arm. "Are you all right? You're as white as a sheet."

"I'm fine," Erin lied. "I'm going out to the duplex — and I think I need to go alone."

She cut through the kitchen and out the back door. As it closed behind her, she broke into a run. Her stomach churned. What had Will said to Luke that would make him pack up and leave? What if she never saw him again?

The duplex where Luke had stayed was stripped bare of his presence — the sheets folded on the bed, the towels in the laundry basket, Luke's clothes, boots, and toiletries gone. Except for the folded note, torn from a yellow pad and tucked partway beneath a pillow, it was as if he'd never been there.

Erin's hand shook as she picked up the folded paper with her name on the outside. She'd believed, in her naivete, that she'd found a man she could love. But it had all come down to this — an empty room and a folded note.

Bracing herself to have her heart broken, she opened the note. The message was brief, only a few lines.

Erin,
I care for you too much to stay and cause trouble. One day you'll realize that my decision to leave was best for both of us. I will never forget you.

Luke

Fighting tears, she refolded the note and stuffed it into her pocket. She couldn't stand the thought of going back to the house to face Rose, Carmen, and possibly her father. Instead she crossed the yard to the stallion barn, went inside, and opened Tesoro's stall. Her stallion nickered a greeting and thrust his elegant head toward her. She spoke to him, pressing her face against his neck. When the tears threatened to come, she found a brush and began grooming his satiny coat, over the withers, down

246

the shoulders, and along the back. The big palomino quivered with pleasure.

Don't cry. Erin focused on the rhythm of the brush and the response of her horse. *Don't cry. You're a big girl now. You're going to be all right. . . .*

"Erin."

She didn't recognize the male voice behind her until she turned and saw Deputy Roy Porter standing at the entrance to the stall. Partway behind him, half hidden in shadow, was Rose.

Erin's throat had gone dry. What if something had happened to Luke? She forced the words. "What is it? Tell me."

"Something's happened to your father, Erin," Roy said. "He was shot on his way home."

My father? Shot? Erin's knees went weak as she grasped at denial. *No!* There had to be a mistake! Nobody would shoot Will! He was too strong, like a rock — her rock.

But surely he'd be all right. She would go rushing into the hospital to find him sitting up in bed, smiling at her, joking about his wound and warning her not to hug him too tightly.

"Where is he?" she asked. "How badly is he hurt?"

Rose came forward, her face a mask of

247

anguish. She took Erin's hand, gripping it painfully with her small, strong fingers. "Will's dead, Erin," she said. "Somebody killed him."

The next hours passed in a blur of pain-induced shock. Erin functioned like an automaton, doing what had to be done. She was the boss of the Rimrock now. Private grief would have to wait.

Sky was on the mountain with the cattle. When Erin called his cell phone from the office, there was no answer — service was spotty at best up there. She left a voice message and another message with his wife, Lauren. Rose had offered to make the call to Beau. Erin insisted on doing it herself, even though giving Will's brother the news almost broke her.

"Are you all right, Erin?" he asked.

"I'll have to be all right, won't I?"

"I'll be on the next plane out. We've got to find the bastard who did this."

Erin ended the call and sank into Will's big, old leather chair — the chair that had long since conformed to the shape of the rangy, muscular Tyler men. The yearning to see her father again and beg his forgiveness for walking out in anger from last night's supper table was like a cry inside her. How could she have known she would never hear his voice or see his face again?

Outside, the sheriff had arrived. He and Roy were already interviewing the ranch hands who'd been around that morning. They'd talked to Erin and Rose as well, and to Carmen, who'd been the last to see Will before he left for town.

Erin knew that the lawmen wouldn't tell her everything they learned. But it was hard to imagine anyone on the ranch wanting to kill her father. Will was — had been — a tough boss, but he was liked and respected by all the men. Could his murder — and that was the word Erin would have to get accustomed to — have something to do with the strange figure she and Luke had seen prowling around the ranch? She had mentioned that to Roy again, but he'd been dismissive of the notion. The killer, whoever it was, had known that Will would be coming back from town, and had set up an ambush to shoot him.

The office door stood ajar. Sheriff Harger gave a light rap, then walked in without an invitation. A heavyset man in late middle age, with a thick, iron-gray mustache, he'd grown up in Blanco County. He knew every inch of the land and most of the people who lived on it.

"I'm right sorry about your dad, Erin," he said. "What a god-awful shock, that somebody would shoot a man like Will."

Erin murmured a polite thank-you, but something told her the sheriff hadn't come inside to offer condolences.

"I've been talking to the hands," he said. "Two of them told me they heard a big row in the barn this morning between Will and the farrier he'd hired — a man named Luke Maddox."

Erin's stomach clenched. Luke would never do anything to hurt Will. But the fact that they'd had an argument a few hours before Will was murdered had to look suspicious.

"From what I heard, it was Will doing the shouting," the sheriff said. "He was telling Maddox to keep away from his daughter. Do you know anything about that?"

Erin rose to her feet. "Yes. Luke and I wanted to spend time together. He insisted that I tell my father first. I did. My father didn't like the idea."

"Did you know about the argument?"

"Not until now. Rose and I were working on her land all morning. You already know that."

"And Maddox? What happened to him?"

Erin felt a wave of nausea. She knew

where this interrogation was leading, but all she could do was tell the truth. "He took his gear and left," she said. "When I came back to the house, he was gone. He left a note with Carmen for my father. It's right there, on the desk."

Harger unfolded the yellow note paper. "It's just his hours and where to send the check — some kind of facility in Oklahoma. So far, at least, it doesn't make sense that he'd plan to kill a man who owed him money."

"Of course it doesn't. Luke had no reason to shoot my father."

"But what about you as the reason? Pretty young girl, in line to inherit a ranch, and her father standing in his way. That strikes me as reason enough."

Erin's heart plunged. Knowing the sheriff would want to see it, she pulled the other note out of her shirt pocket. "He left this for me, in the duplex where he was staying."

Harger studied the note, saying nothing.

"See?" Erin's desperation was rising to panic. There was no way Luke would have murdered her father. But the sheriff clearly thought otherwise. "Read the note again," she pleaded. "He was saying good-bye. He never meant to come back here."

"Maybe, maybe not." The sheriff took two plastic bags out of his vest pocket and bagged each note as evidence. "Right now, there's only one thing I can tell you for sure. I need to find Mr. Maddox and ask him some serious questions. If I don't like the answers, he's going to find himself facing a charge of premeditated murder."

CHAPTER TWELVE

The TV news crew arrived in their van, swarming over the yard, cornering the cowboys and the sheriff for interviews, and ringing the front doorbell again and again. Rose volunteered to go out and fend them off. Fierce as a miniature Rottweiler, she ordered the crew off the porch, informing them that there would be a statement later, and meanwhile they were to respect the family's privacy.

Erin watched the nightmare from the office window, peering like a fugitive between the closed slats of the venetian blinds. The reality of Will's death was just beginning to sink in. Never again would he walk in through the front door. Never again would she sit across from him at breakfast, sharing plans for the day ahead. The hundreds of things he did — the hiring and firing, the financial decisions, the supervision of the men, the marketing of the cattle and so much more — all would fall to her. But the avalanche of responsibility was nothing compared to her grief. She had loved her father. He had been her refuge, her rock. To lose him was unthinkable.

Don't cry. You won't be able to stop.

Through the blinds, she could see the sheriff talking to a reporter on camera. Was he mentioning Luke — putting out the word that he'd quarreled with Will and left the ranch? Had he already put out an APB on Luke's rig?

Luke was an innocent victim of circumstance. Erin knew that. But the sheriff had zeroed in on the perfect suspect and showed no signs of backing off — while the real killer, whoever he or she might be, was getting away with murder.

The jangle of Erin's cell phone broke into her thoughts. She glanced at the caller ID. It was Kyle. Her first impulse was to ignore the call. But sooner or later, she'd have to talk to him. It might as well be now.

"Hi, Erin. Did you get my flowers?" His voice was cheerful. Clearly he hadn't heard the news.

"Yes. Thank you. They're lovely."

"You sound a little off. Is everything all right?" he asked.

"No. My father is dead. He was murdered

this morning." For Erin, saying the words drove the reality deeper, like a hammer pounding in a nail.

"What?" Kyle gasped. "Did you just say what I thought you said?"

"He was shot, ambushed, at the turnoff to the lane. That's all I was told."

Kyle was silent as the news sank in. Then he spoke. "Oh, my God, I can't believe it. Not Will. I can imagine what you're going through. Don't worry, Erin, I'm here for you. I'll be right over."

"No!" The last thing she needed was Kyle fussing over her, most likely pushing his own agenda. "The sheriff's here. The press is here. Beau will be coming, and I'm still trying to reach Sky. I can't deal with you right now, Kyle. I can't deal with *us.*"

"All right. But you're going to need a man in the time ahead. I want you to know I'll be there for you."

"I can't talk now, Kyle. I have to go."

Erin ended the call before he could say anything else. She couldn't think about Kyle now. She was still in shock from her father's death. And she had too many questions on her mind, such as who might have hated Will enough to set up an ambush, lie in wait, and shoot him when he stepped out of his truck. The person who'd done it was still out there, free and unsuspected; but she couldn't count on Sheriff Harger to find the real murderer. Not when he'd already pinned the blame on Luke.

Finding the truth, and clearing Luke of almost certain charges, would be up to her. She would make it her job to find answers, starting with the mysterious, long-haired prowler who could still be haunting the ranch.

From Marie's vantage point in the escarpment, the buildings and vehicles looked like miniature toys, the humans like insects. But even without the cheap, cracked binoculars she'd stolen from a thrift store, she could tell that something big was going on at the Rimrock.

Early that morning, she'd seen the two women take the dirt road north in the brown station wagon. About an hour later, Will Tyler's pickup had headed toward the highway. Soon afterward, the farrier's distinctive rig had pulled out of the yard and disappeared in the same direction. Around noon, the women had returned. And now this.

She lifted the binoculars to her eyes and fiddled with the adjustment. There was no way to get a good focus, but she could make out the sheriff's big, tan SUV parked next to the porch, and the news van a few yards away. A reporter was interviewing a stocky man who was probably the sheriff, with a cameraman and another man with a microphone hovering close. Marie remembered the old news adage, *If it bleeds, it leads.* Only one thing would bring the law and a news crew clear out here — a violent death.

Too bad the victim wasn't the little Tyler bitch. That would save Marie the trouble of killing her. But she'd seen Erin Tyler and the older woman walking back to the house after the sheriff arrived. It had to be somebody else. Will's truck was still gone, and Sky was nowhere to be seen. Unless it was one of the cowhands, it had to be one of them.

Not that it mattered. She didn't much care about Will; and Sky, although he was family, had shut her out of his life before she went to prison. Either way was no skin off her nose. But she might have to rethink her plan for the girl. With so many people around, including the law, the risk was too great. For now, all she could do was wait for a better chance. But Marie's patience was wearing thin. She needed to dispatch the girl, inform Stella, retrieve the stashed bricks of heroin, sell them, and head for the border. The longer she stayed around, the greater the risk of getting caught for violating parole and sent back to Gatesville.

But what if there was another way? What if she could find Stella's drug stash on her own?

How hard could it be? Stella had lived in a rented apartment. She wouldn't have hidden the heroin there, or in her car, which was long gone. And she wouldn't have hidden the bricks on open land or in the escarpment. There was too much chance of their being found. Just one hiding place made sense — the only piece of property Stella had owned — the Blue Coyote.

Having worked there and lived upstairs, Marie knew every inch of the old bar. If the heroin was there — and it had to be — she would find it. All she had to do was get inside with tools and time to look.

Stella had sold the bar to Abner Sweeney to pay her legal costs. Stella and Abner had been friends. As sheriff, he'd skated the edge of the law by doing her a few so-called favors. Maybe if Marie told him that Stella needed her to find something personal . . . But no, that story would never fly. Abner might not be the brightest bulb in the pack, but he wasn't an idiot. She couldn't expect him to look the other way while she tore the place apart searching for illegal drugs.

She would have to go in late at night, after the bar was closed. And she'd have to make sure that no one saw her and lived to tell about it.

Luke had told himself that leaving Erin was the best thing he could do for her. Still, with every mile he drove, the pain of missing her deepened. Over the years, he'd enjoyed a few brief relationships — interludes that had always ended when he moved on. Until Erin came into his life, he'd been satisfied with things as they were. But being with her had made him want more — waking up every morning to the sight of her beautiful face, filling a home with love and the laughter of children.

But he should have known he wasn't made to have those things. He was a temporary kind of man — and Erin was a forever kind of woman.

He'd written the truth in his note. He would never forget her.

Driving since morning, he'd picked up northbound Interstate 27 in Lubbock and was coming into Plainview when he felt the need for a break. At the foot of a handy off-ramp, he found a small diner. Leaving his rig in the parking lot, he went inside, used the restroom, and ordered coffee and apple pie at the counter.

While he was eating, his gaze wandered to the TV mounted on the wall. A regional newscast was just coming on. Luke gave it half an ear until a familiar name arrested his attention.

"Will Tyler, a prominent Blanco County rancher, was shot and killed near his ranch this morning. The unidentified killer, who ambushed Tyler on the road from Blanco Springs, is still at large. But Luke Maddox, a temporary worker on the Rimrock Ranch, has been named as a person of interest by the county sheriff."

There was more, but Luke didn't wait to hear it. Knowing better than to draw attention by rushing, he peeled a bill out of his wallet, laid it on the counter, walked out into the parking lot, and climbed into his truck. After the initial shock of the news, his first thought was for Erin and how she must be grieving. He ached to be there for her. But what comfort could he give her when he was, evidently, the prime suspect in her father's murder?

Starting the engine, he drove out of the parking lot. Running would be a fool's choice. It would only make him look guilty. He had to go back to Blanco Springs and try to account for himself.

Crossing to the southbound on-ramp, he headed back the way he'd come. He was innocent of any crime. But given the circumstantial evidence — his relationship with Erin, the scene with Will, and his lack of an alibi — convincing the sheriff would be tough. Luke knew he had a fight ahead of him. But it was the thought of Erin that drove him now. If she believed in his innocence, he could get through anything. But what if she didn't? What if she'd already judged him guilty?

He was on the freeway, somewhere between Lubbock and the exit to the Blanco Springs highway, when he saw the flashing red and blue lights in his rearview mirror. He pulled off the road and stopped. It was time to face whatever had to be faced.

The sun was getting low when Erin heard the screech of Sky's arriving truck outside. She rushed onto the porch to meet him as he vaulted out of the cab and took the steps two at a time. He was rank with sweat and coated with dust, but as she flung her arms around him, he felt like the only solid thing in a world that was crumbling around her.

He held her as he might hold a child, patting her back in a vain effort to comfort her.

261

"My phone wasn't working," he said, releasing her. "Lauren gave me the news about Will when I walked in the door. We're all in shock, but we're your family, Erin. We'll get through this together."

"Beau's coming," Erin said. "He told me he'd be on the next flight."

"Good. Maybe he can help us find out who did this awful thing."

"The sheriff thinks it was Luke. Did Lauren tell you that?"

"Lord, no! I can't imagine Luke killing anybody. He's one of the gentlest men I know. And he had nothing against Will."

"Not according to the sheriff. Luke and my father had an argument this morning. Then, after Dad went to town, Luke packed up and left."

"An argument? What about?" Sky asked.

"Me."

Sky looked puzzled, but only for a moment. "You . . . and Luke?"

"I love him, Sky." Erin had never said those words before but she felt the truth of them like a burning flame inside her. "I love him and I know he's innocent. But I don't know how to prove it."

"Oh, blast it, Erin." Sky shook his head. "This is getting complicated. Where's Luke now?"

"I have no idea. He could be in jail — or on the road, maybe without even knowing what happened. . . ." Erin's voice broke.

Rose came out of the kitchen. "Heavens to Betsy, Sky, you must be starved," she said. "I sent Carmen home and warmed up some of the stew she made last night. Sit down at the kitchen table, and I'll bring you a bowl."

"Thanks. If you don't mind, I'll clean up first. Something tells me it might be a long night." He disappeared into the half bath off the kitchen where generations of Tylers had washed up before meals.

"You sit down, too, Erin," Rose said. "I know you might not have much appetite, but you've got some tough times ahead of you. You're going to need your strength — that means getting some nourishment in you."

Erin sank onto a chair. Rose was right. If she didn't eat she would be even more fragile than she felt herself to be. But the bowl of savory beef stew Rose set before her, accompanied by a thick slice of buttered bread, seemed more like medicine than food. She would have to force it down.

Sky took his seat across from Erin. Rose dished up two more bowls of stew, poured some fresh coffee, and joined them. No one, not even Sky, felt much like eating, but they went through the motions as they talked.

There would be a funeral to plan — but by now the family had that down to a routine. It could wait until they knew when Will's body would be released by the medical examiner. He had died of a single gunshot wound to the head. But the sheriff would want to recover the bullet or at least determine factors like range and trajectory before returning the remains to the family. The medical examiner would also determine how long Will had been dead. But since he'd been seen leaving town around twelve thirty and had never made it home, the time would be an easy guess.

The thought of Will on the autopsy table sent a cold shudder through Erin's body. This was her father. How could she even imagine what was happening to him? Willing the thought away, she tried to focus on the question Sky was asking her.

"Whoever set up that ambush would have known that Will would be coming back from town. How many people were aware that he'd be on the road?"

"He told Carmen where he was going," Erin said. "Luke would have seen him leave — but so would anyone else who was working around the place. Someone who was already in town could have seen him there, too. Whoever it was must have been crazed with hate to commit such a cold-blooded act — planning it ahead, laying that tire on the road that led to our ranch, then lying in wait and . . ." Erin pressed her hands to her face as if to stem a surge of tears. Will had been a good man. But there had always been people who envied, even hated, the Tylers. The question was, who had hated Will enough to kill him?

"Does Luke own a gun?" Sky asked.

"Doesn't everybody in these parts? Yes, he has a .38. He used it to shoot a rattlesnake when we were checking out the wash where Jasper was found."

"Well, let's hope the sheriff has the bullet that killed Will. If the ballistics don't match Luke's gun, that'll go a long way in clearing him."

"So you believe me, that Luke couldn't have killed my father?"

"Luke strikes me as a decent man. I'm not saying he's the man for you, but without solid evidence, I won't believe he's a murderer." Sky broke off a chunk of bread and used it to sop up the gravy in his bowl.

Sky's guarded reply to Erin's question was not lost on her. But for now it would have to be enough.

"There's somebody else," she said, changing the subject. "Somebody's been prowling around the ranch. I don't know what they want, but Luke and I caught a glimpse of a man above the horse paddock — tall and thin, with long hair, maybe dressed in black, though it was hard to tell. And we thought we heard a motorcycle starting up, far away."

"A man? You're sure?" Sky was suddenly alert, seeming almost wary. "Is there any chance it could've been a woman?"

"I hadn't thought of that. But we found a boot track above the paddock and one just like it in the wash where Jasper died. Oh — and Jasper's pistol and money were missing."

"Did you tell the sheriff?"

"I told the deputy — Roy Porter. I knew him from school. He said the wash was a hangout for smugglers and illegals, and whoever robbed Jasper was probably just passing through. But I took a photo of the print we found in the wash, just in case."

"Do you still have it?"

"I do. It's on my phone. Hang on. I left it in the office. I'll get it."

Erin left the table and hurried to the office. She couldn't help being intrigued by Sky's reaction to her story. Did he know

266

more than he was telling her?

She found her phone. It took only a few seconds to scroll to find the photo of the boot print. She carried the phone back to the kitchen and handed it to Sky.

"I hadn't thought of it before," she said, "but the boot that made that print is narrow enough to be a woman's. If it is, she's no fashionista. That long, pointed toe looks like something out of the nineteen seventies."

Sky didn't respond. He was staring at the photo as if he'd seen a ghost.

"What's wrong?" Erin asked. "Do you recognize something?"

"Maybe," Sky muttered. "But what I'm thinking doesn't make sense. When Beau gets here, tell him he needs to make a phone call for me. I'll tell you more later, depending on what he finds out. Right now —" He pushed his chair back from the table. "I meant to stay longer but I need to go. Thanks for the stew, Rose."

"You're leaving so soon?" Rose asked.

"Sorry. I need to get back to Lauren and the kids. I don't want to leave them alone tonight. And, Rose, you may want to stay in the house with Erin. I can get one of the men to come in if you want."

"I'll be here with my gun. I can probably

outshoot any man on the ranch," Rose said. "At least I've had more experience. We'll be fine. But I wish you'd tell us what's got you so fired up."

"I can't be sure until I have Beau call Gatesville Prison," Sky said. "But I remember those cockroach kicker boots on a relative of mine. If she's out of prison and hanging around here, it could only mean one thing — trouble."

Luke sat at the table in the interrogation room, with the sheriff and deputy seated across from him. He was doing his best to appear calm. But dread was a cold fist clutching at his vitals. When the highway patrol had picked him up, he'd been confident that he could explain his way out of this mess. But he was just beginning to realize how much trouble he was in.

"Am I under arrest?" he asked.

"That depends." The sheriff, a big, walrus-like man, toyed with his mustache. "It depends on the evidence we find and the way you answer my questions."

"I have nothing to hide," Luke said. "I know how this looks, but I didn't do anything to Will Tyler."

"Then why did you follow Will after he left the ranch?"

268

Luke willed himself to stay calm. He knew the sheriff was trying to rattle him, asking him the same questions again and again, hoping he'd slip up and change his story.

"I told you, I didn't follow Will. He left for town or wherever it was he went. I finished my chores, took the time to pack my gear, and headed straight for the highway. By then, Will had been gone for at least an hour."

"Any way to prove where you went? Any gas or credit card receipts?"

"I told you that, too. The tank was almost full when I left the ranch. All I bought was coffee and pie in Plainview, and I paid with cash. Could I have made it that far if I'd taken the time to set up an ambush, lie in wait for Will, and shoot him?"

"How did you know Will was ambushed?"

"It was on the news. I was headed north when I stopped in Plainview to eat. That was when I saw the broadcast. And that was when I turned around and headed back here. I was driving south when I was stopped. You know that, too."

"What did the newscaster look like?"

"Blond, maybe — hell, I don't remember. All I remember is hearing the news."

"Did you see any TV shots of the ranch, or any interviews with folks there, like your girlfriend?"

"I didn't stick around long enough to see, and she's not my girlfriend. It wasn't going to work out between us. That was why I left the ranch."

The sheriff leaned back in his chair, took a toothpick from behind his ear, and chewed on the end of it. "That not working out bit — it was because her father objected, wasn't it?"

"You already know that."

"I do. And I know that it gave you a motive for shooting Will. Get the father out of the way, and you can get the girl and the ranch. Motive, means, and opportunity. You had all three." The sheriff glanced at his deputy, a red-haired kid who didn't look old enough to be out of high school. "Roy, show Mr. Maddox what you found in his truck."

As if he'd waited for this moment in the limelight, the young deputy produced Luke's .38 in a plastic evidence bag. "I found this under the front seat," he said. "It looks to have been fired since it was last cleaned. One bullet is missing from the cylinder."

"And we know that Will Tyler was killed with a single shot from a large caliber weapon," the sheriff added.

270

"Oh, hell!" Luke exploded, losing his patience despite his best effort. "I used the gun to kill a rattler. Erin was with me. You can ask her."

"I'll do that — though she might lie to cover for you," the sheriff said. "And I'll also check your hands for gunshot residue. Not that I expect to find any. A man plotting a careful murder would have thought to wear gloves."

"Fine." Luke had had enough. "Do what you have to. I know the circumstances look bad, but you won't find a shred of solid evidence against me, because I didn't do anything."

"So you say." The sheriff rocked forward, the front legs of his chair thudding against the floor. "But I think we've got enough to hold you for now — and we know that you're capable of violent behavior, Maddox. We did some checking on your background. Just three years ago, you served six months for assault against a man who'd hired you."

Hidden by the shrubbery at the far corner of the parking lot, Marie waited for the last customer to leave the Blue Coyote. She didn't have a watch, but the height of the moon told her it was after midnight. Even at this hour, the night was warm. She was sweating beneath the black leather jacket and jeans she'd worn to blend with the dark shadows. She'd even smeared her face with soot and covered her hands with the black silk glove liners she kept ready in her pocket. She couldn't take a chance on being seen. There were too many people around who might remember her from her waitressing days. The ugly scar on her face was hard to forget.

A buzzing mosquito lit on her cheek. She felt the prick as it sucked her blood. But she didn't move as the blue neon coyote on the sign out front went dark. Abner Sweeney came out through a side door. Turning, he used a key to lock the dead bolt behind him, then walked around to the back of the building and drove away in his SUV.

Marie waited a few more minutes to make sure he wasn't coming back. Then she approached the building, keeping to the shadows. There was no outside security light and no alarm system — she'd already checked for signs of those things. Still, it paid to be careful.

The front entrance and side door, which led to the office where the safe was kept, were locked with dead bolts. But the door at the top of the outside back stairs, used by generations of pleasure-seeking men, had simply been boarded up, which implied that the door itself didn't have a secure lock. Marie was carrying a canvas satchel with a few tools in it, including a small flashlight and a short crowbar. She also had the pistol she'd stolen from the old man in the wash — which she hoped to heaven she wouldn't need. All she wanted was to find the heroin and hit the road. Accomplish that, and she'd be free. Erin Tyler could live her privileged little life, and Stella could burn in hell.

Moving like a shadow, she crept up the back stairs. This would be the riskiest part of her plan. Here she would be exposed, with no way to hide. And prying off the boards could make enough noise to attract attention. But short of breaking a window, there was no other way in. She would have to trust to stealth and luck.

A half dozen scrap boards were nailed at angles to the door frame. Keeping low, Marie started at the bottom. Using the crow bar, she found getting them loose was easier than she'd expected. Whoever had nailed them in place hadn't taken the time to do a good job. Once she'd freed the first three boards, she was able to reach through to the doorknob, push the door inward, and crawl in through the space she'd created, dragging the tool bag behind her.

Once inside, she closed the door, stood, and turned on her flashlight. With luck, any person looking up from the ground would see only the higher boards that were still in place.

The door opened into a dingy hallway. Off to her left was the stuffy, urine-scented room where she'd slept when she worked here. Unlike the waitresses before her, she hadn't entertained men up here. A few of the bar's customers had been bold enough to pat her skinny bottom, but one look at her face had been enough to scare them off. That little room had been miserable, but not as bad as Gatesville. No matter what happened, Marie reminded herself, she would never allow herself to be hauled back there. She would die first.

But right now she needed to find Stella's heroin stash.

The hall ended in an inside stairway, descending into the bar. Marie made her way down, trying to think like Stella, with the law closing in, a half-million-dollars' worth of heroin on her hands, and no fast way to sell it. Where could she hide it? Not upstairs. The second floor was too flimsy. In the office, maybe? Under the floor, beneath the filing cabinet, or better yet, under the heavy iron safe?

Lost in thought, and with her eyes and the light on the sagging wooden steps, she almost slammed into the solid door at the bottom of the stairs. This was something new. Marie shoved against it, twisting and rattling the knob, but nothing budged. The door was securely locked from the other side. This was why no one had bothered to secure the door at the top of the outside stairs. It was no longer possible to get into the bar that way.

Swearing, Marie gave the door a final kick and turned around to go back the way she'd come. That was when a blinding light flashed on from the top of the stairs. Her dazzled eyes could make out the silhouette of a man standing in the open doorway, half shielded by the remaining boards.

"Blanco County sheriff," a young voice called out. "Drop your weapon and come out with your hands up."

Trapped in the stairwell, with no way out, there was only one thing to do.

In a lightning move, Marie drew the old man's pistol, aimed up at the dark figure, and fired.

CHAPTER THIRTEEN

Beau had caught a red-eye flight from DC and picked up a rental car at the airport. Erin and Rose, who'd both slept fitfully, if at all, were up before dawn, having coffee in the kitchen, when he walked in.

Erin jumped up and ran to him. As he held her close, murmuring words of comfort, she fought back her tears. She'd needed Beau to come. But she couldn't just fall apart and let him take over the situation. She had to show him that she could be strong. That's what her father would have expected of her.

She eased away from Beau and stepped back. Now she could see that he looked exhausted, his face unshaven, his bloodshot eyes set in shadow. The news of Will's death must have been as hard on him as it had been on her — maybe even harder, because the two brothers had missed their last chance to make peace.

"Thank you for coming, Beau," she said, taking charge. "Sit down and have some coffee. I know you're tired, but we need to talk."

Beau filled a mug from the carafe on the counter. As he took a seat, his gaze fell on the pistol that Rose had laid on the table, but he didn't ask about it. "So get me up to speed and tell me what I can do," he said.

Erin told him everything she knew about Will's trip to town, the ambush, and the shooting. "The medical examiner still has his body," she said, forcing herself to talk about it as if this were some stranger, and not her father. "We can't plan the funeral until we know when it will be released."

"What about arresting the bastard who shot him?"

Erin had known the question was coming, but it still landed like a blow. Roy had called her late yesterday, as a friend, to let her know that Luke had been picked up and was being held as a person of interest in the shooting.

"The sheriff is holding Luke," she said. "There's some circumstantial evidence against him. But I know he didn't shoot my father. He couldn't have — he wouldn't have."

Beau gave her a knowing look. "What

277

makes you so sure, Erin?" he asked gently. "Is there something you aren't telling me?"

"Only because I haven't had time," she said. "You need to hear it all."

She told him from the beginning, how she and Luke had fallen in love over Will's objections, and how Will had ordered Luke to leave her alone. "That was when Luke decided it would be best for all concerned if he were to leave," she said. "After Dad left for town, Luke finished his chores, packed his gear, left notes for Dad and for me, and drove away."

"And where were you all this time?"

"She was with me," Rose said. "We left early to build a fence around my grandpa's grave. When we got back to the ranch, it was about noon. By then, both Luke and Will were gone. Later, when the sheriff talked to the cowboys, two of them claimed they'd heard Luke and Will arguing in the barn — though it seems Will was the angry one."

"And because Luke was on the road, he has no alibi for the time of the murder," Erin added. "But he didn't do it, Beau. You've got to believe me."

"All right, I'll believe you — for now. Has Luke been charged?"

"I don't think so. Roy said they were just

holding him."

"What about evidence?" Beau asked. "Have they recovered the bullet?"

"Not as far as I know," Erin said. "But they're not telling me much, and I can't talk to Luke."

Beau sipped his coffee. "I take it you're asking for my help."

"You're a federal officer. The sheriff will listen to you."

Beau nodded. "Fine. I'll do what I can to get Luke released. But the best way to clear him would be to find the real murderer."

"You can help us there, too," Rose said. "For starters — show Beau the picture on your phone, Erin."

Erin already had the photo on display. She slid it across the table to Beau and told him where and how she'd come to take it. "Sky thinks it might belong to his cousin, a woman named Marie Fletcher."

"I remember her, all right," Beau said. "Years ago she took a potshot at Jasper and almost killed him, but she was never arrested for it. Last I heard, she was doing time in Gatesville for armed robbery."

"We're hoping you can call the warden and find out whether she's still there," Rose said.

Beau finished his coffee. "I can do that.

279

But even if she's out, why would she set up an ambush and murder Will? She barely knew him."

"That's a good question." Erin rose and began clearing away the cups. "But she's the only lead we have. What if she was being paid — you know, like a hit man?"

"It's possible. I'll call the prison as soon as the office is open. If she's still behind bars, we can throw out that theory. For now, I wouldn't mind a shower and a change of clothes. Then, as soon as it's light out, I want a look at the crime scene." He stood, stretching his arms and flexing his back.

"One more thing before you disappear, Beau," Rose said. "I've talked with Luke. He strikes me as a fine man — and certainly not a murderer. Anything you can do to help clear him will earn my gratitude as well as Erin's."

"I'll keep that in mind." Beau walked out of the kitchen, picked up the suitcase he'd left in the dining room, and carried it down the hallway. Watching him go, Erin felt the dark weight of doubt. Beau's line of work — dealing with drug traffickers — would make anyone cynical. He'd seen the worst side of humanity, and he'd learned to expect the worst of people. What if he hadn't believed her when she'd told him Luke was innocent? What if he was so intent on justice that his real focus would be on proving Luke's guilt?

Leaving Rose in the house, she went outside to help with morning chores. No matter what danger or tragedy hung over the ranch, there were still animals needing food and water, barns that needed cleaning, and cattle that needed to be rounded up and culled for early market. Sky would see that the work ran smoothly. And his wife would see that the routine bills were paid and the ranch books were kept up to date. But Erin knew that the big decisions would be up to her. The Rimrock was her responsibility now. She would have to use what she'd learned, from Will, from Jasper and Sky, and even from her grandfather, to run it like a Tyler.

By the time the chores were done, Beau had come outside. He beckoned to Erin and to Sky, who was helping out before joining the hands on the high pasture. "I made that call to Gatesville Prison," he told them. "Marie Fletcher was paroled early on good behavior three weeks ago."

"Good behavior?" Sky shook his head. "That doesn't sound like the Marie I know."

"There's more," Beau said. "It seems she's AWOL. She was supposed to stay in the area and report to her parole officer every week to start with. The warden says she hasn't shown up once, which means she's most likely on the run."

"Did you tell him we'd seen signs of her?"

"Not yet. I wanted to talk to you first. If she's here, what do you think she wants? Revenge?"

"Against me or Lauren, maybe. But not against Will. That doesn't make sense — unless, as Erin suggested, somebody was paying her for a hit."

"What about Stella?" Even saying the name gave Erin cold chills. Being kidnapped by Stella Rawlins had been the most terrifying experience of her life — and it was her father who'd come to her rescue. Would that give Stella reason enough to want Will dead?

"I didn't think to ask the warden about Stella. But she was sentenced to life without parole. Unless she escapes, she'll die behind bars. But even if she wanted a hit on Will, where would she get money? And how would she get it to Marie on the outside? There's got to be a simpler explanation." Beau glanced at his watch. "By the time I get to town, the sheriff should be in. I'll find out as much as I can."

"And try to bring Luke back," Erin said. "If he hasn't been arrested, they can only hold him twenty-four hours — isn't that the way the law works?"

"As far as I know. We'll see." Beau's answer was noncommittal. Erin understood. If he had any doubts about Luke's innocence, Beau wouldn't want him on the ranch — or anywhere around her.

"If there's any news worth reporting, I'll call you," he said, and strode to his car. As he drove away, Erin's lips formed a word of silent prayer.

Please . . .

As he drove into town, Beau couldn't help observing that no matter how many times he left, Blanco Springs always seemed to call him back. He never wanted to live here again. Neither did Natalie, whose memories of the town, and her abusive first marriage, were far worse than his own. They both liked their suburban DC lifestyle, with its manicured neighborhoods, good private schools, and world-class cultural events. But every time he came back here, he came home — to the simple houses with their rusty old trucks and dead-grass yards; to the Blue Coyote, the Burger Shack, and the one-show movie house; to the rancher's son and high school track star he would never be again. Whether he liked it or not, Blanco

Springs, like the Rimrock, was in his blood.

The sheriff's office and the jail were part of a sprawling, brick complex that also housed the court and shared city and county offices. At this early hour Beau had expected the place to be quiet. He couldn't have been more wrong.

There was an air of frenetic activity about the place. The tan county vehicles were parked out front, and the city constable's black and white car was just pulling up, along with the ambulance that was used to transport bodies to the morgue. Beau had no idea what was going on until he walked in the front door and almost collided with the bulky form of Sheriff Cyrus Harger.

"Beau." The sheriff didn't offer a handshake. "I'm sorry, you've come at a bad time. One of my deputies, Roy Porter, was murdered last night. He took a call about a break-in at the Blue Coyote. This morning, a neighbor walking his dog spotted him dead at the top of the back stairs. Hell, he was just a kid. But he loved bein' a cop." Harger wiped his eyes. "No trace of the sonofabitch who killed him, but we're thinking it might be the same low-down skunk who shot your brother. Bullet wound looks a lot the same."

"I'm sorry." Beau shook his head. Only in

Blanco County would a rookie cop be allowed to answer a call without backup. But that wasn't why he was here. "So does that mean you're letting Luke Maddox go?" he asked.

"For now. But he's still a person of interest. He's been warned to stay close. I guess he can go back to the Rimrock if you'll have him."

"If it'll make you feel any better, you can release him to my custody," Beau said.

"Oh, that's right. You're one of those federal cops. FBI, right?"

"DEA. While I'm here, I want to ask about my brother's remains. How soon — ?"

"Ask me in a couple of days. Things are crazy right now." The sheriff turned away and rushed outside to meet the TV news van that had just swung into the parking lot.

Beau walked back down the hall to find Luke at the counter, getting his personal things back. He looked red-eyed, rumpled, and unshaven after spending the night in lockup. The two men acknowledged each other with curt nods. "Are you all right, Maddox?" Beau asked.

"For now. I'm getting the keys to my rig back, but they're keeping the pistol for evidence. I guess that means I'm still a

285

suspect."

"You've been discharged to me," Beau said. "You can stay at the Rimrock, wherever you were bunking before. You can even go back to work if Erin wants to let you. She's the boss now."

"Fine. And thanks." Luke wasn't smiling. "You won't have any trouble from me."

"I wasn't expecting any. Where's your rig?"

"Out back. I'll see you at the ranch."

Beau was waiting for Luke to assure him that he wouldn't simply take the keys and run. But that assurance didn't come. Evidently, Luke Maddox considered his word to be enough. Beau found himself respecting, if not liking, the man for that.

Beau drove out of town. At the junction with the highway, he glanced in his rearview mirror. He could see Luke's pickup and trailer following a few blocks behind him.

Was this the man who'd planned Will's murder and carried it out in cold blood? So far, he wasn't acting like it. But for all Beau knew, he could be putting on a front. Now he was bringing Luke home to Erin, who was clearly in love with him. If he turned out to be the murderer, her tender young heart would be shattered forever.

"So help me God, Luke Maddox." Beau addressed the oath to the man driving the

286

truck behind him. "If I find out you killed my brother and destroyed my niece, I'll do anything to bring you to justice — even if I have to kill you myself!"

Marie wiped the pistol clean and dropped it into a deep, narrow ravine that was little more than a crack in the rust-hued earth. She hated losing a good weapon, but she couldn't risk being caught with a gun that could link her to the shooting of the young deputy. That unlucky accident would buy her a one-way ticket to death row.

She'd known he was dead as soon as she reached him and saw the bleeding hole where his heart would be. The poor, dumb kid hadn't even been wearing a flak vest. He should've known better, Marie had told herself as she stepped carefully around the pooling blood. For an instant she'd been tempted to take the 9mm Glock that had fallen from his hand, or to rifle his wallet for much needed cash. But that would've been stupid. Resisting the urge, she'd swung over the railing, dropped to the shadowed gravel surface below the outside stairs, scuffed out any tracks, and made what she hoped was a clean getaway.

Now, in the vermin-infested shack that served as her hideout, Marie weighed her options. She had no gun, nor did she have enough cash to buy another weapon on the street. She could steal one, but that might be too risky. Maybe she should just cut her losses and head for the border. At least she'd be alive and free.

But being rich in Mexico meant having access to anything she wanted. Being poor in Mexico — along with being foreign, alone, and ugly — was no better than being dead.

She'd had some setbacks, but it was too soon to give up. After the break-in and the shooting, the Blue Coyote would be under close watch. But maybe the drugs weren't there after all. Maybe Stella had hidden them somewhere else. Or maybe she'd need some kind of password, to let Abner know that she had Stella's permission to search.

She wouldn't know for sure until she'd carried out and reported the hit on Erin Tyler. Even though the gun was gone, there were plenty of other ways to get rid of the girl.

It was time for Plan B, whatever that was.

Just after making the turnoff to the Rimrock, Beau pulled off the gravel lane and stopped his rental car. Driving behind him, Luke could see the yellow crime scene tape ahead. This, then, was the place where Will Tyler had been ambushed and shot.

Stopping a few feet behind Beau, Luke climbed down from the cab of his truck. Beau hadn't asked him to get out, but he wasn't about to wait for an invitation. If any vital piece of evidence could clear him, he wanted to make sure it hadn't been missed.

Beau was already out of the car, standing next to the yellow tape but not trying to cross it. He made no objection when Luke came up beside him. The two men stood in silence for a moment, gazing at the flattened grass where Will's body had fallen.

"Did the sheriff happen to mention whether they'd found the bullet?" Beau asked. "I was hoping he'd tell me, but he was too busy for questions."

"I'm guessing they didn't. Otherwise, they wouldn't have let me out until they'd run ballistics to compare it with my gun. I was hoping they could do that. It would go a long way toward clearing me."

"That's your only gun?"

"Yes, and it's legal." Luke's gaze swept the open rangeland, dotted with scrub and carpeted with parched, yellow grass. The graveled lane was bordered on both sides by a shallow bar ditch. To the east, perhaps a half mile off, lay the house and outbuildings of the syndicate-owned ranch that had once belonged to the Prescott family. A red-tailed hawk, circling overhead, was the only thing moving in the cloudless sky. "Where do you think the shooter was?" he asked.

"Somewhere beyond the left side of the road, I'd guess, since Will was hit climbing out of his truck to move that tire," Beau said. "They'd need some cover — but that patch of mesquite out there would've worked, and it's close enough. The shooter would've needed a pickup to haul that big tire and dump it in the road. Then he would've had to hide the pickup, come back, and wait for Will. Lord, can you imagine the cold planning that must've taken?"

Luke wondered whether Beau was trying to make him squirm with those words. But he could hardly blame the man for being bitter and suspicious. Will had been Beau's brother, and though he'd heard that the two weren't on good terms, the lifelong bond between them would still run deep.

"I'm guessing the sheriff took the tire," he said.

"Yes, and Will's pickup, too," Beau responded. "The investigation team will go through every inch of that truck. If the bullet's there, they'll find it. Let's go. I called

Erin to let her know we'd be coming."

Beau climbed back into his car. Luke drove behind him, his thoughts churning. Beau had phoned Erin, so she'd know he was coming back to the ranch. Beyond that, he had no idea what to expect from her. Would she be cold? Angry? Would she defend him, or maybe even attack him?

He tried to tell himself it wouldn't matter if things had changed between them. But he was lying to himself. Erin mattered. She mattered more than anything in his wretched, solitary life. And now he'd probably lost her for good.

His eyes searched for her as he drove into the yard, but she was nowhere to be seen. Only Rose was waiting, alone, on the porch. Beau parked below the steps and went into the house. Rose followed him.

Luke drove past the house, parked his rig at the side of the duplex. He'd left the place unlocked, with the key on the kitchenette counter. Hopefully, he'd find things unchanged. He could carry his duffel bag inside, clean up, grab a beer if the fridge hadn't been emptied, and maybe catch some sleep before facing the afternoon — and Erin.

She hadn't come out to meet him or even been waiting on the porch to see him arrive. Not a good sign. But if she hated him for leaving, or because she thought he'd killed her father, or maybe both, he couldn't blame her. She was in pain — and some of that pain was his fault.

His duffel was behind the front seat. Slinging the strap over one shoulder, he climbed out of the cab, locked the truck, and mounted the steps to the front porch. The doorknob turned in his hand — at least he wouldn't have to ask for the key. And after a night in jail, this place would feel like a five-star hotel.

He pushed the door open, stepped inside, and dropped the duffel on the overstuffed chair. The window blinds were closed, veiling the rooms in shadow. As his sun-dazzled eyes adjusted to the dimness, Luke became aware that he wasn't alone. Braced for anything, he walked into the bedroom.

Erin was sitting on the side of the bed. Without a word, she stood and walked toward him.

"Erin —" He couldn't read her emotions. "Erin, I'm so sorry." He knew that the words were meaningless. Nothing he said could touch what she must be feeling now.

Standing close, she met his gaze. He saw the tears in her eyes. "Don't talk," she said. "Just hold me."

He drew her against his chest, cradling her in the circle of his arms. She breathed in tiny sobs of relief, her body trembling like a frightened child's. His lips brushed her hair, kissed her forehead, kissed the tears from her closed eyes. The tenderness that stirred in him was like no force he'd ever known. He would give his life to protect this woman — even if it meant having to protect her from himself.

"If you hadn't come back, I don't know what I'd have done," she murmured.

"You'd have carried on," he said. "You're strong, Erin. That's just one of the things I love about you. But we need to talk. There are things you need to understand. Sit down."

He eased her away from him, lowering himself to sit beside her. The temptation to stretch out on the bed with her lying in his arms was almost too strong to resist. But he knew where that would lead, and he didn't trust his self-control.

"You know I'm not the one who killed your father, don't you?" he asked her.

"I never thought you were. Not for a moment."

"Listen to me, then," he said. "I'm still a person of interest. The sheriff let me go, but only because he was dealing with another murder that happened while I was locked up. There's still plenty of circumstantial evidence against me — and there's one more thing, something I haven't told you."

Her blue eyes were steady and trusting as she waited for him to go on.

"Three years ago, I punched a man who was beating his horse with a whip. I tried to stop him, but when he wouldn't quit, I hit him hard enough to break his jaw. That one punch cost me six months in jail on an assault charge. I'd do the same thing again. But having a violent crime on my record is one more strike against me. I could be arrested and charged anytime, Erin. I won't have that hanging over you and me. Until I'm cleared we can't be together."

She laid a hand on his arm. "I love you, Luke. And I'll fight to prove that you're innocent. But what if the worst happens? What if this time, now, while you're here, is all we'll ever have? I don't want to waste a minute."

Lord, she was so young, so unaware of how easily lives could be ruined. Loving him could destroy her. How could he make her understand that?

"Listen to me," he said. "I love you, too. And if I had my way, there'd never be a reason to let you go. But you have to stay clear of me. If we're seen together, that will only strengthen the case against me and damage you, too. People could claim that I killed your father to get my hands on you and the ranch, and that you went along with it."

Her dismayed expression told him he'd finally gotten through to her. "Oh, Luke!" she said. "That's awful! So unfair!"

"But it could happen. You know it could. We can't let it." He stood, took her hand, and pulled her up to face him. "All we can do is hope the person who killed your father is found and arrested soon. Once that happens, maybe we can move on to whatever's next." He lifted her hand to his lips, planted a kiss on her palm, and closed her fist around it. "Now go. Behave as if there's nothing between us. Get through the funeral. Focus on running the ranch. You might even want to go out with Kyle if he asks you. Time will pass, and we'll get through this. All right?"

"All right." She took a few steps toward the front door, then stopped and turned back. Their eyes met — and suddenly she was in his arms again, clinging to him, returning his hungry, desperate kisses. For a long moment, he held her close, memorizing the feel of her eager body against his, every sweet curve and hollow. He wanted her like a drowning man wants air — wanted to touch and kiss every part of her, to be inside her, feeling that warm, moist silk around him. But it wasn't going to happen. Not now. Maybe not ever.

Gently he eased her away from him. "Go," he ordered her. "Go before you get us both in trouble. I love you, Erin."

"And I love you. Whatever happens, Luke, I'll always love you."

Tearing her gaze away from him, she left.

"So when are you going to see your girl again?" Hunter Cardwell demanded. "You can't wait too long. With her father gone, she's going to need a man. That man had damn well better be you."

Kyle nodded as he finished his beef stroganoff and crumpled his napkin next to the dinner plate. It seemed his father always used mealtimes as an occasion to harangue him. Mostly he closed his ears to the tirade, but right now Hunter was making sense. Erin had been putting him off. He needed to call her, make some excuse to see her again, and take things from there.

"Don't worry, Dad, I'll figure something out," he said. "Erin's been pretty busy, and she's grieving for her father. It's not exactly a good time to ask her out on a date."

"Hell, it's the best time. She's vulnerable. She needs comfort. That's when you make your move."

"I said don't worry, Dad. I'll call her."

"Have you heard any more about the investigation? Is that farrier still the prime suspect?"

"How should I know?" Kyle shrugged, relieved that his father had changed the subject. "From what I heard, they let him go after that deputy was shot and killed."

"But the bastard could still have done it. It could just as easily have been somebody else who shot the deputy."

"That's my guess, too," Kyle said. "At least the sheriff must still be keeping him around. His rig's still parked at the Rim-rock."

"You've been to the Rimrock?" Hunter asked.

"Just drove past, that's all. Somebody's got to keep an eye on the place. Might as well be me."

"Fine." He turned to his wife, who sat at the foot of the table. "Damn it, Vivian, there's a food smudge on this spoon. How many times do I have to tell you to rinse the silverware before you put it in the dishwasher? What if we had company? Lord,

I'd be embarrassed to death!"

We never have company, Kyle thought, but he knew better than to speak up.

Kyle's mother didn't answer. Since Will Tyler's death had come on the news, she'd seemed to shrink into herself. Kyle suspected that she'd had a thing for Will. But if she had, it had been nothing more than a harmless crush. She would never have been bold enough to act on her feelings — although if she had, he wouldn't have blamed her.

Hellfire, he couldn't wait to get out of this house and away from his shitty parents. Right now, marrying Erin sounded like a great idea — big house, control over a ranch, and doing all the things with Erin that he'd done with that blond whore.

He would have to work on that — and he would start by giving Erin a friendly call.

CHAPTER FOURTEEN

Deputy Roy Porter's funeral was held two days later. Most of Blanco Springs' citizens turned out to honor their fallen hero, killed in the line of duty. Officers from other local branches of the law formed a procession to accompany the casket to the cemetery. Though it wasn't a military funeral, a bugler from the high school band played taps at the graveside, leaving folks dabbing at their eyes.

Kyle had invited Erin to attend the service with him. Since they had both known Roy, she'd seen no reason not to go. It wasn't really a date. They would be out in public. And being seen with him, especially by the sheriff, would help quell the idea that she was still involved with Luke.

As they stood with the crowd at the graveside, a few yards behind Roy's distraught parents, Kyle kept a possessive grip on her hand. Erin let him. It was a show — a lie for the sake of appearances. She didn't like herself much right now, but she would do anything to protect the man she loved.

She blinked away a tear as Roy's casket was lowered into the grave. It was against all justice that a promising young man should lose his life in such a senseless way.

Erin had known Roy since the year she was in kindergarten and he was in first grade — a nice boy, quiet and well behaved. Once when she'd dropped her library book, he had picked it up and handed it back to her. Otherwise, they'd had little direct contact, but Roy had been there. She'd watched him grow up, change from a gangly, freckled boy to a polite young man. He'd been an Eagle Scout and played baseball, though he'd never been a star. She couldn't recall his ever having had a steady girlfriend. Only when he'd joined the county sheriff's team as a deputy did he seem to have found himself. Roy had clearly loved being a cop. And now he was gone.

Life was a throw of the dice. Some people got what they wanted, whether they deserved it or not. Others had to settle for what they had. Still others, like Roy, got everything snatched away just as they were about to grasp it.

Life was a gamble. Not death. Death took

everything.

The medical examiner had released Will's body to the mortuary in Lubbock. The funeral would be held two days from now. Maybe when she saw him laid to rest, next to her mother, the reality of her father's death would sink home, and she'd be able to move forward. Now it was as if he'd just left the house, and she was waiting for him to come back.

People were walking away from the grave now, headed for their cars. Kyle was still clasping Erin's hand when the sheriff approached with a purposeful stride.

"Erin, I just wanted to check with you." Cyrus Harger was never one to waste time on polite chitchat. "Is Luke Maddox still at the Rimrock?"

Erin pulled her hand away from Kyle's. "He is. He's been working, shoeing our horses to get them ready for the roundup."

"Any trouble from him?"

"Absolutely none. He keeps to himself, minds his own business. Why? Is everything all right? Have you learned any more about who shot Roy and my father?"

"You're assuming it was the same person. Abner thinks the sonofabitch who broke into the Blue Coyote and shot Roy had known about the inside stairs, maybe from

301

years ago, but not about the door at the bottom. He got trapped in the stairwell and, when Roy showed up, he had to shoot his way out.

"The motive at the Blue Coyote was robbery. Shooting Will was a whole different can of beans. The killer knew him, and had reason to want him dead. Sounds to me like two entirely different crimes, committed by two different people."

Erin's heart contracted. So Luke was still a suspect in her father's murder. The sheriff might even be planning to lock him up again.

"Luke had nothing against my father," she said. "He had no reason to kill him."

"That's not what I heard," the sheriff said. "Going by what those two cowpokes told me, you and Luke must've had something pretty hot going on."

Erin was conscious of Kyle standing next to her, hearing every word. She could sense the tension in him, hear the rush of his breathing.

"That's not true, Sheriff," she said. "Luke and I were friends. We liked each other. But it's over now. He left the ranch because he didn't want to cause trouble for me. By the time my father was killed, Luke was miles away."

"So he says. But he can't prove it."

Desperation surged. "Why are you so set on Luke? Ask Sky about his cousin, Marie Fletcher. She's out of prison and hasn't checked in with her parole officer. I took a photo of a boot print I found near the ranch. Sky thinks it's hers."

The sheriff brushed away a fly that had settled on his mustache. "Roy did mention that to me. I'll look into it." His cell phone rang. "We'll take this up again later," he said, turning away to answer the call.

Kyle caught her hand as they walked to the beat-up ranch pickup he was driving in place of the wrecked SUV. His grip was hard and possessive, his mouth a thin-lipped line. He didn't speak as he opened the door of the cab to let her climb in.

Erin waited as he walked around to the driver's side. Maybe this was a bad idea, riding home with him. Last time he'd been angry with her, he'd almost gotten them both killed. The sheriff should have waited to speak with her alone, but Cyrus Harger was about as sensitive as a buffalo bull at a tea party.

Kyle didn't speak until the truck was on the road out of town. "What were you thinking, Erin, cozying up to that pile of trash? I thought you had better taste."

Erin knew better than to defend Luke. "I told the sheriff it was over. If that isn't good enough for you, that's your problem. You don't own me, Kyle Cardwell."

He drove in silence for a couple of miles, probably wondering how to put their relationship back on the right track. Finally he gave her a smile.

"You always did have an independent streak," he said. "But you're going to need more than that to run the Rimrock. You're going to need a man by your side — a man who knows the business. I've got an associate degree in ranch management, and I've worked with my father for years. I'm practically his right-hand man. I know everything there is to know about running a ranch."

"Are you suggesting that I hire you?"

"Funny girl. No, I'm suggesting that you marry me."

She should have known where this was leading. Erin sighed. "We've been down this road before, Kyle. I'm not ready to get married — not to anyone."

"I know what you said. But that was before your father died." He turned down a side lane that wound between drought-parched hay fields and branched off. The main branch cut back to the highway. The other, which Kyle had chosen to follow, ended in a thicket of willows, fed by a mucky seep. The place was known as a popular teenage make-out spot. But this time of day, it would likely be deserted.

Erin stirred uncomfortably on the worn bench seat of the old pickup. "My father raised me to take over the Rimrock and run it," she said. "I never planned on losing him so soon, but I'm ready to step up and do my job. That's what he'd expect of me."

"But you'll be alone." Kyle pulled the truck under the willows, far enough that the branches hung like a curtain over the windshield. "You may know a lot about cows and horses, but people will try to take advantage of you. They'll try to win your trust so they can manipulate or cheat you. You'll need a man to protect you and help you make decisions." He turned toward her in the seat. "If you'll let me, I can be that man."

His look roused Erin's wariness. She'd always been able to manage Kyle and stop him from going too far. But something about him had changed. The familiar eyes that gazed at her had taken on a predatory gleam. Suddenly, without knowing why, she was uneasy.

"Let me show you the man I can be," he said. "Let me show you what I can do. You'll like it — women always do. And when we're

305

married, we can do it all the time."

Alarm flaring, she edged toward the door. "I don't want to stay here, Kyle," she said. "Start this truck and take me home."

"Not until you've given me the chance to change your mind." He reached for her, his hand clasping her arm, jerking her toward him. "No," she said. "I'm saying no — hear me?"

She began to struggle, trying to thrust him away, but he was stronger than she was. He shoved her down on the seat. The black sleeveless dress she'd worn for the funeral fastened down the front. His free hand grabbed a fistful of fabric and yanked. A button popped off, clicking as it struck the dash.

"No! Stop it!" She twisted like an eel, trying to get away as his hand slid up her leg. She'd worn sandals, with no stockings. His touch on her inner thigh triggered a surge of rage and fear that she hadn't felt since her kidnapping six years ago. Her knees jabbed but missed the vital target.

He laughed. "Stop fighting. It'll be great! You'll see!"

"You idiot!" She ground out the words between her teeth. *"You stupid, stupid jerk!"*

Fury gave her strength. She worked an arm free, doubled her hand into a fist, and slammed it hard into his eye.

He yelped and swore, reeling backward and holding his hand to his eye. Erin used the instant of distraction to grab the door handle, shove the door open, and tumble out onto the soft, muddy ground. By the time Kyle had recovered enough to climb out of the truck, she had scrambled to her feet, ducked under the wire fence, and was running across the field, toward the main road.

At first she was afraid he'd come after her. He was faster and stronger than she was, and between her sore ankle, her flimsy sandals, and the rough ground, she knew she wouldn't get far without needing to stop. But evidently Kyle had had enough. As she ran, stumbling every few steps, she could hear him shouting across the distance.

"It's that bastard Maddox, isn't it? You'll be sorry, you lying slut! Both of you!"

Erin made it to the road and began walking along the rim of the bar ditch. Her knee was skinned, her feet were raw, and one sandal had a broken strap, and she was still about ten miles from the ranch. In the blistering sun, with no water, she'd pass out before she made it. Her only hope was that someone would come along and offer her a ride.

If only she could call for help. But she'd left her cell phone at home in her purse. Beau had gone to Lubbock to make the final funeral arrangements. Sky was on the mountain, and Rose had borrowed the station wagon to take some measurements on her land. At least Carmen might be home to take a message and get her some help.

But without her phone, none of that made any difference. She felt like a helpless fool. Maybe she should just find a shady spot and wait. Sooner or later, somebody was bound to come along. Only neighbors and towns-people drove this way. She'd be fine, as long as it wasn't Kyle.

But what if it was? What would she do?

She was struggling with that question when she heard the faint throb of an engine coming from behind her. Turning, she could see the glint of sunlight on polished metal. No, it wasn't Kyle. The truck he'd borrowed today was old and red. This was a newer pickup, a blue one.

Deciding to take a chance, she stood by the roadside and held up her thumb.

The blue truck, which she couldn't place at first, slowed down. The glare of the sun on the windshield hid the driver's face from view. But when the passenger door opened and a deep male voice said, "Erin, are you all right? Get in," she felt reassured. Only as she climbed inside the air-conditioned cab and closed the door behind her did she recognize her good Samaritan.

It was Hunter Cardwell, Kyle's father.

She huddled on the seat, painfully aware of her muddy knees, her broken sandal, and the missing button on her dress. Whatever he must be thinking, it couldn't be much worse than the truth.

He gave her a worried glance as he drove. "What are you doing out here, Erin? Lord, you could have died of heat stroke if I hadn't come along. There's water in a cooler behind the seat. Grab yourself a bottle. Then you can tell me what happened."

Erin reached back and found a water bottle, twisted off the cap, and took a long drink. The cold liquid, spilling down her hot, dry throat, sent a shudder through her body.

"Better?" he asked.

"I think so." She'd been aware of Hunter Cardwell for as long as she'd been dating Kyle. But they'd never really interacted until now. He was a handsome man, even better looking than his son. But she sensed an almost feral quality about him, an air of un-predictability that set her on edge, especially now.

309

She did not want to be here.

"So tell me what happened, Erin," he said. "I thought you were with my son."

"I was." No, she couldn't tell him the whole story. "We . . . uh, had a fight. I told him I could find a ride home. I was wrong."

"That was foolish, Erin. Alone out here in the heat, anything could have happened to you. What did Kyle do to make you leave him like that?"

Squirming inwardly, Erin looked down at her hands. "Oh, just the usual thing, acting like he's qualified to run my life. I won't be treated like a child."

"So why did you act like a child and run off? You're a nineteen-year-old girl, Erin. You need somebody to look after you and manage your affairs now that your parents are gone. Kyle is very capable — he even has a degree in ranch management, and he's been working with me for years. More important, he loves you. All he wants is to make you happy."

Something clicked in Erin's mind. The man sounded just like his son — same argument, even some of the same words. Was it a coincidence, or was something darker going on? Whatever it was, she wouldn't let this man think she could be controlled.

Erin straightened in the seat. "Don't

underestimate me, Mr. Cardwell. I was raised to run the Rimrock. I don't need a man or anyone else to look after my affairs. I'm quite able to look after them myself. And if I need advice, I have an excellent foreman whose wife handles the ranch books. One thing I don't need right now is a husband."

"But you're a woman. You'll have needs. And you'll want a family."

"There's plenty of time for that. I won't be pushed into anything before I'm ready. That's what I told Kyle — and it's what I'm telling you. If Kyle's in such an all-fired rush to get married, I'm sure there are plenty of girls who'd be happy to accommodate him."

But none with her own ranch.

Erin almost said the words, then stopped herself. She didn't need to antagonize this man. She only needed to make him understand that she wouldn't be pushed around.

They had turned onto the graveled lane and were coming up on the spot where her father had been shot. The yellow crime scene tape had been left to sag uselessly between the leaning stakes. Here and there, broken ends fluttered in the light breeze. Erin averted her face as they passed it, struggling against the picture in her mind — Will stopping, getting out of the truck . . .

311

She forced away the rest of the image.

Most people would have driven around the tire in the road. Will had stopped and gotten out to move it aside. The killer had known what he would do. Whoever had murdered her father was no stranger — which likely ruled out a hit. Will's murder had been very personal.

"I'm sorry about your father," Cardwell said. "My wife and I will be going to the funeral, of course."

"Thank you."

"Does the sheriff have any idea who might have killed him? Any suspects?"

The knot of tension tightened in Erin's stomach. "None that he can back up with evidence. Right now he's busy looking for the person who shot Roy."

"I hear that farrier's back on the Rimrock."

The knot pulled tighter. "Yes, he's back at work."

"He could be the one who killed your father. How can you trust him?"

"Because I don't think he's guilty."

"If you believe that, you're a naive young girl. This is exactly why you need someone to look out for you."

Erin looked at the road. Through the haze of dust and distance, she could make out the barn and the windmill of the Rimrock. "You can let me out here," she said. "I'll be fine to walk the rest of the way."

"Don't be silly. I'll drive you all the way to the house."

He sped up as if he expected her to try to jump out of the truck. "We'll be there in a jiffy," he said with a smile.

"Thanks." Erin finished her water bottle.

As they neared the house, he slowed down. "Before you go, I need to say something." He glanced at her to make sure she was listening. "Kyle's young. I know he's got some growing up to do. But he's got a good heart, and he loves you. Here's the thing. If you're having a hard time with him, you can talk to me. I'll always listen and understand. I don't just want to be your father-in-law. I want to be your friend."

The truck was pulling up to the porch. Choosing to ignore his words, she opened the door. "Thank you for the ride, Mr. Cardwell." She closed the door and forced herself to walk slowly and calmly into the house.

Luke had gone back to work, shoeing the horses that would be used in the upcoming roundup. He'd forbidden Erin to help him or even to come by and watch. Instead he reported to Sky, who, in his typical fashion, never mentioned a word about Luke's legal predicament or his relationship with Erin.

He was grateful for the work. At least it kept him occupied. But the thought that the sheriff could show up at any time, cuff him, and haul him back to jail on a murder charge was enough to make him break out in a cold sweat. The circumstances — the confrontation with Will and the lack of a solid alibi — were damning enough. But that assault conviction in his past was the capper. Unless evidence could be found that would clear him, he was dead meat.

The real killer was out there, maybe close by. But as long as the sheriff had a likely suspect and, with a little more evidence, could wrap up the case and take the credit, he wouldn't want to waste time looking for anybody else.

Luke paused to swig water from the bottle he kept close by. The temptation to run was a constant urge. Leave everything. Just disappear into another life with another identity. But that would be a sure admission of guilt. The only way to prove his innocence — and to be with Erin — was to stay.

As if the thought could summon her, he looked across the yard and saw Erin climbing out of an unfamiliar blue pickup that

314

had pulled up to the house. She was dressed in black — probably for the funeral of the young deputy who'd been killed. But even at a distance he could tell that something was wrong. He could almost sense her struggle as she climbed the front steps, head up, limping slightly, as if trying to hide pain.

He wanted to go to her. But that was out of the question.

As the truck backed up and turned around, he tried to see the driver. The sun's glare on the windshield made it difficult to get a good look, but he could tell it wasn't Kyle. Did she have a new man in her life? But he'd be a fool to ask that question. Erin wasn't his property. Even if she loved him, he hadn't earned the right to call her his.

As she disappeared into the house, he turned away and went back to work, shaping a shoe for a sturdy dun gelding. His hammer blows rang across the yard as he pounded the steel shoe on the anvil. At least Erin would hear the sound, know he was close by, and that he was doing his best to watch over her.

Vivian sat frozen at the foot of the table, willing herself not to break. She'd witnessed countless mealtime arguments between her husband and her son. Most of the time

315

she'd managed to stay uninvolved. But this time Hunter's fury had pulled her in, with no way out.

"Tell me the truth, Vivian!" His fist crashed onto the table, rattling the plates and cutlery. "Who were you sleeping with when this dolt was conceived? I know it wasn't me! There's no way somebody like me could've fathered such a clueless idiot!"

"Look at him." Vivian spoke calmly, knowing he wanted her to cry and crumble. Her icy self-control was the only weapon she had against his rages. "You know very well he's your son. There's no need for you to say those terrible things."

"Stop it, both of you!" Kyle shot to his feet. His swollen left eye looked like an overripe plum. "Stop talking about me as if I'm not here! I'm an adult, for Christ's sake! At least treat me like one!"

"Then start acting like one! I asked for one thing — get that girl to marry you! I even paid for a lesson with that whore so you'd know what to do when the time came. And what do you do the next time you're with little Miss Tyler? You manhandle her till she fights you off and runs. I don't know what the hell you are — mentally defective maybe. But one thing you're not is a man. Maybe you should stick with those damn porno sites on your computer and leave real women alone."

Vivian stifled a gasp. She'd actually believed her son when he'd said he was taking an online course. She'd never checked his computer because she wanted to respect his privacy. And the lesson Hunter had mentioned — what else could it be? What a stupid, naive fool she'd been.

Trembling, she rose from her place at the table. "I'm going to my room," she said. "You two can finish this without me."

"Stay right there!" her husband snapped. "I'm not finished with you! You're the one who raised this namby-pamby excuse for a man. You always coddled and spoiled him. You always protected him when he had to face something hard. Now look at him. Look at what you've done. This is your fault!"

Shattered, Vivian gripped the back of her chair. She'd tried to be a good mother. She'd tried to shield her son from his father's vicious browbeating. Had her well-meant protectiveness made Kyle weak? She could only blame herself.

Hunter swung back toward his son. "I have one question for you. Can you fix this mess and get the girl back? Answer me!"

"It wasn't my fault." Kyle's voice bordered

on a whine. "It's that bastard Maddox. He's turned her head. As long as he's around, there's no chance Erin will have me."

"I didn't ask you whose fault it was," Hunter said. "I asked you if you could fix it. So can you?"

Kyle hesitated; then his head came up. His jaw took on a determined thrust. "Yes," he said. "I can fix it."

Hunter nodded. "That's more like it," he said.

Dressed in her lacy pink nightgown, Vivian sat on the edge of the bed. The house was quiet. Kyle had gone up to his room, probably to do things she'd resolved not to think about. Hunter had gone out to check on a colicky mare that the vet had treated earlier. But he'd be back soon. And he'd take out his frustrations on her, in bed.

At least for now, she had an interlude of peace and quiet — time to calm her screaming nerves, time to think about Will and to mourn what could never be.

Strange, she felt closer to him now than she had when he was alive. It was almost as if she could feel his spirit near to her, giving her comfort, even returning her love.

She had kept the pages she'd written about their make-believe affair. They were safely hidden in a plain manila envelope that she'd slipped between the king-sized mattress and the box springs, as far under as she could reach. Hunter would never have a reason to look there.

The news of Will's murder had rocked her world and banished her hope of anything real between them. But it hadn't stopped her from loving him. She had hidden the pages before his death and hadn't looked at them since. But she would keep them always. Maybe, in her memory, what had been make-believe would become real.

The urge to read those pages again, imagining herself in Will's arms, was almost unbearable. Maybe, just for a moment . . . But no. Hunter was due back soon. She couldn't risk the danger of discovery. As unloving as he was, he was very possessive of her. He had even threatened to kill her if she ever cheated on him. Better safe than sorry.

Good advice, she told herself as she heard the front door open and close. As Hunter's footsteps approached the bedroom door, she slipped beneath the covers, lay back on the pillow, and prepared herself for what she knew would be more like punishment than lovemaking.

CHAPTER FIFTEEN

Erin lay in bed, staring up into the darkness. The glowing numbers on her bedside clock read 1:45. She'd been trying to sleep for almost three hours. But it was no use. Even though she was physically and emotionally exhausted, the thoughts in her head, swirling and clashing like the winds of a tornado, refused to let her rest.

All nerves and movement, she sat up and swung her legs to the floor. The house was quiet. Beau was asleep in his old room. He would be flying back to DC after Will's funeral. For now, Rose had moved into the old housekeeper's quarters off the kitchen. Soon she'd be going home as well, to prepare for the permanent move to her land on the creek. Then, except for Carmen coming in to work, Erin would be alone in the house, maybe for a long time to come.

But it was the thought of Luke that was keeping her awake. The terror, the worry, the burning love that filled every part of her. How much longer would he be in her life? How would he bear it if he lost his freedom for something he hadn't done? And how would she live if she lost him?

Dressed in the oversized cotton tee she wore as a nightshirt, she thrust her feet into leather slippers and wandered out onto the porch. The night was warm and clear, the stars a spill of diamond points across the ink-black sky. Insects hummed in the darkness. A coyote call, echoing from the foot-hills, touched her heart with melancholy.

Luke's rig was parked outside the duplex. The windows were dark. Was he sleeping after a long day of working in the heat, or was he awake and restless, just as she was, fearing what the next day would bring?

Now that the sheriff had concluded that Will's murder and Roy's weren't committed by the same person, Luke was almost sure to be arrested and jailed again. It was only a question of when. For all she knew, it could be as soon as tomorrow.

The next few hours could be all the time they had left.

Suddenly she was moving, crossing the porch, hurrying down the steps, keeping close against the house where, she knew, her movements wouldn't trigger the security light. Luke had told her to keep away from him. But a wall of fire couldn't have stopped her now. She had to go to him — to offer him the one gift she had to give, and to hold the memory of that giving forever.

The night breeze fluttered the thin shirt against her body. She felt its soft warmth on her skin and thought of Luke, touching her, loving her. In the quiet darkness, she could hear her own beating heart.

She passed the shelter of the house and crossed the open ground. The moon and stars lent enough light for her to see Henry, hunting in the backyard. She left him in peace and moved on.

As she mounted the front porch of the duplex, a shiver of doubt swept over her. What if he wasn't here? What if she offered herself and he sent her away like a naughty child being banished to her room? What if he'd met some woman in town and called her, and . . .

Stop it!

Summoning her courage, she tried the doorknob. The door was locked.

She rapped lightly on the wood, once, then again. Agonizing seconds passed before she heard a stirring inside, the faint creak of floorboards, the metallic click of a sliding lock. The door opened cautiously at first, then swung inward. Luke stood framed in the doorway, his hips wrapped by a hastily grabbed towel, which he clutched with one hand.

There was no need for questions. An unspoken understanding flowed between them as they faced each other in the darkness. With his free hand, he pulled her inside, closed the door and locked it before gathering her close. "Damn it, Erin," he whispered, his mouth brushing her forehead. "This isn't the way I wanted it to happen."

"It doesn't matter. I just want it to happen." She kissed him, her lips parting and softening against his. His body smelled of clean soap and felt like rough velvet through her thin shirt. Her trembling fingers reached down for the hand that held the towel around his hips and pulled it free. The towel caught between them for an instant, then dropped to the floor. He stood naked in her arms, his erection jutting hard against her belly. There was no fear in her, only wonder, desire, and a sureness that, whatever might happen in the days ahead, she was meant to be his.

He kissed her, tongue probing deep, igniting heat, hands raising the hem of her shirt to clasp her buttocks and pull her against him. Need rose in her, hot and hungry and raw. Her body molded to his, thrusting against the sweet contact that sent pleasure rippling through every part of her. She shuddered with the first release. Then, sensing that there was even more where that came from, she pushed again.

Luke groaned. "I think we're in the wrong place for this," he muttered, sweeping her to the bed.

By the time he lowered her to the pillow, Erin's shirt was gone. She lay looking up at him in the faint moonlight that filtered through the blinds, loving the sight of him as he leaned over her — the muscular shoulders and arms, the mat of black hair that narrowed below his chest to trail down his belly, and most of all his face, his expression blending love, tenderness, and anguish. Neither of them spoke of it, but he knew, as she did, that if things went wrong, this could be their last night together.

Raising a hand, she ran her fingers down his cheek. He turned his head and kissed them, then bent to nuzzle her small, firm breasts. Taking his time, he nibbled and sucked each nipple to an aching nub. She gasped with pleasure as each small tug deepened the pain of wanting him inside her. Luke was an experienced lover — that was a given. It would be like him to prolong her first time, heightening her pleasure and making sure she was ready. But the urge to give herself was more than she could hold back. She thrust her hips against him, needing, demanding.

He moved away for a moment, and she knew he was protecting her. *Stop,* she wanted to say. *Having your baby would be a joy. It would leave me with a part of you forever.*

But she knew better than to speak the words. Luke was a responsible man. He would never allow such a thing to happen. Not even if she begged him for it.

He returned to her in the bed. She opened to him, her arms, her moisture-slicked thighs, all wanting, all welcoming. His fingers stroked her, preparing her, parting the delicate layers. "Yes . . ." she murmured. "Now . . ."

He shifted between her legs. Her little cry as his hard length slid inside her changed to a murmur of bliss as he began to move. Swimming in new sensations, she moved with him, letting him carry her to a climax that was like ten thousand flowers all bursting into bloom.

Afterward, warm and contented, she lay in his arms. She was his woman now, and

325

he was her man — and for this moment, everything was as it was meant to be.

Before the first stirrings of dawn, they made bittersweet love again. Then it was time for Erin to leave. Knowing she mustn't be seen with him, she gave him a last, lingering kiss, slipped out of bed, and found her shirt and slippers. By unspoken agreement, neither of them had mentioned what lay ahead. There were too many fears, too many unanswered questions. She simply paused at the door, whispered, "I love you, Luke," and stole out into the darkness.

The house was blessedly quiet. Crossing the parlor and tiptoeing down the hall, Erin made it all the way to her own bedroom before the tears spilled over.

It was midmorning when the sheriff's tan SUV drove into the ranch yard and pulled up to the house. Luke, who'd been working since dawn, willed himself to ignore the new arrival. But the sick feeling in his gut told him that his worst fears had come to pass. And there was nothing he could do about it.

Erin and Will's brother, Beau, had come out on the porch. They waited as the sheriff and a deputy climbed out of the vehicle and mounted the steps. Now they were talking.

Beau turned and pointed across the yard, toward the pen where Luke was preparing to shoe his third horse of the day.

If Luke hadn't known for sure why the sheriff had come, he knew it now.

Erin was standing back, letting her uncle do the talking. That was as it should be. Any reaction on her part — any effort to defend him — would only make matters worse.

A memory flashed in his mind — Erin in his arms, giving him her love and her sweet, virginal body. Maybe it had been unfair of him to take what she'd so willingly offered. But he wasn't sorry. Whatever happened, he would carry the memory like a secret treasure.

He could only hope she felt the same. If she had regrets, he would never forgive himself.

The sheriff and the deputy climbed back into the SUV, drove across the yard, and stopped next to the barn. The two of them, both armed, got out and walked toward the shaded pen where Luke was bent over the shoe he was shaping on the anvil. The sheriff unlatched the gate, swung it partway open, and stepped through with the deputy behind him.

When Luke could no longer ignore the

pair, he straightened and turned around. He was nearly a head taller than the burly, middle-aged sheriff, and he was holding a hammer, but he knew better than to resist what was about to happen.

"Put down your weapon, Maddox," the sheriff said, drawing his pistol.

Weapon? Luke dropped the hammer to the ground.

"Turn around and put your hands behind your back. Deputy —" He nodded toward the other man.

Luke did as he was told, but the feel of the steel cuffs clamping around his wrists sent a jolt of panic through him. He wanted to fight. He wanted to run. Anything but to submit to this humiliation.

"Luke Maddox," the sheriff said, "you are under arrest for the murder of Will Tyler. You have the right to remain silent. Anything you say can and will be used against you in a court of law. . . ."

The sheriff rattled off the Miranda rights in an expressionless voice. When he'd finished, he motioned to the deputy to put Luke in the back of the vehicle. The skinny, taciturn deputy gave Luke a shove — something he might not have done if Luke hadn't been under restraint.

As the door was about to close, Luke

leaned toward the sheriff, who was still standing outside. "One question, if you don't mind, Sheriff Harger," he said.

Harger scowled. "You can ask it, but I don't have to answer."

"Just this," Luke said. "You let me go once, in part because you had no solid evidence. What changed your mind? Why are you arresting me now?"

The sheriff's scowl deepened. Luke knew he had no right to ask the question. But he needed to understand what had happened and what he was facing. A city cop would know better than to share information. But this small-town sheriff liked to talk. He might enjoy revealing more just to watch his prisoner squirm.

"All right, I'll tell you," Harger said. "We had an eyewitness come forward — a witness who claims he saw you unloading that big tire from the back of your trailer and leaving it in the road."

Luke swore silently to keep up his courage. But inside, he'd gone cold with fear. It was as if he could feel the jaws of a trap, closing around him. "Whoever your witness is, he's either mistaken or lying," he said. "As I've told you, I wasn't there."

"Well, the witness recognized your rig. With that trailer behind the truck, it's pretty

329

hard to mistake."

Which would suggest that the claim is a lie, Luke thought. "How reliable is your witness?" he asked.

"Very. In fact, I think he was even an Eagle Scout. And he lives close enough to have been in the area. His claim is totally believable."

The sick tightening in Luke's gut told him he already knew the answer to his next question, but he asked anyway. "You've told me that much. Can you tell me who it was?"

Harger hesitated, then shrugged. "I don't see why not, since you'll find out sooner or later. It was the neighbor's son, Kyle Cardwell."

Erin stood on the porch as the hulking, tan SUV took Luke away. Until now, she'd managed to keep a tight rein on her emotions. Falling apart with the sheriff looking on would only have worsened Luke's case. But now that the sheriff's vehicle had vanished in a cloud of dust, those emotions broke free.

"We've got to do something!" Wheeling like a cornered animal, she turned from Beau to Rose, who'd come out onto the porch. Neither of them spoke.

"He didn't do it! You know he didn't!

330

You've got to believe me!"

Rose came forward and laid a gentle hand on her arm. "I believe you, dear. Luke is a good man. But what can we do except wait and let justice take its course? He'll have a lawyer —"

"Only a public defender — not a *good* lawyer. Beau, you must know some of the best defense lawyers in the country. Who can I call?"

Beau shook his head. "I know some good lawyers, Erin. Unfortunately, you could never afford their fee, especially with the ranch in such dire straits."

"I'd do anything!" Tears blurred her eyes. "I'd even sell Tesoro!"

"Even that wouldn't be enough," Beau said. "And I have a feeling that Luke wouldn't want your help, especially that kind of help. He strikes me as a proud man."

"But we could at least hire somebody local — somebody good —"

"You aren't listening, Erin." Beau exchanged glances with Rose. "I know you want to help Luke. But there's nothing you can do. You've got enough troubles of your own right now."

"What — ?" Erin stared at him. "I know things are tight, with the drought and all. But we've survived hard times before.

Surely —"

"Come with me, Erin." Rose took her hand. "Beau, would you excuse us for a few minutes? We need to have a private talk."

Beau nodded, his expression knowing. "I'll be right here."

Rose led Erin inside and down the hall, into the ranch office, with its view of the ranch yard, the barns, and the escarpment beyond. Erin had spent her share of time in this room, sitting at the antique desk that had passed through three generations of Tylers before her. But only now, as she took her seat in the big leather chair, its surfaces worn soft and thin from long use, did she feel the true weight of the responsibility that had fallen on her shoulders.

On the wall next to the door, in a leather frame, hung a photo of her grandfather, Bull Tyler, taken when he was about fifty years old — a man in his prime, handsome in a rugged way, his demeanor cocksure, as if he knew he could take on the world and win. The photo had been posed for a magazine article, at a time when Bull was already a legend.

"What do you think he would say to you?" Rose's question broke into Erin's thoughts. She'd taken the chair on the opposite side of the desk.

"I only knew him when he was old," Erin said. "But I think he would say what he said then — *Land and family. Family and land. Nothing else matters.* Is that the reason you brought me in here?"

"I wish it was. No, dear, there's something you need to understand before another day — or even another hour — goes by."

"All right. I'm listening."

"Your father was my good friend," Rose said. "He confided in me — things that I need to pass on to you now. Things he would have told you himself if he'd been given the chance."

"Are you saying my father was keeping secrets from me?"

Rose settled back in the chair, hands in her lap, fingers stirring restlessly. "I think you know how much he loved you. He wanted to spare you the burdens he carried, to give you time to have fun and enjoy your life as a young girl. But toward the end, he knew he couldn't wait any longer. He had to tell you the truth."

"But he never got the chance." Erin felt her father's loss like a knife through her heart. "So now that's become your job. I'm sorry."

"No sorrier than I am," Rose said. "You know that when Will bought out Beau's share of the Rimrock, he had to borrow the money from the bank."

"Yes, I know that. And I know it was a hardship for him. That's one reason that he and Beau were barely on speaking terms. But we've made the payments for the past three years. I know it hasn't been easy, but we've always managed."

"Yes, you have. But this year has been different. This drought has been the worst ever."

"I know. That's why we're getting ready to sell off surplus cattle and horses."

"There's something else, Erin. Something your father was planning to tell you, probably on the day he died. The bank didn't give him easy terms on that loan. This year a balloon payment is due by the end of December — two hundred thousand dollars."

Erin stifled a gasp. She felt the color drain from her face.

"At the time he signed on the loan, Will didn't have much choice," Rose said. "He was hoping the years would be good ones and he could raise his profits enough to make the payment. But you know what happened. This has been one of the worst years ever for the ranch, and the year before wasn't much better."

"So we don't have the money." Even speaking the words felt like a sentence of doom.

"According to what Will told me, there's barely enough in reserve to pay monthly expenses until the stock can be sold off. And even if you sold everything, it wouldn't cover the payment. As of October first, if the bank doesn't get their money, they'll foreclose on the ranch and sell it — probably to the syndicate."

In the silence that followed Rose's words, Erin struggled to grasp what she'd just heard. She'd known the ranch was in trouble, but as she'd said earlier, they'd survived tough times before. However, this was more than a tough time. This was losing the ranch where four generations of her family had lived — the only home she'd ever known, the legacy she'd hoped to pass on to her children and grandchildren. This was unthinkable.

"What about Beau?" she asked, grasping at straws. "I know he never meant for this to happen. Couldn't he lend me back some of the money he took for his share?"

Rose shook her head. "For one thing, your father had too much pride to ask him. But even if he'd asked, Beau used the money to buy a nice home in the country near the

335

DC area, and to build a clinic for his wife's veterinary practice. There's not enough cash left to make a difference."

Erin's hands clenched into fists. She'd just lost her father. She was on the verge of losing the ranch, and she was in no position to help the man she loved.

She could feel shock turning to rage. She wanted to curse and pound the desk. She wanted to scream and cry. Why hadn't her father shared his worries sooner? Life hadn't prepared her for any of this. It wasn't fair.

Bull Tyler's steely eyes gazed down at her from the photograph on the wall. In her mind, she could hear his voice as she remembered it, roughened by pain and the alcohol he'd turned to after the terrible riding accident that had broken his spine and left him wheelchair bound.

Hell, of course it's not fair! Life isn't fair! Grow up, Erin! Be a Tyler. Figure out what has to be done and do it. Land and family. Family and land. That's all that matters!

The words lingered in Erin's mind as she reached deep inside herself for strength — Tyler strength that was as much a heritage as her beloved ranch. *Land and family. Family and land. Figure out what has to be done and do it!*

Wherever those words had come from,

Erin knew they were all the wisdom she had. She raised her head and took a deep breath. "Tell me everything you know, Rose," she said.

Rose shifted in her chair, leaning toward the desk. "When Will drove into town for the last time, he mentioned that he was going to the bank to ask for an extension. If that's where he went, I'm guessing he was disappointed. The bank would have no reason to help a man who's over a barrel — especially if they've got a cash buyer waiting."

"And I can't believe they'd help me either," Erin said. "But I'll need to talk to someone there. At least they might tell me about their conversation with my dad. If I knew what was said and what time he left there . . ." She paused, thinking. Could there be a connection between her father's visit to the bank and his murder? Maybe the syndicate wanted him out of the way so they could buy the Rimrock when the bank foreclosed.

"Let's go back outside and talk to Beau," she said. "The funeral isn't until tomorrow. Today, while he's here, I could use his help."

Beau readily agreed to help Erin piece together the events leading up to Will's murder. Hopefully, their search would yield some clues. Finding the real killer would be their one best chance of freeing Luke.

They started at the bank. Much as Erin wanted to be seen as an independent woman, she had to admit that having a federal agent with her, asking questions, made it easier to get answers.

Sim Bartlett, the bank president, admitted that Will had come by the morning he was killed. Sim had kept him waiting, partly in the hope that the rancher would give up and leave. He'd known what Will wanted and what his answer would be. Why go through the painful scene again?

"Finally I had no choice except to talk to him," Bartlett said. "It was the same conversation we'd had before. Will wanted an extension on the payment. I had to tell him no."

"Was anything said about the syndicate buying the ranch?" Erin asked.

Bartlett hesitated, but a stern look from Beau was enough to keep him talking. "Now that I remember, there was a mention of it. When I said that a man from the syndicate had questioned me about buying the Rimrock, Will looked like he'd been gut punched. My guess is that he'd been planning to sell them some of the land bordering the old Prescott Ranch. Since they were more interested in taking over the Rimrock, that wouldn't have been an option." Bartlett shrugged. "I felt sorry for Will, but business is business. I wasn't hired to be nice."

Rage rose in Erin as she imagined her proud, dignified father forced to grovel in front of this soulless man. For now, she held her anger in check. Later, she would have to deal with the bank herself. There would be plenty of time to tell Bartlett what she thought of him.

"Is there anything else you remember?" Beau asked.

"Only that Will left here in a pretty sour mood. He looked like a whipped dog."

Quivering with suppressed anger, Erin climbed back into Beau's rental car. "A whipped dog! That man is a monster, Beau!"

"I agree with you." Beau slid behind the wheel. "But I don't think he had any reason to murder Will. The bastard already had Will over a barrel. All he had to do was wait."

"What about the syndicate? They want the ranch."

"The syndicate is a legitimate investment company, with a decent reputation. They're hardly the Mafia. And they had no reason to kill Will. All they had to do was wait for the bank to foreclose, then snatch up the property at a bargain price. Let's move on. I can guess where Will might have gone next."

Erin didn't need to ask. Her father had never been much of a drinker, but he'd turned to alcohol more often since his wife's death. After the letdown at the bank, he'd have been wanting a drink, or at least a beer.

They parked next to the Blue Coyote and went inside. Erin wasn't legal to be there, but when she walked in with Beau, Abner didn't object. The hour was still early. A couple of out-of-towners sat at a table with their beers. Otherwise, the place was empty.

"I already talked to the sheriff." Abner wiped down the bar with a towel as he responded to Beau's question. "I'll tell you what I told him. Will showed up right after I opened the place, which would've been about eleven. I handed him a Corona, because that was his usual. He paid, took it, and sat in the corner, drinking. He didn't want to talk but I could tell he was hurting bad. After about twenty minutes, he got up and went out to his truck. I heard him drive away. That was the last I saw of him. Damned shame what happened. We had our differences in the past, but Will was a good man."

"Who else was here when he left?" Beau asked. "Was there anybody who might have made a call, or taken a shortcut to get ahead of him on the road?"

"I see what you're gettin' at." Abner hadn't forgotten his own lawman days. "But it was early. The only ones here, besides me, were Shep and Herman." He named a couple of old men to whom the bar was like a second home. "They didn't have phones, and they stayed till the place got busy around noon. Then they left, probably walked home. Neither of them drives anymore. If you're looking for a suspect, I think you can cross them off your list."

"What about Marie Fletcher, Sky's cousin? Didn't she used to work here?"

"Not for me. That was when Stella owned the bar. But I do remember her. Toughest woman I ever knew. Nobody messed with Marie. Too bad. She must've been pretty before her face got cut. Might've had a whole different life without that."

"You know she got out of prison, don't you?"

"I know. And it wouldn't surprise me a bit if she'd been the one to shoot that nice, young deputy. Probably came here to rob the place and got stuck in the stairwell. That's what I told the sheriff. But I wish him luck trackin' her down. Cyrus is out of his league with that one. She's Comanche, and a helluva lot smarter than he is."

"What are the chances she might've killed Will?"

Abner shook his head. "Doesn't make sense to me. She didn't have anything against Will. And killing in broad daylight doesn't strike me as her style. She'd more likely do it at night, like a cat."

"Anything else you can tell me?" Beau asked.

"Just that I'll be shutting down the Blue Coyote for Will's funeral tomorrow. That'll be a big one. Will had a lot of friends."

"Yes," Beau said. "A lot of friends and at least one enemy."

CHAPTER SIXTEEN

"Well, no surprises so far." Erin fastened her seat belt as Beau drove away from the Blue Coyote. She'd hoped, at least, to learn something that might help Luke. But that hope was already beginning to fade.

"It's too soon to get discouraged." Beau seemed to read her mood. "Think of putting a jigsaw puzzle together — a piece here, a piece there, and at some point you begin to see the whole picture."

"Or maybe you never do," Erin said. "Not if too many pieces are lost. My dad got turned down by the bank. He stopped by the Blue Coyote for a beer, then headed home and died on the way. That's all we've learned. And it isn't enough."

"So we keep trying," Beau said. "Right now I'm going to the jail to talk to the sheriff. I want you to stay put in the car. He's apt to tell me more if you're not with me."

343

"What about Luke? Will you be able to see him?"

"He's probably still being processed. But that's not why we're here." Beau pulled into the parking lot of the city and county complex and found a shady spot in the farthest corner. "Wait for me here. I'll leave the keys so you can turn on the AC if it gets too hot. I'll try not to be too long."

"It doesn't matter. Take the time to find out everything you can."

Beau left, and Erin settled down to wait. Time crawled past. The sun climbed higher in the sky, shrinking the patch of shade that kept the car's interior from turning into an oven. People arrived and left. Still there was no sign of Beau.

She imagined herself bursting into the jail, demanding to see Luke, maybe even taking him at gunpoint and whisking him off to someplace safe, like Mexico. Silly schoolgirl fantasies. The reality was, there was nothing she could do.

By the time Beau showed up, Erin had the car running with the air-conditioning on high. Beau climbed into the driver's seat. His grim expression scared her. She forced herself to ask the question. "What did you find out?"

Beau shifted into reverse and backed out

344

of the parking spot. "Plenty. Most of it not so good. You may want to write this down when we get home."

"Fine. But tell me now. How's Luke?"

"I don't know. I didn't see him. But I spent enough time with the sheriff to get some answers."

"I'm listening." Erin steeled herself as he turned the car up Main Street, in the direction of the highway.

"Luke's being arraigned in the morning. His lawyer, a woman, has been assigned, but she has yet to show up. She'll work with him to prepare the case for the grand jury, if it gets that far. I'm guessing she'll want to talk to you."

"And I'll want to talk with her. What else?"

"The medical examiner determined that Will died sometime between eleven-thirty and noon. I'm guessing the lawyer will try to prove that Luke was somewhere else, but so far he has no alibi.

"The bullet is still missing. The medical examiner didn't find it, and there's no sign that it hit Will's truck, which means that either the shooter took it, or it's still at the scene."

More bad news, Erin thought. A ballistics test could confirm that the bullet hadn't come from Luke's gun. That would go a

345

long way in establishing reasonable doubt.

"Can I go to the place where Dad was shot and look for it?" she asked.

"Maybe. But if you find it, you mustn't touch it. Otherwise the prosecutor could claim that it was planted at the scene." Beau glanced at her as they turned onto the highway. "There's one more thing, Erin. You're not going to like it."

"So far I haven't liked anything I've heard. How can they hold Luke when they don't have a scrap of solid evidence against him?"

"I asked the sheriff the same question. He told me an eyewitness came forward, someone claiming they saw Luke unload that big tire from his trailer and leave it in the road."

Erin's heart dropped. "That's impossible."

"Is it, Erin?"

"What are you saying, Beau?" she demanded. "You can't believe that Luke would murder my father!"

"I believe what fits," Beau said. "Luke left the ranch sometime after Will went to town — Carmen should be able to confirm the time. When the police picked him up on the freeway, fifty miles from here, he was headed back toward Blanco Springs. He claimed to have turned around in Plainview, more than a hundred and fifty miles away. If that was true, he couldn't have shot Will and made it that far before the news came on TV. But what if he lied? What if he just went partway, waited somewhere, and then headed back, knowing he'd be picked up? It could've happened that way. He could have killed your father, Erin."

The sense of betrayal burned like acid. "Luke would never do such a thing! I don't believe you!"

"That's because you love him. And love can make you see things in a different light. I'm saying this because I don't want you hurt. You have to prepare yourself for the truth."

"I know the truth. And I don't believe that witness. Did the sheriff tell you who it was?"

"He did." Beau glanced at Erin as the car slowed for the turnoff to the Rimrock. "It was your old boyfriend, Kyle Cardwell."

"Your lawyer's here, Maddox." Through the bars the deputy cuffed Luke's wrists before opening the cell and leading him to the interrogation room, where he chained the cuffs to a ring on the table. Luke bore the humiliating treatment with as much patience as he could manage. But he was all raging fury inside. He knew whose lie had put him here, and he knew why.

It would be all too easy to blame Erin's

innocent love for putting him here. If she'd kept her distance, Will wouldn't have taken him to task that morning, and Erin's jealous boyfriend wouldn't have claimed to witness something that never happened. But even if he tried, he couldn't fault her. Her love had been the sweetest, truest thing he'd ever known. And whatever happened, last night would remain the happiest memory of his life.

"Wait here," the deputy said. *As if he could get up and leave.* Alone in the bleak room, Luke willed himself not to appear nervous. He could almost feel the eyes watching him through the one-way glass. His assigned lawyer would be a public defender, probably young and inexperienced. Well, he would have to make the best of that. He certainly couldn't afford to pay anyone halfway competent. All he could do was pray for a miracle. Otherwise, he'd be spending the rest of his life behind bars, maybe even on death row.

What would happen to his grandmother if he went to prison? He had some money in a savings account. Maybe the lawyer could help him arrange for it to go to her care.

But now he was getting ahead of himself.

A click of the doorknob riveted his attention. The deputy opened the door to reveal a stocky figure, silhouetted against the light. Only as the door closed behind her and Luke saw her more clearly did he realize he was seeing a woman.

She appeared to be in her sixties, plump, with frizzy, dyed red hair. She was wearing a sleeveless, flowered sundress that showed her fleshy, suntanned arms and stretched tight over her ample bosom. Instead of a briefcase, she carried an oversized red leather purse.

She walked toward the table, her carved wooden cane thumping on the floor. Remembering his manners, Luke stood. The chain locking his cuffs to the table kept him from straightening to his full height, but at least he'd made the effort.

"No need for formalities. Sit down, Mr. Maddox," she said, plopping onto the folding chair across from him. "My name's Pearlina Murchison. You can call me Pearl."

As Luke sat down again, she laid her purse on the table, opened the clasp, and slid a manila file out onto the table. He took a moment to study her. Her jowly face was freckled from the sun. Behind thick, tortoiseshell glasses, her blue eyes were sharp and alert. When she leaned closer, Luke could smell the strong stench of cigarette smoke.

"I've only had a few minutes to read up on your case, Mr. Maddox," she said. "My first impression is that we've got a tough fight ahead of us. But I'll give it my best shot."

"That's all I'm asking," Luke said.

"Fine. And you don't need to say it. I'm not what you expected. But believe me, this isn't my first rodeo. I worked in Chicago, in the Cook County prosecutor's office, for twenty-eight years. When my health couldn't take it anymore — bad heart — I came home to Blanco, where I grew up. I'm pretty much retired now, but I help out the court when they need me. So let's get started. You're familiar with attorney-client privilege?"

"Yes. I'm afraid this isn't my first rodeo either."

"So I see." She glanced at the file, which lay open on the table. "So, since you understand that everything you tell me here is confidential, I'll just ask you straight out. Did you ambush and kill Will Tyler?"

"Absolutely not."

"Okay, so let's hear your side."

Luke told her the whole story, including his relationship with Erin and his decision to leave the Rimrock. Only one detail was left out — their night of lovemaking. That was too personal to share.

"So the girl believes you're not guilty of killing her father?"

"That's right. I'm sure she'll want to talk to you."

"And the so-called witness was her boyfriend until you came along?"

"That's right."

"Fine." Pearl closed the file and slid it back into her purse. "You'll be arraigned in the morning. You'll plead not guilty. After that we'll work on three possible lines of defense: Number one, if the bullet can be recovered and tested, it won't be a match for your gun. Number two, the witness had reason to lie about what he saw. And number three, we can hope to prove that you were too far away to have committed the crime. Got it?"

"Got it." Luke had a good feeling about the woman. At least she was experienced. But that was no guarantee she could clear him of murder.

"All right, then." Pearl stood and gathered her things. "Don't get your hopes up. I've seen stronger defenses than yours fall apart, but we'll give it our best shot. See you in the morning."

With that, she walked out, the thump of her cane echoing down the hall.

351

Will Tyler's funeral filled the Congregational Church and overflowed into the parking lot. The service was informal, with friends who'd known him invited to get up and say a few words. Several did, including Rose, who spoke about the early days when she'd known him as a boy.

Erin had glimpsed Kyle with his parents, taking their seats in the back of the chapel. Now she kept her face forward, focusing her attention on the service. But it was as if she could feel his gaze boring into the back of her head. She hadn't spoken with him since the discovery that he was the sheriff's witness against Luke. But this was the time to honor her father's memory. Any nastiness with Kyle would have to wait.

She listened as Will's friends told stories about his honesty, his fearlessness, and his generosity. Will Tyler hadn't been a perfect man, but he'd been a good man, passionate in his devotion to his ranch and his family.

By the time the closing hymn was sung, there was scarcely a dry eye in the place. The congregation stood with a rustling of motion. With what was left of the family — Beau, Sky, Lauren and their children, and

Rose, who'd been included — Erin followed the casket out the door to the waiting hearse. Kyle was still watching her — she could sense it, like a fly crawling on her skin. But that couldn't be allowed to matter.

Later on, after Will was laid to rest beside his beloved Tori, she would deal with Kyle, the bank, the sheriff, the ranch, Luke's lawyer, and everything else that had been laid on her inexperienced shoulders. Right now, all she could do was say a loving good-bye and try to carry on as her father would have expected.

Most of the townspeople went home after the church service. The closer friends and family followed the hearse to the Rimrock for Will's burial in the family cemetery. The little plot, on the crest of a low hill, looked dry and desolate in the summer heat, the sparse grass yellowed, the ground baked hard, the granite headstones hot to the touch.

The oldest grave was that of Williston Tyler, who'd settled the land and fathered a son by a wife who'd died young. His son, Virgil "Bull" Tyler, who'd built a hardscrabble ranch into a family empire, lay next to his beloved Susan. Now Will would be there, too, beside Erin's mother.

Other spaces were empty. Would she lie in one of them someday? Erin wondered. Would Luke? Or would this sad little square of land be gobbled up and sold to the syndicate, along with the rest of the Rimrock, when the bank foreclosed?

The thought triggered a burst of hot emotion. She couldn't lose the ranch. She owed it to these people, and to generations to come, to keep the Rimrock in the family. Somehow, whatever it took, she would have to find a way.

Back at the house, guests gathered for a late buffet of drinks, fresh rolls, donated salads and casseroles, and Carmen's chocolate cake. When Jasper had died, it had been Will who'd greeted people and accepted their condolences. Now, with Will gone, Beau packing the car for the trip home, and Sky tending to the ranch, that duty fell to Erin.

Most everyone was kind, squeezing her hand, introducing themselves if she didn't know them, and offering what passed for comfort. Aside from a nagging headache, she was holding up well, or so she thought, until she looked across the room and saw Kyle and his parents making their way toward her. From where she stood, she could see the swollen, purpled flesh that ringed his left eye.

Something inside her shrank and hardened. Why hadn't these toxic people stayed home? They hadn't been friends of her father's and, after her last encounter with Kyle and his father, they certainly weren't friends of hers.

But she was at the center of attention in what amounted to a public gathering. She knew better than to make a scene. That would come later, in private, when she confronted Kyle about lying to the sheriff.

Close up, Vivian Cardwell looked drained. Her striking green eyes were bloodshot, her makeup caked on her colorless face. Erin had sensed that she had had a harmless crush on Will. Was she grieving for him, or was there something darker behind her haunted look?

Her hand gripped Erin's, the fragile bones almost digging into her flesh. "I'm sorry, dear," she said. "So very sorry. Your father was a fine man."

"Yes, thank you," Erin murmured, extricating herself. Hunter Cardwell was next, his big hand swallowing hers, his wolf-eyed gaze strangely intimate. "My condolences, Erin," he said. "We're here for you anytime you need us."

Kyle's arms went around her in a possessive hug. Erin stood cold and rigid in his embrace. He seemed unaware that she knew about his lie. But that would change. "We need to talk," she said, speaking close to his ear.

"Yes, we do. I'll call you." He released her, smiled, and moved on with his parents, leaving her with a cold lump in the pit of her stomach.

"Are you all right, Erin?" Rose had stayed nearby. "You look pale. If you need to go and lie down, I can cover for you. I'm sure everyone will understand."

Erin raised her head and squared her shoulders. Part of her wanted to do as Rose had suggested. But this was no time to appear weak. She was in charge of the ranch now. She needed to be stronger than she had ever been in her life.

"I'll be fine," she said. "I'll have to be, won't I?"

By the time the last of the guests were gone and the remnants of the buffet were cleared away, it was late afternoon. Heat waves rose from the gravel in the ranch yard. Clouds roiled above the escarpment, but the moisture they appeared to bring was only virga — the ghostly rain that evaporated long before it reached the ground.

Dressed in jeans once more, Erin sat in the ranch office, feeling small in the big leather chair that the Tyler men had filled so masterfully. An hour ago she had said good-bye to Beau, who'd invited her to call him with any questions or concerns, but hadn't offered any help beyond that. She was on her own.

The yellow pad on the desk was covered with scribbled notes, ideas, and reminders that she was attempting to organize into a meaningful list. Tomorrow she would go to the bank and take the death certificate the mortuary had given her. Will had listed her as beneficiary on all the ranch accounts, but she would need to make sure they were properly transferred and her signature authorized.

So cold. Words and numbers had taken the place of her fierce, loving father who would never hug her again, never talk with her over breakfast, never ride with her on a mountain trail or teach her how to rope a steer. In the past five months she had lost the three most important people in her life — her mother, Jasper, and now Will. And she could only honor them all by carrying on alone, not just for herself but for the Rimrock family — all the good people who'd made a life and a living here.

357

While she was at the bank, she would face Sim Bartlett and tackle the question of an extension on the balloon payment. The bank president would no doubt turn her down. But she was determined to let him know that she was in charge now and wouldn't stand for being bullied.

And then there was Luke.

Giving way to fear, she pressed her hands to her face. Tomorrow morning Luke would be arraigned on charges of first degree murder. But she couldn't be there for him. She couldn't visit him in jail or even call him. Any contact would only strengthen the prosecution's case against him.

The court should be able to tell her how to reach his lawyer. She would call the woman, maybe arrange a meeting, and tell her everything she knew about the circumstances. Beyond that, all she could do was pray.

Putting her emotions aside, she returned to sorting her notes, listing items in order of urgency. She was making a start when her cell phone rang.

Kyle.

Telling herself that now was as good a time as any, she took the call.

"Still mad at me?" he asked, his manner as brash as ever.

Erin warned herself to be cautious. "That depends," she said.

"You told me we needed to talk. Want to go for a ride?"

No more rides! "I'm pretty busy," she said. "Why don't you just come over? We can sit on the porch and have a beer."

"Playing it safe, are you?" He laughed. "Fine. Now? Or would you rather wait till tonight?"

"Now's all right."

"You don't sound very excited."

"Think about it, Kyle. Think about the last time we were together and what you did and said."

"Hell, woman, you socked me in the eye. I was in pain."

"Like I said, we need to talk. You can come over or not. It's up to you."

Fifteen minutes later the old ranch truck pulled up to the house and Kyle climbed out. Erin met him on the porch with a cold Bud Light in each hand. She handed him one as he came up the steps. "Sit down," she said.

He lowered himself into the chair that had always been Will's. Erin stifled the urge to insist that he move. What difference would it make now?

"So, are you ready to apologize for black-

359

ing my eye?"

"Are you ready to apologize for being a jerk, or should we just call it a draw?" Erin sat down in the chair that she'd placed three feet away. When she thought of what he'd done, she could barely stand the sight of him. But she had to get through this. She had to make it clear that she knew he'd lied about Luke.

He put his boots on the rail, popped the tab on his beer can, and tipped it to his lips. "Sorry about your dad," he said. "I mean it. I really do. What an awful tragedy for you." He studied her over the rim of the can. "I guess that makes you the boss, doesn't it?"

"For whatever that's worth." Erin set her can on the porch without opening it. Why not tell him the truth? Maybe it would cool his ardor if he knew she was going to be landless and poor.

"I still say you're going to need a man in your life," Kyle said.

"Only if he's rich." She took a perverse pleasure in giving him the news. "My father died owing the bank a balloon payment of two hundred thousand dollars. If I can't come up with it by the first of October, I won't have a ranch to boss. The bank will foreclose, and probably sell the place to the syndicate. Maybe your father knows something about that."

"Lord, no." Was he surprised or just playacting? "My father just works for the syndicate. He's not one of the big shots. Otherwise, I'd ask him to help you out."

"So," Erin asked, "do you still think I'll need a man to help me manage my fortune?"

"That's not fair, Erin. You know I'd take you with the clothes on your back — or without them."

She ignored his attempt at a joke. "Right now I'm more interested in finding out who killed my father."

"I thought that was settled. The sheriff's arrested your farrier, Luke Maddox. The man's got guilt written all over him."

"How can you say that? The evidence against him is all circumstantial."

"Then you haven't heard. An eyewitness saw him putting that tire in the road to set up the ambush."

"How convenient that someone just happened to be there. Can you tell me who it was?"

"I think you know," he said. "It was me. I was alone in my upstairs bedroom, looking out the window, when I saw that rig of his stop on the road."

"That road's at least a half mile from your

house. How could you see anything clearly?"

"I couldn't at first. But I had a feeling something fishy was going on, so I got my binoculars out of the closet and opened the window for a better look. It was Maddox, all right, and he was rolling that big tire out of the back of his trailer. He left it in the road and drove off. I'm guessing he hid the rig out of sight on some farm road and snuck back around to wait for your dad."

Erin knew that he was lying. There was no way Luke could have committed the murder. But Kyle's story gave her chills, not because it might be true, but because it was plausible — just plausible enough for the sheriff to accept.

If she'd been frightened for Luke before, she was terrified now.

"Are you prepared to tell that story in court, under oath?" she demanded.

"Sure. I don't see why not, since it's true — unless you can talk me into changing my mind. I could always say I made a mistake, leaving Maddox to take his chances."

Erin's pulse slammed. Would Kyle stoop to blackmailing her?

"How do I know you aren't lying?" she asked.

"You don't. You weren't there. As I recall, you were off somewhere with Rose. You'll

362

have to take my word for it, just like the sheriff did." He was leering at her, his face wearing the lazy, lopsided grin that she'd once thought was cute. Now all she wanted to do was punch that grin off his insolent face, maybe take out a couple of front teeth in the process.

Freezing her emotions, she stood. "You need to go, Kyle. If you're lying to me, and if you lied to the sheriff, we can never be friends again."

He took time to unfold his legs and rise to his feet. One hand crushed the half-empty beer can, shooting a stream of yellow liquid onto the porch before he tossed it at her feet. "You know how to find me, Erin," he said. "And when — not if — you do, I'll be waiting."

Toward dawn, Marie approached the abandoned line hut, after a nightly ramble that included a quick check on the Rimrock and some foraging in the dumpsters behind the Burger Shack and Shop Mart. As she neared the ramshackle building, her tingling danger senses told her that someone had been there. When she left her bike and approached her hideout, her flashlight beam found the tracks of a four-wheel-drive SUV and the kind of low-heeled boots that troopers tended to wear. There was no vehicle in sight, but someone could still be inside, waiting for her to return.

Time to go. Now. She'd left nothing in the vermin-infested shack except some clothes, a few snacks, and her bedroll, which could easily be replaced. The important things — her dwindling supply of cash, the burner phone she'd stolen, her flashlight, first-aid supplies, and cigarettes — were in the panniers on her bike. Nothing else was worth the risk of getting caught, especially if they got her for killing that cop in the stairwell of the Blue Coyote. For that, she wouldn't just be returned to Gatesville. She would end up on death row.

Cursing her rotten luck, she made it back to her bike and wheeled it a half mile down the trail before starting it up. The engine coughed and roared as she shot down the back road. She'd learned to be careful. But one stupid split-second decision had put the cops back on her trail — and they wouldn't give up, not when she'd brought down one of their own.

Abner Sweeney must've remembered her. Or Sky might have noticed some sign that she was around and called the sheriff. Then there was that little Tyler bitch taking a picture of her footprint. For two cents she would kill them all. Too bad she'd ditched the gun she'd taken off the old man. She could use it now. Stealing another one would take time, caution, and luck.

Where to go now? That was the question. With no drugs or cash, Mexico was out. Staying around here had become danger-ous. But her only hope of a secure future lay in killing Erin Tyler and getting Stella's stash.

Lubbock might be the best solution. She knew neighborhoods where it might be pos-sible to disappear among the brown-skinned population. She'd even had some connec-tions there before her prison sentence. If they hadn't moved on, they might be will-ing to help her in exchange for a few favors. It wasn't the best solution, but for now it would have to do.

When the heat died down, she would be back. And next time she wouldn't fail.

Gunning the machine, she mapped out the network of backroads in her mind. The rising sun found her headed north, roaring toward the city.

CHAPTER SEVENTEEN

The next morning, when the bank opened, Erin was waiting at the door. The single teller let her in, but she had to wait another half hour for the account manager to show up. She sat on a folding metal chair, thinking about Luke, who would be facing the judge for his arraignment this morning. She tried to imagine the dread, the humiliation, he must be feeling — the indignity of standing before the court in chains. Luke's strength and dignity would be sorely tested today.

It was a given that he would be held without bail, at least until the grand jury met to decide whether the case should go to trial. After that, he could be jailed for weeks, even months, while the case was prepared. What would time as a prisoner do to him? Would he remain the gentle, honest man she'd fallen in love with? Or would he become hardened, bitter, and distrustful?

Erin was saying a silent prayer when the account manager walked in from the rear of the bank and sat down at her desk.

The woman, who'd worked school lunch before getting the bank job, remembered her and beckoned her over.

"I'm so sorry about your father, dear," she said. "And so soon after losing your mother, too. My, you're going to have a lot of responsibility on your shoulders. But don't worry, we can help you with that. I imagine you're here to transfer the accounts to your name. Did you bring the death certificate?"

"I brought everything." Erin took her paperwork, including the death certificate, power of attorney, and most recent statements, out of the briefcase that had belonged to her mother. "When we're done here, I need to speak with Mr. Bartlett," she said.

"I'm sure you do. He already knows you're here." As the woman printed out the documents that needed to be signed and notarized, Erin looked past her, toward the glass-fronted office at the back of the bank. She could see Sim Bartlett in a suit and tie, sitting behind his massive desk as if he were president of some Fortune 500 corporation instead of a small-town bank whose employees could be counted on the fingers of one hand. He was a big frog in a tiny pond, and she would not allow him to intimidate her.

When the accounts had been transferred, Erin was escorted back to Bartlett's office. The room behind the glass was furnished like an old-time men's club, the walls darkly paneled with heavy molding at the top, the furniture massive and expensively made. A gilt-framed photo of Bartlett shaking hands with the previous governor of the state hung on one wall. Bartlett, a stocky man whose silver hair was too sculpted not to be a toupee, rose behind his desk and extended his hand.

Erin had never spoken with the man. But the thought that this pretentious old goat had made her father's last days miserable made her want to turn her back and walk out.

Instead she accepted his handshake and his invitation to take a seat. "Thank you for seeing me, Mr. Bartlett," she said, meeting his gaze.

"My condolences for your loss." Bartlett had not attended Will's funeral. "I hope you understand that this meeting is just a formality. It doesn't change the terms of the loan on your ranch or the fact that the payment will be due as stated in the contract."

"I wouldn't have expected anything else," Erin said. "But I want you to know that this isn't over. I'll be exploring every alternative I can find. Nobody's taking my ranch."

He gave her a condescending smile. "Knock yourself out, my dear. I'll be interested in seeing what you come up with — and in watching you fail."

"Have a nice day, Mr. Bartlett." Erin stood, turned away, and walked out.

She made it to the sidewalk out front before her knees began to shake. The battle lines had been drawn. At least she'd stood up to the wretched man. But standing up was one thing. Making good on her word was something else.

There were other lenders, she reminded herself. Not here in Blanco Springs, but in the city. Surely, with the ranch as collateral, she could find a bank that would refinance the loan on easier terms. She would start her search in the next few days. Right now, she needed to find Luke's court-appointed attorney.

When she told the court receptionist about her connection to the case, the woman murmured her condolences, scrawled a name and phone number on a notepad, tore off the page, and handed it to

Erin. "She's probably left for the day. But that's her cell phone, so you should be able to reach her. She's a character. You'll see."

After walking out into the sunshine, Erin sat on a bench and studied the paper the woman had given her. *Pearlina Murchison.* The receptionist had said she was a character. But maybe that didn't matter. What did matter was that Luke's life was in this woman's hands.

Erin entered the number on her phone and waited for the ring.

"Hello?" The voice sound old and hoarse. A heavy smoker, maybe.

"Ms. Murchison, my name is Erin Tyler."

"Yes. I know who you are. Luke said you might want to talk to me. Can we meet now?"

"I was hoping we could. Tell me where."

"Can you come to my house? I only live a few blocks from the courthouse, but I don't get around so well, and I just got home." She gave Erin directions.

A few minutes later, Erin parked at the curb. She recognized the small brick house now. For as long as she could remember, it had stood vacant, the windows boarded, the yard overgrown with weeds. But now she could see that the place had been cleaned up. The yard, though dry, had been mowed.

The front door was painted a cheerful lime green. Spider plants hung in macramé slings over the covered porch, where a figure in a flowered sundress overflowed one of two large rattan chairs. Two cats dozed on the low steps. Three more sprawled in the shade of the porch.

Good grief, was Luke being defended by a crazy cat lady?

"Sit down, dear. You can call me Pearl." The woman hauled herself to her feet. Erin noticed the cane propped against the chair and the pack of Marlboros on the side table. "I've got some cold sodas in the fridge. I'd offer you a beer, but I've been sober for six years, so I don't keep temptation around."

"Maybe later, thanks," Erin said. "Right now I'd rather just talk to you. How is Luke?"

Pearl lowered herself to the chair again. "About how you'd expect. He's a proud man. Reminds me of a caged lion. He told me to make sure you stayed away."

"Yes, we agreed that it might hurt his case if I showed up. But it's hard, not being able to see him. All I can do is make sure you have everything you need for his defense."

"I spent most of the night studying his file and looking for anything that might help — insomnia is just one of my complaints. Did

371

you know about the previous assault charge?"

"Yes. Luke punched a man for abusing a horse. He told me he'd do it again in the same situation."

"And the witness? The one who claims to have seen him unloading that tire?"

"He was my boyfriend before Luke came along. I can't disprove his claim because I wasn't there, but he's got to be lying. Last night he even hinted that he might change his story if I'd go back to him."

"Would you be willing to testify to that in court?" The blue eyes that peered at Erin through tortoise-framed glasses were sharp and intelligent.

"Certainly, but what he said was only implied. It might not be enough to convince a jury."

"You may be right, but at least it's an option. The fact that the victim was your father, and that you still believe in Luke's innocence, should carry some weight. Are you sure you wouldn't like a soda?"

"If you'll let me get it, and one for you, too," Erin said.

"Thanks. These old legs aren't what they used to be when I was Miss Blanco County of 1972. I'll take a root beer."

Erin got up and went inside through the

screen door. The interior of the little house was cluttered but clean, with sagging, well-worn furniture facing an old-style TV. One entire wall was covered in bookshelves — their contents running the gamut from law, to science, history, and literary classics. One shelf was filled with well-worn paperback romance novels. Two more cats lounged on the chair, a tabby on the back, a ginger on the arm.

The Formica table in the kitchen was littered with open files, newspaper clippings, and old law books, scattered around an open laptop computer. Passing the table on her way to the fridge, Erin couldn't help noticing some familiar names and faces. It appeared that Pearl had been researching Luke's case in depth — the people involved, the crime scene, the sheriff's records, the witness accounts, and legal precedents in similar cases. The lady was doing her homework. Cats or no cats, Pearl Murchison was the real deal.

With renewed respect, Erin took a root beer and a Diet Coke from the fridge and carried them outside. The cat Pearl had been stroking jumped off her lap as Erin sat down again.

"Answer one question for me." Pearl popped the tab on her root beer and sipped it as she talked. "If you weren't in love with Luke Maddox — and I'm assuming you are — would you still believe that he didn't murder your father?"

The question shocked Erin for an instant, but she answered without hesitation. "I've seen Luke at work. I've seen his gentleness and witnessed his integrity. There's no way he's a killer. That aside, it makes no sense at all that he'd kill my father. It would have cost him everything he valued. Besides, he wasn't even there. Is that good enough for you?"

"For now. So let's move on. What I'm hoping to do here is prove to the grand jury that there's no case to take to trial. For that we need to do at least one of two things — either prove that Luke couldn't have committed the crime, or prove that someone else did. Are you with me so far?"

Erin nodded.

"Here's where I need your help," Pearl continued. "As I see it, there are two conflicting claims. According to the medical examiner, and confirmed by Abner Sweeney, who saw him leave the bar, your father was killed between eleven-thirty and noon, when somebody spotted his empty truck from the main road. Your ex-boyfriend claims that sometime before that he saw

Luke setting up an ambush. Luke's version of the story is that he left the Rimrock around ten — a time confirmed by your housekeeper — and that he made it all the way to Plainview before he heard the news on TV and turned around."

"That's right. He stopped at a diner off the first exit. As soon as the news came on, and he heard they were looking for him, he turned around and headed back."

"That's what he told me," Pearl said. "But here's the thing. After Luke was picked up and booked the first time, the sheriff faxed a copy of his driver's license to the Plainview police. They took the picture to that diner to confirm that he'd been there. Nobody in the place remembered seeing him or his rig."

"No!" Erin stared at her. "He said he was there! Why would he lie when he knew it would be checked?"

"You tell me," Pearl said. "I called the TV station. The first news about the crime came on at one o'clock that day. If we can place Luke in Plainview at the time of that broadcast, he's in the clear. If not, he's in trouble."

Erin shook her head in disbelief. "Something's wrong. Could the police have gone to the wrong diner?"

"There's only one. It's called Sam and

Edna's and it's not a chain. There's a water tower behind the parking lot. The Plainview police confirmed the name and the exit number. There was no mistake."

"No surveillance cameras?"

"One. But it was broken weeks ago and never fixed."

"Something else, then." A black cat jumped onto Erin's lap. She stroked it absentmindedly, her thoughts churning. A mistake had been made — but how? The answer could literally mean the difference between life and death for Luke.

"What about the time?" she said. "Luke was there at one o'clock — maybe a few minutes before, enough time to order. By the time the police got there with his driver's license it would have been later in the afternoon. What if the shift changed? Different servers and probably different customers . . . ?"

"Bingo." Pearl was smiling. "That's just what I was thinking. That's why I called the place before you came. The diner is open round the clock. The morning shift is from five o'clock to one."

"So someone could've seen Luke before the shift change. How do we find out?"

Pearl rose to her feet, leaning on her cane. "Just one way, honey. I don't drive anymore.

But you do. If we go now, and maybe break a few speed limits, we should be able to make it before the shift change. Are you with me?"

Erin dumped the black cat off her lap and stood. "We'll need a picture," she said.

"No problem. I've got a copy of his mug shot from the jail. Just let me grab my purse and lock up."

Once they hit the freeway, Erin stomped on the gas pedal. The old station wagon had been well maintained over the years, but it had never been built for speed. She pushed it as hard as she dared. Maybe this trip would turn out to be a waste of time. But the shift change was the only idea that made sense. Anything that could free Luke was worth a try.

But over the past few days, as she'd grown older and sadder, one thing had become clear. Even if she could save Luke, she couldn't own him. As Pearl had described him, he was like a caged lion. And there were many kinds of cages. Luke loved her in his way. But he also loved his freedom.

The drive to Plainview took less than three hours. Pearl chatted most of the way, talking about her years as a prosecutor in Chicago. She'd had some amazing experiences, but Erin was too distracted to listen closely. Her heart drummed in her ears, blurring the sound of Pearl's voice, as she watched for the Plainview exit sign.

Her pulse kicked to a gallop as she swung the car onto the off-ramp. Where the road leveled off, she could see the diner on the right, and the water tower behind it. A couple of long-haul semis were parked on the far side. *SAM AND EDNA'S.* She could see the sign out front as she pulled into a space. The dashboard clock said 12:46.

Erin helped Pearl out of the car. The peak lunch hour was ending as they came up the sidewalk. A man who looked like a truck driver held the door for them to go in. Erin thanked him.

The counter, where Luke had claimed to have sat, was empty. Pearl sank onto a stool and fumbled in her red purse for the photo she'd brought.

The waitress behind the counter, whose name badge read *Marge,* appeared to be about fifty, with graying hair pulled up into a bun. She looked tired, but still managed a friendly smile. "What can I get you?" she asked.

"Nothing right now." Pearl laid Luke's photos, showing him face-on and in profile, on the counter. "We're hoping someone

378

here remembers this man. He claims to have been here about this time on Friday."

Marge took the photo. "Oh, heavens, yes!" she exclaimed. "How could I forget that face, and those eyes? But these are mug shots. What on earth has he done?"

"Nothing," Pearl said. "That's what I'm here to prove. Can you tell me everything you remember about him?"

"Let's see . . . I want to get this right."

"Do you mind if I record your statement?" Pearl fished a small, old-style cassette recorder out of her purse. "If what you say can be verified, you'll be saving a man's life."

"Really? Uh . . . sure." Marge suddenly looked self-conscious.

"It's all right," Pearl said. "Just say what you remember. I'll help if you get stuck." She switched on the machine.

Marge cleared her throat. "Like I said, he came in just before I got off shift. It was coming up on one o'clock. He sat down at the counter. Handsome man, I remember. The other girls were stealing looks at him, too, sort of giggling. I gave him a menu. He pushed it away. Said to just give him a cup of coffee and a slice of that apple pie in the case behind the counter."

"So you did?" Pearl prompted as Erin

379

listened, barely breathing.

"I did," Marge said. "I turned away to get his order. When I put the pie and coffee on the counter, he was watching TV. The one o'clock news had just come on. I wasn't paying attention to it myself. But all of a sudden he put down his cup and stood up. I asked him if everything was all right, but it was like he didn't hear me. He just took a bill out of his wallet, dropped it on the counter, and walked out. Hardly took two bites of that pie. But here's the strange part. When I picked up that bill, I saw that it was fifty dollars! Fifty dollars! My stars! I don't think he even looked at it. That's why I remember him, even apart from his bein' such a feast for the eye."

Pearl switched off the machine. "Thanks," she said.

"Did I do all right?" Marge asked.

"You did perfect, honey," Pearl said. "You don't happen to have that bill, do you?"

"Why, I just might. When I first found it, I thought sure he'd realize his mistake and come back, or at least call. So I put it in an envelope and stuck it under the tray in the cash register. If nobody's moved it, it should still be there." She opened the cash drawer and lifted the tray. "Here it is!"

Erin had cash in her shoulder bag. She

found two twenty-dollar bills and a ten. "Here," she said, thrusting the cash at Marge. "Keep it for yourself. I know that's what Luke would want."

"Wait," Pearl said. "I want a picture of you, Marge, with that bill. Then we'll take it."

Pearl snapped a couple of pictures with her phone. Then she took the bill, zipped it into a plastic evidence bag from her purse, and tucked it away.

"I hope you'll let me know what happened to that poor man." Marge picked up her purse, which was stashed below the counter.

"I promise to let you know," Erin said. "When this is over, he might even want to come back here and thank you in person."

"Well, now, that was time well spent," Pearl said as Erin helped her into the car. "If nothing else goes wrong, when I present this evidence to the sheriff, we should have your Mr. Maddox cleared and out of jail by morning, if not sooner."

Erin slipped into the driver's seat, started the car, and pulled onto the southbound freeway. "It sounds like wonderful news. But after all the awful things that have happened lately, I know better than to celebrate too soon. Can they get Luke's fingerprints, or maybe DNA, off that bill?"

"Not easily, and probably not anytime soon, especially since the bill's an old one that's been handled a lot. But just having it will back up Marge's account. That should be plenty for a solid alibi. Luke couldn't have killed your father and shown up at that diner in Plainview an hour later. Don't worry, dear. Everything's going to be all right."

"Yes. Thank you so much, Pearl," Erin said. But she knew that even with Luke free, everything was far from all right. She would still be dealing with the drought and the bank loan. And the most troubling question of all remained to be answered.

Who had murdered her father?

"You can go, Maddox." The sheriff shook his head as he unlocked Luke's cell. "Your alibi checked out yesterday when a waitress at that diner recognized your photo. The court's dropped all charges." He tossed Luke a plastic bag with his clothes and boots inside. "Put these on and toss that jumpsuit in the laundry bin on your way out. The clerk up front will have your wallet, your keys, your phone, and your gun."

Groggy and red-eyed after a sleepless night, Luke shoved the hated orange jumpsuit down off his body. Maybe he was dreaming. Maybe he was about to wake up to the real nightmare that he was still a prisoner, caged in this damned cell, charged with a murder he hadn't committed.

He couldn't just be free to go. He didn't have that kind of luck. But before the dream ended, he was going to get as far away from this place as he could.

Everything was here — shirt, jeans, boots, even the belt they'd taken right away so he wouldn't hang himself with it. He needed a shave and a shower, but it wasn't going to happen here. Raking his hair out of his eyes, he tossed the jumpsuit and, with an armed deputy watching, strode up to the window to collect his other possessions. Too bad his rig was at the Rimrock. Otherwise he could just take it and go — get the hell out of Erin's life. He loved her to the depths of his restless soul. But he was no good for her. He'd already caused her far more pain than she deserved.

The truth had come to him in the dead of a dark night. Erin was young and bright, with a promising future. She needed to be free to meet the right man and make the right choices. He was older and had already seen too much of the dark side of life. Even if he didn't end up in prison, he needed to be man enough to walk away before he ruined her life.

Now, from the shadows of the hallway, he could see her. She was standing in a shaft of morning sunlight that fell through the high window of the jail's reception area. Dressed in jeans and an old denim jacket with the sleeves cut out, she looked like an angel, her golden hair framing her face like a halo.

As he walked into the light, she saw him. A little cry escaped her lips. She flung herself toward him, wrapping her arms around his neck. Despite his best intentions, Luke couldn't have kept her back if he'd wanted to. He held her close, letting her kisses flood him with the joy of being with her and being free.

As their embrace broke, he realized they weren't alone. Several people, all strangers, were seated in the row of chairs that lined the wall. The ones he could see looked as if they were trying not to smile.

"Erin, we've got an audience," he murmured.

"I know." She was beaming with happiness. "We don't have to hide anymore, Luke. I don't care if the whole world knows I love you!"

He stifled a groan. Leaving this passionate, vulnerable woman was going to be the most painful thing he'd ever done. But right now his gear and his rig were all back at the ranch, and she was his ride. He would find a way later.

"Let's go," he said, guiding her toward the door. "We can talk on the way."

"Fine. I'll drive." She let him open the car door for her and waited while he went around to the other side. He could tell her on the way home that he was leaving, and explain the reasons why if she'd let him. Then there'd be nothing to do at the ranch except maybe clean up, collect his things, and go. Erin would be angry and hurt, but someday she'd be grateful that he'd left.

As he settled into the passenger seat, she handed him a sealed envelope. "This arrived for you yesterday," she said. "I brought it because I thought it might be important."

Luke turned the envelope over. It bore the name and return address of the care facility where his grandmother was staying. Had he forgotten to send them the monthly check? He could've sworn he'd mailed it on the first of the month, before all the craziness at the Rimrock.

While Erin drove, he ran his thumb under the sealed flap of the envelope and drew out the single-page letter, unfolded it, and read the terse, typewritten message.

Dear Mr. Maddox:

We regret to inform you that your grandmother, Mrs. Edith Webster, passed away peacefully on August 13 of this year. An attempt was made to notify you by phone, but since we were unable to reach you, in accordance with her wishes, her earthly remains were cremated two days later. . . .

There was more, including a statement of how much he owed them for the remainder of her care and the cremation service. He would read it in more detail later, send a check, and ask them to save the ashes for him.

"Bad news?" Erin asked as he slipped the letter back into the envelope.

"My grandmother. She died last week." Surprisingly, he choked on the words. "She meant a lot to me. I'd planned to go back to Oklahoma and see her after I finished the work at the Rimrock. Now it's too late. . . ." His eyes blurred with tears. *"Damn,"* he muttered.

"I'm so sorry." She reached over the console and squeezed his hand. "I know how it feels. I'll always regret that the last words I said to my father were angry ones. Now I can never take them back and tell

386

him how much I loved him."

Luke didn't answer. His throat felt as if a fist had closed around it.

Her fingers tightened around his hand. "I never want to have that regret again. That's why I'll never let you go without telling you I love you — even if I can't hold on to you, even if you're planning to leave me for good. Your last memory of me will be telling you that I love you."

She was ripping him apart inside. "Erin —"

"No, listen." Her eyes were on the road, her expression a sad smile. "I'm a big girl, Luke. I know you're a man who has to be free. You never promised me you would stay, not even when we were making love. If I wake up some morning and find you gone, I'll understand, and the memories I keep will be the good ones. There's only one thing I'll ever ask of you — and I'm asking now."

Luke waited in silence, sensing that what she said would be the key to everything.

"Just this," she said. "If you go — or when you go — I want you to promise me that you'll never come back."

387

CHAPTER EIGHTEEN

Dinner that evening was a small celebration. Carmen had made her specialty — chicken enchiladas and chiles rellenos with refried black beans. Erin had invited Sky, his wife, Lauren, and Luke to join her and Rose for the meal. There was also a place set for Carmen, who would eat with them once the food was served and take some leftovers home to her husband.

Luke couldn't remember the last time, if ever, that he'd eaten a meal with cloth napkins and matching china. Sitting quietly while the conversation buzzed around him, he let his gaze linger on each person at the table — Sky, lean, dark, and chiseled, smiling at his stunning, auburn-haired wife; Rose, a wise, graying elf; and Erin, at the head of the table where her father would have sat, sadness lingering in her soft blue eyes. This was the Rimrock family now. And for tonight, at least, he was part of it. For how long? he wondered. Would he go back to being hired help tomorrow? Would he settle into place as Erin's lover, or would he simply load his gear and leave?

Erin's words in the car had thrown him. He'd expected her to make womanly demands on his freedom and pout if he resisted. Instead, with surprising strength, she had left the door wide open. He could stay or he could go. But his decision would be final.

The longer he waited, the more painful that decision became. He loved Erin and wanted to do what was best for her. His better judgment was telling him to leave before he got in any deeper. But his heart was whispering a very different message. He wanted her, in his arms and in his bed. But was he willing to settle for being her nighttime man? If not, he had some hard choices to make.

The conversation at the table had turned to the subject of finding Will's killer. Now that Luke had been cleared, the sheriff's investigation would be back to square one.

"My father would want me to put the past aside and move on," Erin said. "But how can I? I can't sleep at night, knowing the person who committed that awful crime is still out there."

389

"What about that woman, Marie?" Rose asked. "She's already wanted for the murder of that poor young deputy. Isn't it possible that she shot Will, too?"

"I've thought about that," Sky said. "But Marie had nothing against Will and nothing to gain by shooting him. And the way he was killed, in broad daylight, that isn't her style."

"That's pretty much what Abner told Beau," Erin said. "Roy was killed in a break-in, most likely a robbery. He was in the wrong place at the wrong time. But my father's murder was planned. It had to be personal."

"Another thing that argues against Marie," Sky said. "That tractor tire was big and heavy. She couldn't have moved it without help, or at least access to a truck. Whoever set up that ambush would've had a way to get the tire onto the road."

"And they'd have known that my father would be coming back that way," Erin added.

"Plenty of people would've seen Will in town," Rose said. "The folks at the bank, the ones in the Blue Coyote, and anybody who saw him in passing could have figured out that he'd be going home later."

"But they wouldn't have known he was in

town until they saw him." Erin had put down her fork, her meal forgotten. "The person who ambushed and shot my dad had to plan ahead. Whoever it was would've needed to know where Dad was going and when he planned to be back, so they could be ready."

"Ay, Dios mío!" Carmen's fork clattered onto the table. Her face had gone pale. "I forgot until just now. That day, as Mister Will was leaving in his truck, the office phone rang. By the time I got in there to answer it, he'd driven away."

"But you did answer the phone, right?" Lauren asked.

"Yes." Carmen paused, struggling with the memory. "There was a man on the phone. He asked to talk to Will — called him by name. I said Mister Will had gone to town. Then he asked how soon Mister Will planned to be back. I told him" — her voice broke — "I told him he shouldn't be more than a couple hours. Oh, no!" Breaking into sobs, Carmen pressed her hands to her face. "What if I shouldn't have said that? What if it was my fault — my fault that Mister Will died?"

Erin sprang out of her chair and wrapped an arm around the cook's shoulders. "No, Carmen! It wasn't your fault. You did what anyone would have done."

Sky rose from his place and moved around the table. "Listen to me, Carmen," he said. "Nobody is blaming you for this. But maybe you can help us. Did the man give you his name? Did you even recognize his voice?"

"I . . . don't know." Carmen's sobs were ebbing. "At the time, I didn't give it a second thought."

"Take your time." Sky offered her a glass of water. "Maybe it was nothing. Maybe it was just a call. What did he say when you answered the phone?"

Carmen sipped the water, her eyes closed. "It's coming back," she said. "He was friendly. He knew my name. He said 'Hello, Carmen, this is . . .' Sorry." She shook her head. "I'm trying."

"It's all right. Take your time," Sky said.

She opened her eyes. "I remember now," she said, pausing as if to make sure. "It was the neighbor, the man who runs the syndicate ranch — Mr. Cardwell."

Vivian passed the bowls of pasta and meat sauce around the table and waited for the first verbal blow to fall. For as long as she could remember, Hunter had used the evening meal as a forum to lay down the law to his wife and son. Over the years,

392

she'd grown accustomed to his criticism and sarcastic barbs. But lately — over the past week or so — they'd gotten steadily worse. Lectures had become vicious rants, most of them over trifles.

Was something wrong with him, or were these dark spells her fault? Hunter had always insisted that she brought out the worst in him. At some point, she'd begun to believe it.

She was adding Italian dressing to the salad when Hunter started in on Kyle. When her husband was finished with their son, it would likely be her turn.

"I heard on the news that Maddox was released from jail this morning," he said. "It appears that his alibi checked out after all. He's been cleared of all blame."

"Uh-huh." Kyle twirled a length of dripping spaghetti onto his fork and captured it with his mouth.

"Damn it, stop stuffing your face and listen to me!" Hunter snapped. "What kind of moron are you? You lied to the sheriff about seeing Maddox unload that tire from his rig. Now you're in trouble and you don't seem to give a shit."

Kyle swallowed his food. "I didn't lie. I made a mistake. There's no law against that. It's only perjury if you lie under oath."

"Maybe you won't be arrested. But anything you say or do reflects on our family. Nobody will ever trust us again. Hell, I could even lose my job over this. And what about the Tyler girl? You said you were going to fix that."

Kyle shrugged. "I gave it a shot. But that's over and done with. Erin's with Maddox, and she won't even talk to me. But you won't care, once you hear what she told me about the Rimrock's money troubles."

"I knew that Will Tyler was having a struggle," Hunter said. "But if you were to marry the girl, you might be in a position to ask the syndicate for help."

"No, I mean like *big* money troubles. She's going to lose the ranch. The bank will foreclose after the first of October. Once that's done I'm betting they'll sell the property to the syndicate."

"Well, if that's what happens, maybe the syndicate would hire you to manage the place." Hunter waited for a response. When it didn't come, he pressed his son harder. "Why not? You've got the degree and the experience."

"Great," Kyle said. "Then I'd have a chickenshit job just like yours."

Hunter lunged to his feet, upending his chair as he stood. Vivian stifled a scream as his big hand slammed the side of his son's head. Kyle reeled sideways, choking and cursing before he righted himself.

"Kyle, are you all right?" Vivian was genuinely scared for him.

"No," Kyle whimpered. "I think my eardrum's busted. My head's ringing. Need to lie down."

"Don't be a bawl baby. Stay here like a man and finish your food." Hunter sat down again and poked his spaghetti with a fork. "If you can call this slop food. Vivian, why in hell's name can't you learn to cook pasta al dente? You always boil it to mush. And it's cold. Why can't you serve it hot?"

"It was hot when I put it on the table," Vivian said.

"Don't you dare contradict me!" A sweep of Hunter's hand sent his plate crashing to the tile floor, splattering food and broken china in all directions. "You can't cook or help with the ranch work or even be out in polite company without embarrassing me. All you're good for is being a slut. A filthy, lying slut who'd let any man on top of her."

Vivian stared at him, speechless with horror. He'd said some awful things to her but he'd never gone this far before.

Still unsteady from his father's blow, Kyle pushed back his chair and stood. "I've had enough," he said. "I'll be out of here as soon as I can pack my things. Maybe if I get away from you two, I can figure out how to become a decent human being."

A startled look flashed across Hunter's face, but he swiftly masked it. "Go on," he snarled. "You can even take that old shit-bucket of a truck you've been driving. I don't care what you do. I've never believed you were my son anyway."

"Kyle!" A cry was torn from Vivian's throat as her son headed for the stairs. "Don't go! Don't leave me!"

He turned with one foot on the bottom step. "I love you, Mother," he said. "But I won't stay around and be part of this sick mess anymore. If you can't stand up to your husband, maybe it's time you thought about leaving, too."

As Kyle disappeared upstairs, Hunter stood. Kicking a piece of broken china out of the way, he strode to the front door. "I'll be back soon, Vivian," he said. "And when I walk in the door, I want to see this place cleaned up and you in our bed."

After he'd gone, Vivian cleaned up the kitchen, not because Hunter had told her to, but because she couldn't stand to look at the mess. Her face burned with shame as she swept the china shards into a dustpan and mopped up the spatters of spaghetti sauce. From upstairs, she could hear the sounds of Kyle packing to leave. She wouldn't try to stop him. Her son was right. If she'd been mistreated by Hunter, it was because she'd allowed it. His abuse would stop only when she refused to tolerate it.

By the time she'd finished mopping the kitchen floor, putting away the leftovers, and loading the dishwasher, it was dark outside. Kyle was running cardboard boxes and stuffed trash bags out to the truck. Standing in the kitchen, she watched him. She understood that he wanted to be gone before Hunter returned. But why couldn't he stop and talk to her, or at least look at her?

Never mind — she knew the answer to that question. He was determined to go, and he didn't want anything holding him back, least of all the mother who'd coddled and protected him all his life.

At last, Kyle went out the door and didn't return. When she heard the old truck's engine cough to life and fade with distance, Vivian knew he was gone. She hoped, with a mother's desperation, that he'd be safe and that, somehow, he'd stay in touch with her. But he was a man now. She had to accept that and move on herself.

Dry-eyed and strangely numb, she mounted the stairway and walked down the hall to the master bedroom at the end. Inside, she turned on a side lamp and sat down on the bed, which was covered with a treasured quilt her grandmother had made for her wedding. The drapes, which matched the yellow color in the quilt, were closed, the room stuffy from the heat of the day. She should open a window, Vivian thought, but she felt too drained to get up and move.

What now?

Maybe it was time to look after her own welfare.

With Kyle gone, she would be the sole target of Hunter's rages. And there would be no one here to stop him from getting physical — as he had tonight when he'd struck his son. Hunter was a strong man. If he lost control, she could be in real danger.

Unless she was going to leave — and she had yet to make up her mind about that — she would have to walk on eggshells around the man. Among other things, that would mean complying with his demands in bed.

As she reached under the pillow to get her nightgown, something crackled faintly beneath the mattress. Only then did she remember what she'd hidden there.

She hadn't reread those forbidden fantasies about Will since his death. Somehow, now that he was gone, it just didn't seem fitting. Vivian knew she'd be a fool to keep those blistering pages. If Hunter were to find them by accident, she could only imagine what he would do.

After rants like the one tonight, Hunter usually drove into town, to have a drink and cool off at the Blue Coyote. There was a shredder downstairs in the ranch office. He should be gone for at least another hour. That would give her plenty of time to rip those forbidden fantasies out of her notepad and shred them into sad bits of confetti.

Raising the edge of the quilt, she thrust her arm between the mattress and the box spring. Her groping fingers found the manila envelope that held the notepad. Stretching, she clasped the edge and pulled it free.

Her hand shook as she unfastened the clasp. It was just dawning on her what a dangerous thing she'd done. She should have destroyed the pages after writing them — or better yet, she should have kept her erotic dreams in her head and never written them down at all.

The notepad slid out of the envelope and into her lap. She stared at it, her whole body breaking out in a cold sweat. A wave of nausea washed over her, followed by a surge of panic.

The notepad was blank, the damning pages torn away.

"Is this what you're looking for, Vivian?"

Her gaze jerked toward the open door. Outlined by the light from the hallway, Hunter stood on the threshold. His fist clutched a wad of crumpled pages. "Tonight I called you a slut," he said in a low, quiet voice that was more terrifying than a shout. "You're worse than a slut. You're a whore. But you're my whore, and nobody's going to take you away from me. Will Tyler learned that the hard way."

Vivian struggled to slow her careening thoughts. What had Hunter just said? Had he been the one who'd killed Will?

She forced herself to speak. "When did you find those papers, Hunter? They were mine. You had no business taking them."

"A while ago. And I can take anything I want to in this house. When I first read these —" He shook his fist, crushing the pages tighter. "When I read what that sick bastard Tyler was doing with my wife — *my wife* — I wanted to kill him, and you, too. But no, I came to my senses. I decided to have it out with him — tell him to leave my woman the hell alone. I called him, but the housekeeper told me he'd gone to town. That was when

400

I realized that talking to him wouldn't be enough. I was a man. I had the right to satisfy my honor."

Would that satisfaction include killing her, too? Vivian remembered the loaded pistol that Hunter kept in the drawer of the nightstand. If she could get to it, she might at least be able to save her own life.

"In some countries, you'd get stoned to death," Hunter said. "Lucky for you, we live in a civilized society."

"Listen to me, Hunter," she pleaded. "Those things you read, they weren't real. They were made up, like a story I was writing. Will never touched me except to shake hands. Yes, I was attracted to him. But he barely knew I existed. You killed an innocent man!"

"You're a lying whore!" He took a step toward her, letting the papers fall to the floor. Vivian edged along the side of the bed, toward the nightstand.

"When I thought of you and that bastard together, I wanted to kill you, too. But then I read what you wrote again, and I knew I wanted to do those things to you myself. I wanted to thrill you like he did. I wanted to make you scream and yowl like a cat in heat — like you've never done with me."

Vivian edged closer to the nightstand.

401

"Please don't kill me, Hunter," she begged, stalling for time. "I'm your wife. I'll never tell anybody what you did."

"Shut up! Now that your boy's not around to protect you, I can do anything I want. Keep me happy, and I might not kill you — or again, I might. But I can promise you one thing. You're never going to cheat on me again! Now get your clothes off!"

The drawer was inches away. Hunter wasn't armed, but he was strong and fast. If she didn't move like lightning, he could grab the gun or even strangle her with his bare hands.

She reached for the drawer handle, but not fast enough.

"What are you doing?" he snapped, instantly alert.

"My — that gel I use. I've been dry lately . . . I thought —"

"Forget that. I said, get your clothes off."

Desperate, she tried another tack. "Fine. But if you really want to do what's on those papers, we have to start slow." Willing her hands not to shake, she unbuttoned her shirt and slid her bra straps off her shoulders. The breasts that tumbled out were full and ripe. She'd always been proud of her beautiful breasts. "Suck my tits," she whispered. "Suck me like a baby. You'll see what it does to me, and to you."

He dropped partway to his knees and buried his face against one breast. Lying back, she held his head there, pushing him into her softness to cover his eyes. His mouth was hard, hurting her. But she moaned and squirmed against him, pretending to like it while her free hand crept toward the drawer and pulled it open. Her heart slammed as her fingers closed around the grip of the 9mm Glock. She had one chance. Fail, and she would be a dead woman.

Clamping her hand around the grip, she lifted the gun from the drawer. She had it, but not at the right angle for cocking, aiming, and firing the weapon, and she didn't dare let go to adjust her hold.

"What the devil — ?" Sensing her distraction, he jerked away and saw the gun. Before he could recover, she raised her knees and shoved him backward. He was on his feet in a flash, but the instant's delay gave her time to cock the pistol and get both hands around the grip, police-style.

"You bitch!" He was standing over her where she lay on her back, with the pistol pointed up at him. If he were to reach out and seize her arm, it wouldn't take much effort to twist her aim away and take the gun. There was only one way she could save herself.

Vivian pulled the trigger.

The shot echoed off the walls of the room. A look of surprise flashed across Hunter's face. He reeled, staggered, and went down. Blood flowed from the wound in his side, soaking into the white rug.

He was alive but too badly wounded to get up. She knew better than to shoot him again. The police would question that. But she was no nurse and certainly no hero. Grabbing the pillow off the bed, she pressed it against the wound. "Hold it tight if you want to live," she said. "I've got a phone call to make."

With icy calm, possibly from shock, she picked up the bedside phone and dialed 911. "This is Mrs. Cardwell at the old Prescott Ranch," she told the dispatch operator. "I've just shot my husband in self-defense. . . . Yes, he's alive, but he's losing a lot of blood. Yes, I've put pressure on the wound, but you'll need to send an ambulance. Oh — and call Sheriff Harger. Tell him that Hunter Cardwell just confessed to murdering Will Tyler."

After ending the call, Vivian pulled up her bra and buttoned her shirt. Then she picked up the pages Hunter had dropped and carried them downstairs to the shredder.

The distant wail of sirens woke Erin in the darkness. She stirred in Luke's arms, pulled away, and sat up in bed.

"What is it?" He opened his eyes, instantly alert.

"Listen," she said. "Something's wrong."

He sat up, listening beside her. "They don't sound close. And they don't seem to be getting closer. Maybe something's going on at the syndicate ranch."

"What if it's a fire? It could spread." Erin remembered the terrible wildfires of a few years ago, especially the one that had nearly destroyed the Rimrock.

He kissed her cheek. "What do you say I go out on the porch and have a look?"

"I'll go with you."

"Stay here," he said. "Do you want to cause a scandal?"

"It doesn't matter anymore. Rose isn't fooled, and it's nobody else's business that I'm out here with you."

"Just stay put. I'll be right back."

Wrapping his hips in a towel, he opened the front door of the duplex and stepped out onto the porch. Erin waited, hugging her knees in the bed. Spending the night with Luke, loving him, then drifting off to sleep with her naked body spooned against his, was her idea of heaven. But it was only a temporary heaven. A world of thorny challenges and heartbreaking decisions waited for her beyond the door of this safe little room.

She remembered the words she'd said to Luke, telling him that he could leave anytime, as long as he didn't come back. She'd forced herself to say those words, as much for herself as for him. But the truth was, she had never wanted anything more desperately than she wanted to keep him. She wanted him by her side for life, as her partner, her husband, and the father of her children. But if it turned out that he loved his freedom more than he loved her, she would never force him to stay.

After a few minutes on the porch, he came back inside and locked the door behind him. "No fire," he said. "I didn't even smell smoke. But I did hear sirens, and I may have seen flashing lights headed for the syndicate place. I couldn't be sure. They were too far off. But whatever's going on, it doesn't seem to have anything to do with us."

"That's a relief. Come on back to bed." She raised the covers, giving him room to slide under. Nestling close, she breathed in

406

the warm, clean aroma of his skin. "I don't want morning to come," she whispered. "I want to stay here, with you."

He kissed her. "Morning always comes, love — until the day when it doesn't. I know you're going to have a lot on your shoulders. But you're strong and smart. You'll do your father proud."

"Not if I lose the Rimrock to the bank."

His arms tightened around her. "I know that if you go down, you'll go down fighting all the way. But you mustn't blame yourself for something that wasn't your fault."

"Blaming is a waste of time and breath. Tomorrow morning I'll be sitting down with Sky and Lauren to draw up a financial statement of the ranch's assets and liabilities. With that in hand, I'll start a round of calling on the big banks in Lubbock. My dad only borrowed half the value of the ranch to buy out Beau. The rest is free and clear. With that much collateral, surely someone will be interested in refinancing. That's the last hope."

"You'll make it work," he said. "I have faith in you."

"Thanks." She nuzzled the warm hollow at the base of his throat. "I wish you could come with me."

Erin regretted the words as soon as she'd

said them. The last thing she needed, when approaching bank officials, was a boyfriend in tow. She needed to come across as a capable, independent woman.

"My specialty is horses, not banks," Luke said. "I'll be right here, getting your cow ponies shod for the roundup."

And what would happen after his work was finished? she wondered. Would he leave and move on? Luke was a man who had to feel useful. Hanging around the ranch, working as a common cowhand or looking for things to do, was bound to wear on him. And if she lost the ranch . . . Erin tried to imagine a future without the Rimrock. She'd have nothing — a young woman barely out of her teens, with no job skills beyond handling horses. If Luke were fool enough to marry her, she'd be a burden, following him around from job to job or pining away at home because he was always gone.

It was unthinkable. She wouldn't do that to him.

Luke stirred beside her. "Something tells me you're not going back to sleep," he said. "I can almost feel your mind working."

"Which means I'll be keeping you awake, too, if I stay," she said. "You haven't had a decent night's sleep since your arrest. You deserve better than this. I'm going back to the house. We'll have other nights."

Luke didn't argue as she gave him a long, deep kiss, slipped out of bed, and pulled on her clothes. He was exhausted, she knew, and their lovemaking — she smiled at the memory — hadn't exactly reinforced his strength. He would probably be asleep by the time she was out the door.

"See you in the morning," she whispered, brushing a kiss on his lips. Then she stepped outside, into the night.

Henry slithered across her path as she crossed the yard, patrolling the place for rats, mice, and the occasional rattler. Good old Henry. If someone else took over the Rimrock, they would probably kill him on sight. Before she let that happen, she would trap him and release him into the escarpment.

But she couldn't think of that now. Somehow she would have to find a way to save her beloved ranch.

Tomorrow she would begin.

CHAPTER NINETEEN

Ten days had passed since Luke's release from jail and Hunter Cardwell's arrest for Will's murder. The split-level house on the syndicate ranch stood empty. Vivian Cardwell and her son were both gone without a trace.

Rose, too, was gone. She had flown home to Wyoming to finalize the sale of her house to her brother-in-law. Once that was done, and her possessions boxed and loaded in a trailer, she'd be driving her truck back to Texas, where workers were already clearing the land for the prefabricated log home she'd ordered.

Rose had earned a settled, comfortable future, Erin mused as she gazed out the office window, watching the flight of a red-tailed hawk. Sadly, her own future, and the future of the Rimrock, remained as bleak as the sun-parched landscape outside. She'd applied for the refinance at four different banks. Three of them had already turned her down. The loan officer at the fourth bank had promised to let her know the board's decision by this afternoon. She was waiting for the call now.

Faintly, across the yard, she could hear the *ping* of Luke's hammer as he shaped a shoe on the anvil. It was a comforting sound, a sound she had come to love — a sound she would sorely miss when he was gone.

Things were good between them, more than good, especially the nights when she stole into his bed in the duplex and stayed until just before dawn. His tender, passionate loving had ushered her from girlhood into womanhood. But there were rules between them. He refused to come to her room in the house, and, by unspoken agreement, neither of them talked about the future. It was a closed door, to be opened only when the time came.

The ringing landline phone on the desk jerked her attention back to the present. She glanced at the caller ID. Her pulse broke into a gallop. It was the loan officer from the bank.

Her hand shook as she picked up the receiver. She was braced for another disappointment, but that cruel spark of hope refused to die.

"Miss Tyler?"

"Yes?" She willed her voice not to quiver.

"This is Dan Farley over at Texas First National. How are y'all doing today?"

How am I doing? "That depends on what you have to tell me."

"Well, since you're not in the mood for chitchat, I'll get right to the decision. I'm right sorry, but I'm afraid we won't be able to help you out."

Her heart sank. Why had she even bothered to apply? "Can you tell me why?" she asked. "The value is there, and I'm only asking half of what the ranch is worth."

"Oh, the ranch is fine. We all agreed on that. The problem is you, Miss Tyler. You're a nineteen-year-old girl, barely out of high school, with no credit history. You've never even bought a car — for that matter, you don't even have your own credit card. If you were a man, maybe —"

"This is the twenty-first century. What you just said is called discrimination."

"Well, sorry, miss, that's just the way it is. All I can do is wish you better luck somewhere else."

Erin hung up the phone and slumped over the desk. The four banks she'd tried were the largest and the most likely to make big loans at a fair rate. Now she'd be faced with the second tier of institutions, the smaller banks, loan companies, and credit unions, some of them with tarnished reputations. There was always the chance that they could cheat her out of her property. And then there were private lenders who advertised — a frightening prospect, only for the desperate. She was a little fish in a sea of sharks. But she couldn't give up. She had to keep trying.

She could call Beau and ask him for advice. But no, Beau, through no bad intent, was the cause of this mess. She could understand now why her father had been so angry with him.

She was getting a headache. Right now, what she needed was fresh air and Luke's calming presence. He wouldn't tell her what to do. That wasn't Luke's way. But he would listen while she talked through her problems and arrived at her own understanding.

She loved him for that. And she needed him. She needed his strength and his quiet acceptance of her as the person she was. She needed his arms in the night and his wisdom in all the days of her life. But to tell him that might make him feel trapped. If he decided to stay, it would have to be of his own free choice.

She followed the sound of his hammer and found him in the large pen, under the open shed roof. He had taken off his shirt. His muscular torso gleamed with sweat. A paint gelding was tied to the fence. A half dozen other horses drowsed around the water trough as they waited their turn.

Erin stood by the fence, watching him work, waiting for him to look up and notice her.

After a few minutes he turned and saw her. One look at her face told him what had happened. "They turned you down," he said.

She nodded. "I'm trying to be a big girl about it, but I feel like I've been thrown in a lake and left to drown — and I'm about to go under for the third time."

"Hang on." He came out through the gate, closed it behind him, and took her in his arms. She pressed her face against his chest, inhaling his manly aroma and tasting the salt on his skin. He held her — simply held her, without trying to tell her that everything would be all right. Luke always seemed to know what she needed.

"What now?" he asked, after a brief silence. "I can feel you thinking."

"Just grasping at straws," she said. "Someone in one of the banks told me about this investment group. It's a long shot. They do business loans, not real estate loans. But the ranch is a business."

"So, do you think it's worth talking to them?"

"What have I got to lose? The worst they can do is say no. And there are other lenders, just not as good or as safe as the banks. I can't quit and let the ranch go, Luke. I've got to keep trying."

"I know." He kissed the spot where her hairline peaked at the midline of her forehead. "So when are you going back to Lubbock? You've been running back and forth almost every day. Maybe you need a break."

"No break. There's no point in wasting time. I might as well go tomorrow. Everything's under control here, isn't it?"

"As far as I know. Sky runs a tight ship. The men know their jobs, and so do I."

"Then I guess that's the plan," Erin said. "Want to come to supper tonight? Carmen's going home early, and Rose is gone, so it'll be just you and me."

"Sounds good." He released her with a grin. "I'd better get back to work. The boss lady doesn't take kindly to slackers."

"Go then." She gave his rump a playful slap. "I'll see you tonight."

Erin walked back to the house with a

415

spring in her step. Luke had a way of lifting her spirits and making her feel strong and capable. She still had a load of worry on her shoulders, but for tonight, at least, she would put it aside and enjoy her time with the man she loved.

Deep in the escarpment, the dry night wind moaned through the canyons like a living thing. The crescent moon gleamed like the blade of a silver scimitar against the black night sky. Coyote calls echoed across the foothills.

In the sheltered hollow beneath a ledge, Marie lit a cigarette, leaned back against a boulder, and watched the smoke rise into the darkness.

Three days ago, she'd returned to her vantage point above the Rimrock Ranch. This time she had a faster bike and a gun — both stolen. And this time she was determined to finish what she'd started.

She'd been too cautious in the past. Her resolve to make Erin Tyler's death look like an accident had cost her precious time. And time was running out. She needed to make the hit, collect Stella's stashed drugs, and get out of the country. Faking the murder to look accidental didn't matter now. If the law caught up with her, she'd go down for killing a cop.

The plan she'd come up with was relatively simple but would take split-second timing. For the past two mornings, she'd watched Erin Tyler walk out to her old brown station wagon, dressed for the city and carrying a briefcase. Wherever she was going, probably Lubbock, she would most likely be taking the freeway.

The best version of Marie's plan depended on the little Tyler bitch making the drive again, hopefully tomorrow. If it didn't happen, she could carry out her attack on a different road. But the freeway would make for an easier approach and a faster getaway.

Closing her eyes, Marie rehearsed the plan in her head. The lumbering wagon wouldn't have much speed. It would probably be in the right-hand lane. On her old but sweet Harley-Davidson Dyna Low Rider, which she'd stolen when the owner left his keys on the bar to use the restroom, she'd have no trouble catching up to the wagon and speeding away after the shots were fired — at least two rounds, she calculated. Three, just to be safe. Her helmet, worn with the visor down, would hide her face and hair. By the time the out-of-control car rolled off the freeway or crashed into oncoming traffic, she'd be long gone.

The pistol, a .357 Magnum she'd lifted from the front seat of a parked car, was a cold weight in the shoulder holster she wore under her leather jacket. Marie touched it, as if to reassure herself that it was there, loaded and ready. *Just do it,* she told herself. *Get it over with, get the drugs, and you'll be free.*

Luke had finished morning chores and was washing his hands at the outside tap when he saw Erin come out of the house. She headed for her station wagon, then turned and saw him. As she crossed the yard, he stepped into the barn to give them some privacy.

Balancing her briefcase, she ran to him and flung her arms around his neck. A few hours ago they'd been in his bed together, but she greeted him as if they'd been apart for weeks. He loved that about her — the way she gave herself with total abandon, holding nothing back. As he held her, he imagined waking up to that sweet love every morning, giving her babies, and watching them grow up. Could he be the steady, caring husband she needed by her side? Could he be a good father to their children? Could he love her as freely and trustingly as she loved him?

418

Sometimes, like now, his feelings for Erin were so intense that they scared him. Could he be the man she needed and deserved? Or would his restless nature cause him to let her down and break her heart?

His arms released her. His eyes looked her up and down. She was wearing new jeans and a denim blazer over a pink silk blouse. Her boots were freshly polished. "You're a knockout this morning," he said."

She laughed. "The look I was aiming for is tough, successful businesswoman. Wish me luck."

"You've got all my wishes. Maybe this will be the day when something good happens."

"I hope so. Gotta go." She stretched on tiptoe to brush a kiss over his lips, then turned and strode across the yard toward her car.

Luke watched her walk away, admiring her spunk. He would have given anything if he could take on her burden and make her troubles go away. But there was nothing he could do except be here, and give her refuge when the going got rough.

As she reached the old, brown station wagon and climbed inside, a chill crept over him — a premonition that something wasn't right. Luke had learned to trust his instincts, but this time there appeared to be no cause for alarm. Will's killer was behind bars, and there'd been no sign of the mysterious intruder since the shooting at the Blue Coyote. Sky's cousin had probably left the country.

He could shout at Erin, stop her from leaving, and insist that she stay here. But he knew she wouldn't listen. She would laugh, call him an old worry wart, and drive away.

All he could do was let her go. But he wouldn't take an easy breath until she was safely home again.

Marie cut across the flatlands and along the back roads. At the junction with the highway she idled the bike and waited until the brown station wagon had passed, then followed about two hundred yards behind. Perfect timing, she congratulated herself. Now all she had to do was keep back, out of sight, until the vehicle was on the freeway. At the right spot, she would speed up, come even with the wagon, draw the .357 Magnum, put a couple of shots through the driver's side window, and lose herself in the morning commuter traffic. Mission accomplished.

The plan sounded almost too easy. But she'd rehearsed it in her mind at least a hundred times. The critical part was holding steady when the time came to draw and fire. Do it right, and Erin Tyler would be dead before she knew what had hit her. Do it wrong . . . but she couldn't afford to do it wrong. Not this time.

After the first twenty miles or so, the traffic grew heavier as commuters, heading for work in the city, merged onto the freeway. By now the lanes were crowded enough for her bike to blend in, but moving well enough to allow for speed. Marie could see the station wagon ahead of her, in the right-hand lane, just as she'd expected. The lane next to it was clear. It was now or never.

Adrenaline poured through Marie's body. Her pulse kicked into high gear as she accelerated — fast enough to come even with the wagon, but not too fast for her to aim and fire. She drew the pistol. Now she could see the driver's profile through the side window. It was Erin Tyler, all right. And she was looking straight ahead.

Steering with her left hand and aiming with her right, Marie fired two quick shots. She glimpsed a crimson splatter on the cracked glass, but she couldn't stick around to check the extent of damage. With a roar, the bike shot ahead, moving forward, then to the left, where it zigzagged into the main stream of automobiles. Minutes later, as the city neared, she slowed, secured the gun in its holster, and let the bike mingle with the heavy morning commuter traffic. From somewhere far behind her, she could hear the wail of sirens.

She had done it. She had killed Erin Tyler and made a clean getaway. Euphoria surged. As it filled her like a drug, she raised the visor on her helmet, flung back her head, and shrilled a Comanche war cry.

When he saw Carmen rushing out of the house, Luke suspected that something had happened. When she came closer, and he saw her wild-eyed, stricken face, he knew.

With a silent prayer on his lips, he ran to meet her.

"I just saw it on TV," she gasped, struggling for breath. "They didn't give a name, but I know it was Erin —"

"What happened?" He clasped her shoulders to steady her.

"A driver, shot on the freeway south of Lubbock — brown Chevy station wagon. It rolled down an embankment and crashed at the bottom. They showed the car. It was Erin's. I know it was her!"

"What about Erin? Is she alive?" It was all Luke could do to keep from shaking the poor woman.

"They — they said the driver, a woman, had been air-lifted to the hospital in critical condition. That's all I know. The TV's on in the house. Maybe we can find out more."

Luke released her. "I'm going inside to see what I can find out. Call Lauren. Have her get hold of Sky, wherever he is. Tell them that as soon as I find out for sure it's Erin, I'll be on my way to the hospital."

He raced into the house. The big-screen TV was on in the den, but the news had gone to commercial. Desperately he grabbed the remote and flipped to another local channel. There it was, the shot of the car, upside-down at the bottom of a grassy embankment, its top and side smashed in. Luke caught a glimpse of the license plate. It was Erin's car.

The reporter mentioned the name of the hospital where the driver had been taken. That was all the information Luke needed. Rushing outside again, he said a quick word to Carmen, grabbed his shirt from the fence, shouted to a hand to let the penned horses back into the paddock, and un-hitched his truck from the trailer.

Minutes later, he was roaring out of the yard, trailing a cloud of dust down the lane all the way to the main road.

423

■ ■ ■ ■

Marie took her time, leaving the freeway and winding her way through the streets into the barrio, where she felt safe enough to go to a café and have some coffee. She was still keyed up after the successful hit and escape. She needed to unwind before she tried to contact Stella.

News of the shooting was bound to go statewide. Stella had access to TV in prison. With luck, she would see the broadcast and know that Marie would be calling to get the location of the drug stash.

In the restaurant, which she'd scoped out before going in, she chose a booth with a view of the front door and a direct path to the kitchen and the back alley where she'd left her bike. She felt confident that she'd made a clean escape, but one couldn't be too careful.

The TV, mounted high on the wall behind the counter, was broadcasting a game show in Spanish. When the man brought her coffee, she pointed to the TV and asked, *"Inglés?"*

He glanced around to make sure no one was watching the game show, then nodded and switched the channel, using the remote in his pocket. A local newscast was just beginning, and there, on the screen, was a live shot of the wrecked brown station wagon.

As Marie watched, the camera zoomed in on the driver's side window with two bullet holes in the blood-splattered glass. The reporter's voice droned in the background. ". . . The female driver was air-lifted to University Medical Center in critical condition. . . ."

No! Marie's coffee slopped over, scalding her fingers. *It's impossible! The little bitch is still alive!*

She willed herself to stay calm and finish her coffee. If Erin Tyler didn't die, Stella would know. And all this planning, all this risk, would have been for nothing.

There was no way around it. Unless she wanted to flee the country with nothing, she would have to finish the job.

Luke raced into the emergency room and found the main desk. "Erin Tyler," he told the nurse on duty. "She was shot on the freeway and air-lifted here. What can you tell me?"

"Are you family?" The nurse was maddeningly calm.

"She doesn't have any family. But if she

survives, I'm going to marry her." As soon as Luke spoke the words he felt their truth. To lose Erin would be to lose the future, their love, their family, all they could give each other.

"Just a minute." The young nurse turned away to speak to a supervisor, then came back to Luke. "She's in surgery now. That's all I can tell you. It may be a while. If you want to wait, give me your name, and I'll have the doctor come out and talk to you when he's finished."

"Thanks." Luke gave his name and sat down to wait. He'd never been one for churches, but now his lips moved in silent prayer. *Please . . . please . . . she's my love, my life, my everything. . . .*

Three hours later, each minute an eternity of waiting and worry, the doctor, who looked young enough to be in high school, walked out between the swinging doors. He was smiling — smiling, thank God.

"Mr. Maddox?"

Luke rose to his feet, his legs unsteady beneath him. "Yes, how is Erin?"

"Very, very lucky. The bullet went in at a shallow angle, barely penetrating the skull. She lost some blood, but we were able to remove the bullet and repair the wound,

426

hopefully without any damage to her brain. We won't know for sure until she wakes up.

"Her other injuries were from the crash — broken ribs, a dislocated shoulder, some bruises and lacerations from the glass. Nothing that won't heal in time. You can thank her seat belt for that."

Luke began to breathe again. "There were two shots fired. I saw the car window on TV."

"Evidently the other shot missed. We couldn't find anyplace else where she'd been hit. Again, she's a very lucky woman."

"When can I see her?"

"When we're sure her vitals are stable, we'll move her to a room in the ICU. You can be with her then. But she'll be unconscious."

"For how long?" Fear gnawed at him. What if she didn't wake up at all?

"Hours, at least," the doctor said. "Maybe even days, if her brain takes that long. That's up to nature now. Go get some lunch and some rest. Come back in an hour. You should be able to see her then."

Luke walked out into the parking lot. Food and rest. He wouldn't be interested in either until he knew Erin was going to be all right. Taking out his phone, he called the house and gave Carmen an update on Erin's

427

condition. Then, for the next hour, he wandered aimlessly around the hospital complex, burning off nervous energy and worrying.

At best, Erin's recovery would take weeks, even months. The time lost could cost her the ranch. Maybe Sky could take on the task of finding a loan? At least he was a relative. Luke or one of the more experienced hands could take over as temporary foreman. . . . Never mind, he was getting ahead of himself. But Erin would be devastated if she lost her beloved Rimrock. He could love her and take care of her, but part of her soul would be gone.

Luke hadn't worn a watch, but when he couldn't stand the wait any longer, he went to the hospital's main information desk. They gave him directions to the ICU and the number of Erin's room. He took the elevator and found her at last, white and still, with a bandage on her head, an IV drip in her arm, and monitors attached to a machine that beeped signals above her bed.

A middle-aged nurse was typing notes into a computer on a stand. She gave Luke a smile. "Don't worry. She's been through a lot, but she's a strong girl. Her vitals are good. She just needs a good, long sleep while her brain recovers."

"Can I stay with her?" Luke asked. "I'd like to be here when she wakes up."

"Sure, if you want to. There's coffee at the nurses' station. The restroom's down the hall to your right, around the first corner. Push the call button if she needs anything."

As the nurse took the computer and walked out of the room, Luke found the one comfortable-looking chair and moved it next to the bed. Sitting down, he took her hand in his. Her fingers were cold, but he could feel the pulse at the base of her wrist, beating steadily. She was a strong girl, the nurse had said. He was just finding out how strong. But she was going to need him in the time ahead.

He raised her chilled hand to his lips. "I love you, Erin," he whispered. "I'm not going anywhere. I'll be here for you, always."

As the hours passed, Luke fell into a doze. He awakened to darkness through the window blinds. Someone had dimmed the lights in the room and in the hallway, but he could see that Erin was still sleeping. He could hear the low, regular beep of the monitor and the soft sound of her breathing. A glance at the wall clock told him it was after midnight.

His legs were cramped from sitting in the same position, and he needed a restroom.

Some coffee wouldn't hurt either, if there was any available. Standing, he stretched his limbs and walked quietly out of the room.

There was a light at the nurses' station at the far end of the hallway. The only other sign of life was a person in a baggy custodial staff uniform, wearing a cap and sunglasses and towing a cart with a mop bucket and a trash receptacle. He — or she — appeared to be cleaning the floor, dipping the mop in the bucket and slopping it indifferently back and forth.

Still half asleep, Luke made his way down to the restroom. Minutes later, he was washing his hands, about to leave, when the realization hit him like a lightning bolt.

A cap and sunglasses? In the middle of the night?

He was out the door like a shot, rounding the corner and racing back toward Erin's room. There was no sign of the worker or the cart, but Erin's door had been closed.

There was no lock, thank heaven. He burst into the room to find the so-called custodial worker — tall, rail thin, and wearing boots with long, pointed toes under baggy coveralls — standing over Erin with a pillow, about to press it over her face.

Everything came together in a flash. Luke

430

charged, grabbing the lanky figure from behind. The pillow fell to the floor as they struggled. The intruder, a woman — he could tell from the sound of her gasps and grunts — was surprisingly strong, twisting and kicking and jabbing in an effort to reach the knife that was thrust into her back pocket. Luke grabbed one arm and caught the other, twisting both behind her back, hard enough to dislocate her shoulders if she resisted. A long braid whipped Luke's face as the cap and glasses fell away. He stared, recognition stirring in his brain. The narrow, angry face, the slashing scar . . . *He knew her.*

The years peeled away. He was a boy again, walking into his brother's kitchen, seeing the flash of a knife as it ripped open his wife's face from temple to mouth. *Marie.* It was a common name. Until now it had never occurred to him that his former sister-in-law and Sky's murdering cousin were one and the same.

"Luke." Incredibly, she recognized him. "You saved my life once. Save it again. Please. Let me go."

Luke didn't reply. He could tell her he was sorry, but that would be a lie.

A nurse had appeared in the open doorway. "I've called Security," she said.

"They're coming."

"Fine." Luke forced his squirming captive to the floor, holding her facedown with her hands pinned behind her back. "While you're at it, call nine-one-one. Tell the dispatcher that the police can come and get Marie Fletcher."

432

CHAPTER TWENTY

It was morning when Erin stirred and opened her eyes. The first thing she saw was Luke bending over her. He looked exhausted, his eyes bloodshot and sunk into shadow. His hair was mussed, his jaw dark with stubble. But he was smiling. That was all that mattered.

But everything else was strange — the bed, the room, the pain in her head, and the tubes and monitors attached to her arm. Where was she? What had happened to her?

Luke bent down and brushed a gentle kiss on her chapped lips. "Good morning," he murmured. "Do you know where you are?"

She struggled to think clearly. "Am I in . . . the hospital?"

"You are. You've been through a pretty rough time. Do you remember anything about what happened to you?"

She tried to shake her head. It hurt. A lot. "I don't remember anything," she said.

"You were driving on the freeway when someone came by and shot you through the window," Luke said. "The car rolled down an embankment and crashed. The doctor who took the bullet out of your skull said you were lucky to be alive."

Erin's free hand moved up to touch the bandage on her head. "When did all this happen?" she asked.

"Yesterday. You haven't missed much."

"And you've been here the whole time?"

"Since you got out of surgery. I never want to leave you, Erin. Not ever again."

She gave him a feeble smile. "That suits me fine," she said. "But something tells me I won't be worth much for a while. Strange, all I remember is driving on the freeway. I was on my way to apply for a loan and — oh, no!" She struggled to sit up. "Get me out of here! I've got to get that loan!"

Luke eased her back onto the pillow. "No, you don't. Somebody else will have to see about the loan. I'm going to talk to Sky. Maybe —"

"No, I'm the owner of the ranch. They won't talk to anybody else. And even if they would, they're not going to lend money to somebody who's flat on her back in the hospital. How long do I have to be here? Ask the nurse —"

434

As if summoned, a perky young nurse stepped into the room. "You're awake! Awesome! How do you feel?"

"It doesn't matter." Erin tried to push herself up, but a stabbing pain in her ribs stopped her. She lay back on the pillow. "I need to get out of here. How soon can I be released?"

"Not for a couple more days, at least. And then you'll have to rest at home. You've had some serious injuries, honey. You can't just get up and go running around like nothing's happened. Now, let's check your vitals." She took Erin's blood pressure and looked at the monitors. "Excellent. I think we can take that IV out and move you to a regular room before breakfast this morning. You'll be more comfortable, but you'll still need to stay quiet. I hear your boyfriend was with you all night. He sounds like a keeper. You'd better hang on to him."

"I plan to, if he'll have me." Erin managed a smile.

"Just try and get rid of me," Luke said. "While you're busy with the nurse, I'll go outside to get some air and make some calls."

"Get yourself some breakfast," the nurse said. "The cafeteria's pretty good. And it'll

435

take a while to get Erin here cleaned up and transferred to her new room."

Outside, in the parking lot, Luke took his phone out of his pocket. It was early yet. No one answered in the main house, but Luke did manage to reach Sky and give him an update. "Thank God," Sky said when he heard that Erin was awake. "And thank heaven you caught Marie. I know she's my cousin, but I've disowned her. She deserves to be behind bars. But what I can't figure out is why she was trying to kill Erin."

"Maybe the sheriff will be able to tell us." Luke decided to save the story of his own connection to Marie for another time.

"Oh, something else," Sky said. "Carmen took a call yesterday from a lawyer, a Mr. Shannon White, who said he had some urgent business with Erin."

"Did Carmen tell him that Erin was in the hospital?"

"No. She just told him Erin was unavailable and took his number."

"So he didn't say what his business was about?"

"Only that it was urgent, and private. I've got his number. I'll text it to you. If Erin's feeling up to it later, she may want to call him, or have you do it."

436

"I'll let her know. And thanks." Luke ended the call and checked to make sure he'd received the text. Should he wait to tell Erin? If the lawyer was with the bank, and was handling the probable foreclosure on the ranch, she didn't need more bad news. But Erin was a big girl, Luke reminded himself. She could make up her own mind.

When he saw her again, in her new room, she was sitting up in bed with her breakfast on a tray. Dressed in a clean hospital gown, she was picking at her food, looking as if somebody had died.

"How are you doing?" He kissed her forehead below the bandage. "Feeling any better?"

"Hurting less. They gave me some pills for the headache pain. It's just —" She blinked back tears. "I can't imagine my life anywhere but the Rimrock," she said. "But I'm going to lose it to the bank. I've done everything I can, and I can't do more, especially not from here. I've just got to accept it. But what will I do, Luke? Where will I go?"

You can marry me and let me take care of you. Luke knew better than to say the words. Erin loved him, but this was no time for a proposal. The ranch was everything to her, the land, the people, and the animals. She was mourning the loss as if it were a death — and she'd seen far too much death lately.

Because there was no point in waiting, Luke told her about the lawyer's phone call. "Let's hope it's not more bad news," he said.

"Why not? Most of the other news has been bad. What else could go wrong? Maybe somebody wants to sue me. Would you call him for me, Luke? If he's in town, see if he could come this afternoon. Whatever he wants, we might as well get it over with."

The lawyer had agreed to come at two o'clock. In the interim, Erin had napped while Luke bought some jeans, a shirt, and some underclothes at a nearby mall and used the private shower in her room to clean up. When the lawyer, an elfin, white-haired man in a tailored suit, walked in precisely on the hour, they were waiting for him.

Luke offered him a chair. He sat on the edge, stiffly formal, with his briefcase on his lap. "I heard about your terrible accident, Miss Tyler," he said. "I hope that you'll feel a bit better after you hear what I've come to tell you."

Better? Luke and Erin exchanged glances.

Could it be that this wasn't bad news after all?

"My firm, White, Anderson, and Carruthers, represents the estate of the late Jasper Platt. Mr. Platt executed a will with us several years prior to his death."

Jasper! Something tightened around Erin's heart like an invisible hug when she thought of how much she'd loved the old man.

"I apologize for the delay. It's taken us some time to update Mr. Platt's financial records, but I believe you'll find everything in order. As you're probably aware, Mr. Platt had no descendants, and no living family except a niece. Is that correct, as you understand it?"

"Yes," Erin said. "The Rimrock was family to him. He was one of us."

"So I gather." The lawyer opened his briefcase, slipped out a paper, and put on his wire-framed glasses. "Mr. Platt left a twenty-thousand-dollar bequest to his niece, who has already accepted that amount. The rest of his assets were willed to the Rimrock Ranch for as long as the land remains in the hands of the Tylers and their descendants."

Erin could hear her heart pounding. Jasper hadn't been a wealthy man. His only possessions of any worth had been his truck, his guns, and his ATV. But if he'd left the ranch a few thousand dollars, how kind he'd been to think of them.

The lawyer's eyes narrowed. "As you know, Mr. Platt was a man of few needs and simple tastes. But the Tylers paid him a fair wage as the foreman of the Rimrock. Almost every paycheck he earned, he invested over the years. His bequest to the Rimrock is in the amount of four hundred eighty-three thousand dollars and sixty-two cents."

Erin felt a moment of light-headedness. Then the tears came, flowing like rain down her cheeks. *Oh, Jasper — we loved you so much. You were not of our blood, but you were our father, our grandfather, our dearest friend. And now, again you've saved us!*

Luke reached for her hand and held it tight as the lawyer continued. "I'll leave you with a copy of the will. All that remains is for you to tell me how you want the funds distributed."

"If you can wait until I'm out of the hospital," Erin said, "I'd like to open up a special account for the money. Then you can do an electronic transfer. Is that possible?"

The little man smiled. "Entirely possible, my dear. I may be an old fossil, but this is the twenty-first century. Just let me know when you have the account and we'll make the transfer." He handed Erin a photocopy of the will, with his card attached, shook both their hands, and walked out.

Erin collapsed in Luke's arms and sobbed — healing tears for her mother, her father, Jasper, and the ranch that would stay in their family — hopefully forever. Luke held her gently, taking care not to hurt her broken ribs. Erin had her miracle, and she was his.

As they broke apart and he kissed her tear-streaked face, a deep rumble quivered in the air. A drop of wetness spattered the outside window, then another and another.

Luke walked to the window and raised the blinds to give them a view of black clouds roiling across the sky. "I'll be damned," he said. "It's raining."

EPILOGUE I

Gatesville Women's Prison
Two weeks later

"Here's your gourmet lunch, girl. Eat hearty." Mavis, who was doing time for selling meth, slid the tray through the slot in Marie's cell. Cold hot dogs and canned beans again. Marie would have told the woman to stuff it, but after a week in solitary, any voice was better than the silence.

"Any news from outside?" she asked.

"Just the usual." Mavis wasn't supposed to talk to the prisoners in solitary, but if no guards were around, she didn't mind breaking that rule.

"Listen, I need a favor." Marie pressed close to the bars, keeping her voice low. "Can you get word to Stella Rawlins, tell her I'm here?"

"Stella? Oh, honey, you haven't heard, have you?"

442

"Heard what?" Marie asked.

"Stella passed away last month, in the infirmary. She's gone to hell, or wherever she deserved."

"Oh, damn." Marie had no pity for Stella, but her death meant that even if she'd succeeded in killing Erin Tyler, Stella wouldn't have been around to tell her about the drug stash.

"Somethin' else, I heard," Mavis whispered. "I talked to a girl who was workin' the infirmary when Stella died. Stella wanted to give you a message. She said, 'If that bitch Marie ever comes back here, tell her there wasn't ever any drugs. I told her a lie.' "

Marie sagged against the bars. "That's what Stella said?"

"That's the story I heard," Mavis said. "She said it, and then she died laughin'."

EPILOGUE II

One year later

Erin Tyler Maddox sat on the front porch with her husband, holding hands between chairs and watching the sun set over the escarpment. This year the land was green again. Cattle fattened in the grassy pastures. Blackbirds flitted among the cattails in the marshland. The playa lake where Jasper had loved to hunt wild turkey lay like a mirror, its silver shallows reflecting the fiery sky.

The two of them had just come back from a dinner at Rose's place. This year, the pretty log house was surrounded by vegetable and flower gardens. Chickens supplied eggs not only for Rose but for the Rimrock. And a small herd of goats, which Rose had to fence out of her garden, gave milk that she made into delicious cheese.

"Do you think Rose is lonely over there, alone?" Erin asked, thinking out loud.

"I think Rose is perfectly content," Luke

444

said. "She has everything the way she wants it. Besides" — he patted Erin's rounding belly — "in a few months she'll have a little honorary grandson to babysit and play with."

Erin laughed. "She's so excited about our having a boy. She only had girls, you know. Oh — she mentioned her daughters are coming for Christmas this year. She's going to have a houseful."

"I'd say Rose is doing just fine," Luke said. "And we're going to have a houseful, too, with Beau's family coming for a visit next week."

"I'm so glad they're coming. April will have a blast, running around the ranch with Sky's kids. And I can get some much-needed baby care pointers from Natalie while I enjoy her little one."

"Beau promised to take me bird hunting in Jasper's old spots," Luke said. "We're going to take his old shotgun with us."

"I'm sure Jasper will be with you in spirit," Erin said.

"And I believe that Dad, wherever he is, will be glad we mended fences with his brother. Speaking of Dad and Jasper, do you think our son will be okay with the name we've chosen?"

"Jasper Williston Maddox? He'd better be.

445

He'd better do it proud — and it'll be up to you to tell him what those names mean. Come here, you." He pulled her gently out of her chair and onto his lap.

Erin curled against him, with her head on his shoulder and their baby between them. Things wouldn't always be this perfect, she knew. There would be good years and bad, fences to mend and heartaches to endure. But they knew what truly mattered. In the words that Bull Tyler had spoken and passed down through the generations, *Land and family. Family and land.* Forever.

ABOUT THE AUTHOR

Janet Dailey's first book was published in 1976. Since then she has written more than 100 novels and become one of the top-selling female authors in the world, with 325 million copies of her books sold in nineteen languages in ninety-eight countries. She is known for her strong, decisive characters, her extraordinary ability to recreate a time and a place, and her unerring courage to confront important, controversial issues in her stories. To learn more about Janet Dailey and her novels, please visit JanetDailey.com or find her on Facebook at Facebook.com/JanetDaileyAuthor.